PUFFIN BOOKS

blood red horse

K. M. Grant was born into a large Lancashire family that often found itself caught up in historical events – usually on the losing side. Stories of high adventure, most of them true, were part of everyday life. Married, with teenage children, the author now lives in Scotland and works as a writer and broadcaster. *Blood Red Horse* is K. M. Grant's first novel, and a sequel is currently being written.

blood red horse

K. M. GRANT

PUFFIN

PUFFIN BOOKS

Published by the Penguin Group
Penguin Books Ltd, 80 Strand, London WC2R 0RL, England
Penguin Group (USA), Inc., 375 Hudson Street, New York, New York 10014, USA
Penguin Books Australia Ltd, 250 Camberwell Road, Camberwell, Victoria 3124, Australia
Penguin Books Canada Ltd, 10 Alcorn Avenue, Toronto, Ontario, Canada M4V 3B2
Penguin Books India (P) Ltd, 11 Community Centre, Panchsheel Park, New Delhi – 110 017, India
Penguin Books (NZ) Ltd, Cnr Rosedale and Airborne Roads, Albany, Auckland, New Zealand
Penguin Books (South Africa) (Pty) Ltd, 24 Sturdee Avenue, Rosebank 2196, South Africa

Penguin Books Ltd, Registered Offices: 80 Strand, London WC2R 0RL, England

www.penguin.com

First published 2004
5

Set in Sabon
Typeset by Rowland Phototypesetting Ltd, Bury St Edmunds, Suffolk
Made and printed in England by Clays Ltd, St Ives plc

British Library Cataloguing in Publication Data
A CIP catalogue record for this book is available from the British Library

ISBN 0-141-31706-X

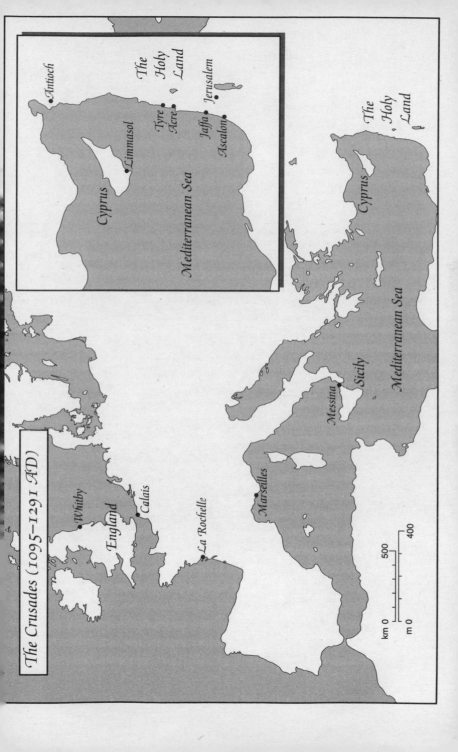

The Crusades (1095–1291 AD)

Antioch

The Holy Land

Tyre
Acre
Jaffa
Ascalon

Jerusalem

Limmasol

Cyprus

Mediterranean Sea

The Holy Land

Cyprus

Whitby

England

Calais

La Rochelle

Marseilles

Messina

Sicily

Mediterranean Sea

km 0   500
m 0   400

for William, Clemmie, Eliza and Cosmo

'the air of heaven is that which blows
between a horse's ears'
Arab proverb

1

Hartslove, 1185

On a warm summer's evening, a very angry twelve-year-old boy was leaning against a chestnut tree, tearing a leaf into small pieces and muttering to himself. He was dripping wet. Running towards him over the grass came a smaller girl, her skirts, which were extremely grubby, hitched up to her knees. Some distance behind her, panting, came a large, elderly woman whose ability to move at any speed other than a bustling walk had long since vanished. The elderly woman was also hampered by a large bundle and the fact that she was shouting as she went, 'Ellie! Eleanor! MISS ELEANOR!'

The girl took no notice. The boy, however, stopped scowling at his shoes and scowled at the approaching parties instead. The girl stood in front of him, wiped her hands on her skirt and demanded, 'What's going on, Will? The courtyard is in an uproar, and Gavin's nose is pouring blood.'

Will glared at her. 'I hate him.'

'I hate him, too,' Ellie agreed, although this was not strictly true.

She always tried to hate Will's older brother for Will's sake. But ever since she'd caught Gavin crying over a little dog of his that had died, she had found this quite hard. Gavin certainly could be mean. Catching her watching him as he mourned his dog, he had loudly ordered the corpse to be thrown into the moat. However, when Ellie ordered the body to be retrieved from the water, she had, rather unexpectedly, found Gavin beside her. She thought he would be angry. Certainly, he never spoke a word, and after the dog had been properly buried by the two of them in the animals' graveyard, he stalked off without a backwards glance. But about a month later she found a small, delicately carved, wooden dog on her pillow. She had kept it in a pocket ever since and, for some reason she could not really account for, never told Will about it. Without either she or Gavin saying a word, she just knew that Gavin wouldn't either.

Ellie tried to offer some comfort. 'Gavin's a horrible bully,' she said, a little more forcefully than was strictly necessary. 'But I still don't know what happened. How did you get so wet?'

'I'll tell you what happened, Miss Eleanor,' said the nurse, who had caught up and, despite being very out of breath, seized William before he could escape. 'But first things first. Now, Master William, let's be having you.' She pulled an extremely uncooperative Will towards her and tried to wrap him in a rough blanket. 'What a to-do!' she said as she began to fuss over his clothes.

'Well?' demanded Ellie, almost stamping her foot with impatience. The nurse waited to reply until she had finished tut-tutting over the state of William's shirt, which was torn in several places.

'Well, Miss Eleanor,' she said at last, 'Gavin saw Master William riding that great big stallion of Sir Percy's and called for everybody to come and look. That's all.'

William found it difficult to protest from underneath

the blanket, but a voice squeaky with indignation made some muffled comments, and a pair of elbows dug into the nurse's ribs.

'It's no good, Master William,' said the nurse, quite unmoved. Her bulk easily flattened the boy against the tree as she, with dexterity born of long practice, removed his wet tunic and handed him a dry one. 'You'll catch your death if you don't change.' She then neatly hooked William's legs from under him, whipped off his shoes and removed his leggings. 'Here. Put these on.'

There was a scuffling and a flurry of activity. Oaths were uttered. The nurse raised her eyebrows. Eventually William emerged, his brown hair tousled and his humour blacker than ever.

'That's not exactly what happened,' he retorted, furiously shaking himself free from the nurse's grasp. 'Gavin did call for everybody to come and look at me riding Sir Percy's horse, but only to make fun of me. '"If you want to see what a flea would look like on a dragon,"' William mockingly imitated his brother, '"come and look at Will." And it was not only the knights who laughed,' he went on, aiming a kick at the pile of wet clothes, 'it was all the servants, too. Anyway, I got my own back if his nose is bleeding. Good.'

'But how did you get so wet?' repeated Ellie.

There was a short, rather painful, pause.

'Gavin threw me in the horse-trough.'

'A very bad boy, that Gavin,' observed the nurse, wringing out William's sopping tunic and folding it neatly. 'A very bad boy indeed.'

'He threw you in the horse-trough?' Ellie tried to compose her face and think of something appropriate to say. 'Maybe he will go to hell.'

Will looked at her pityingly. 'You don't go to hell for that kind of thing.'

'You might,' said Ellie defensively. 'How do you know?'

Will sighed. Here he was being dressed by an aged nurse and listening to a silly girl talking nonsense.

'I'm going to get Sacramenta,' he said, trying to salvage some dignity out of the situation. 'She needs to go out. And nobody can say I look like a flea on a dragon on her.'

The nurse was exasperated. 'But it's nearly dinner time, Master William,' she said. 'We've company. Your father will be angry if you are gadding about on that horse instead of sitting at table.'

'I don't care,' said William and began walking back towards the castle. Eleanor was unsure what to do, but then ran and skipped along beside him. The old nurse watched them both, picked up her bundle and sighed. The children were growing wilder each day. They missed a mother. She pulled out a bottle from under her skirts and took a small sip. Then she tucked William's wet clothes firmly under her arm and set sail for the laundry.

William, with Ellie beside him, strode along in silence for a while. Then, in the distance, the little girl spied a line of monks in white habits filing slowly into the woods that stretched away to the west of the castle.

'Look,' she said, 'there are those monks who are building the new monastery. They must be coming away from their meeting with your father.' She glanced sideways at William, then continued, 'I saw one of them squatting behind a tree this morning. When he saw me, he didn't know what to do so he began chanting the Rule

4

of St Benedict with his eyes tight shut, as if him not being able to see me meant I couldn't see him.'

Will seemed to take no notice, but Eleanor went on anyway.

'So I began to recite Our Lady's Psalter aloud until he was finished and couldn't squat any longer. He cleaned himself up with his eyes still tightly shut but if I stopped, he opened them just a tiny bit to see if I had gone away.' She glanced at William again. 'It was not easy, I can tell you, reciting Ave Marias looking at a monk's behind.'

Will's lower lip wobbled. Then suddenly he stopped walking, threw back his head and shouted with laughter.

'Oh, Ellie,' he said, 'you really are a wicked girl. What would Father say?'

Eleanor pulled down the sides of her mouth and made her voice deep and gravelly.

'Sir Thomas would say: "Eleanor Theodora de Barre, you are the despair of my life. How are we to make a lady of you? Who on earth will marry you and run the great estates you have been left?"'

William, his good humour creeping back, took up the challenge.

'Ah, indeed, Sir Thomas,' he sighed, now imitating the fussy treble of Piers de Scabious, the constable of his father's castle. 'What are we to do with such a pair as Master William and Miss Eleanor? Truly, truly, children are nothing but heartache and nuisance.'

The game was a familiar one. Soon, the pair were engaged in most unChristian mimicry and Will's outraged dignity began to feel less raw.

The horse-trough incident was by no means unusual. Like many brothers, William and Gavin were constantly at war. Their father, Sir Thomas de Granville, appeared almost to encourage it, and their mother, who might have exercised a restraining influence, had died in childbirth when William was six and Gavin was ten. Eleanor's own mother, a distant cousin of the de Granvilles, had also died in childbirth – at Eleanor's birth, as it happened – and her father had been killed fighting for the king. Passed for a while from relation to relation, for the last eight years Eleanor had been living with the de Granvilles, and William had become her special friend. However, even at ten years old, Ellie knew that it was for the land she had inherited as well as out of kindness that Sir Thomas had agreed to take her in. Occasionally she overheard conversations between Sir Thomas and Gavin in which her name was mentioned. She was too wise not to realize that her great wealth meant her destiny lay not with William but with Gavin. Elder sons must get the prize of the wife with the worldly goods. Ellie had always thought this very unfair.

But she was not thinking about that now. She had a much more pressing concern, and that was to stop William going out on his horse and missing dinner, since that would annoy Sir Thomas and spoil the whole evening. This was not only for William's sake. If the monks, whom Eleanor loved to tease, had been complaining about her, she wanted Sir Thomas kept sweet.

'Where will you take Sacramenta?' she asked innocently enough as William became silent once more. 'She is so fast, you could probably gallop to the river bridge and back and still get something to eat.'

'Perhaps,' said William. He kicked at a stone. 'Sacramenta can gallop, I know.' He kicked the stone harder, then began what to Ellie was a familiar complaint.

'But the thing is, much as I love Sacramenta, I want a bigger horse, a destrier. I did not look like a flea on a dragon on Sir Percy's black stallion and I could manage him very well. Nor do I look like a pea on Montlouis. Both those horses would be just the thing for me. Gavin got Montlouis when he was my age, I know he did. So why can't I have one of my own?'

Ellie made sympathetic noises but since she hadn't ever had even the meanest, scruffiest pony to call her own, she also felt entitled to ask, 'But isn't a light, speedy horse like Sacramenta just as good for you at the moment?'

'That's not the point,' replied Will. 'Of course she's good. But for tournaments, a courser like Sacramenta is just not, well, you know, well, just not . . .'

'Not quite strong enough?' offered Ellie.

'That's it. That's it precisely. Sacramenta is lovely but she is just not strong enough.'

'I see what you mean,' said Ellie, and went on: 'Maybe you could talk to Sir Thomas about it this evening. He is always in a good mood when we have company. If we were to catch him at the beginning of dinner before he gets talking to the guests . . .'

William considered. 'You mean not go out on Sacramenta and instead put up with having to sit at the same table as Gavin?'

'Well,' said Ellie, 'if you are polite to Gavin your father would see how grown-up you are. And don't forget, you did make Gavin's nose bleed with your fist.'

William brightened. 'So I did. Perhaps that is a good idea. Perhaps it is silly to cause trouble when I want something. Thanks, Ellie.'

Ellie nodded as William grabbed her and, in just the

way she loved, spun her round and beamed. 'Race you back.'

He set off with purpose. He was not going to be beaten again today, and Ellie, picking up her skirts and shaking out her auburn hair, ran happily after him. Everything would be sunny again.

William waited for her as he approached the drawbridge and they galloped over it together, pretending to be horses snorting for their suppers. William told himself that he only played this game for Ellie's sake but the truth was that horses, whether real or imagined, were his passion and he thought about little else. Whenever he ran he imagined himself on a big, bold destrier, a warhorse clattering home from the battlefield. Even at his prayers, William's mind was in a field or a stable filled with horses that were all his own. The boy had studied the horses in the de Granville stud from birth. He knew more about them and loved them more than any of the servants, even Old Nurse of whom, for all his cursing and swearing, William was fonder than he would ever have admitted.

But now, after the excitements of the day, hunger suddenly overtook him. All he could think about was dinner. Taking care not to even glance at the offending horse-trough, he chased Ellie up the stone steps leading to the great hall, hoping against hope that they had missed the lengthy grace so favoured by Sir Thomas's chaplain, that there would be roast lamb, and that Gavin had a horrible headache.

2

Inside the curtain wall of Hartslove Castle much building was taking place and, in the great hall, the noise of hammering and sawing had provided a backdrop to meals since the spring.

The first Sir Thomas de Granville had come over to England with William the Conqueror in 1066 and, for his pains, was one of the lucky Norman nobles given a sizeable estate in the north comprising wild, purple moors, bristling forests and gentle farmland. The forests were full of quarry to be hunted, and a wide, meandering river provided fish for the table. The first Sir Thomas built several strongholds, but his favourite, and the one in which he spent most of his time, overlooked the river at a spot where the deer loved to drink, hence its name – Hartslove – which he added to his own. The Conquest made the de Granvilles a more important family in England than they would ever have been in France, so it did not take the first Sir Thomas long to decide that he liked his English lands far better than the lands he had left behind. But he also, somewhat to his surprise, found that he quite genuinely liked the people. Indeed, he liked them so much that he chose a wife from among them.

After she produced six sons and three daughters, the first Sir Thomas de Granville of Hartslove was content.

In the wars that followed the death of the Conqueror, the de Granvilles kept swapping sides, supporting one ambitious royal brother, then another. They built more castles and actively, and sometimes violently, made their presence felt as they settled into the fabric of England. However, by the time the civil wars ended with the crowning of King Henry II, years of strife had worn the country down.

And the de Granvilles of Hartslove, too. They had spent too much time fighting and not enough time building. The result was that by the time Gavin and William's father (the fifth Sir Thomas) inherited the estates, although the de Granvilles rode high in the king's favour, Hartslove Castle was more a ruin than a stronghold and no longer fit to defend itself.

But all this was changing. Having buried his father and obliged a greedy younger brother to become a bishop in a suitably distant county, our Sir Thomas set about defeating his own enemies and then began the serious work of fortification, using all the latest techniques. Through his bravery in fighting for the king, he had earned a wife with a large dowry, ropes of hair the colour of corn and a soulful expression. However Sir Thomas's military successes were not matched by success in producing children. After a while, and with the king's permission, Sir Thomas, in the manner of the times, had his marriage annulled.

'Sorry, and all that,' he had said to his weeping ex-spouse as he sent her back to her father. 'It's nothing personal.' Sir Thomas did not, however, return the dowry, and this was one of the reasons that the current programme of castle reinforcement was so important. His first wife's relations were threatening to attack, and Sir Thomas was keen that Hartslove should not be susceptible to marauders.

He had better luck with his second wife. She was plain but productive and, despite her bad teeth, Sir Thomas surprised himself by growing quite fond of her. This wife brought with her lands in the north and produced a baby every other year. It was dreadful when they nearly all sickened and died. But at least the two boys had survived and then, Eleanor had been sent to Hartslove to be raised when she was two. After Ellie's arrival, Sir Thomas felt his family needed no further additions, so when the second Lady de Granville's body finally gave up, Sir Thomas did not bother to replace her.

While his domestic life had sometimes been sad and occasionally troublesome, Sir Thomas had never let it interfere with his duty to his monarch or to his own best interest. He was careful not to take sides unnecessarily during King Henry's frequent squabbles with his fractious children. After the death of Henry's oldest and most rebellious son, he constantly reminded his own two boys that if the de Granvilles wished to survive they must play a careful game with the royal heirs who were left. 'Richard is a tricky soul,' he said. 'Easier for us, perhaps, if he carries on living over the sea in Aquitaine and never comes here. As for that John Lackland, well, the king has sent him off to try his luck with Ireland. But the news from there is not good. I doubt it will be a success. Steer a clever course, my sons, steer a clever course.'

Then he turned his attention to his castle. Hartslove was slowly being transformed into an impregnable new fortress with a circular keep and walls so thick that no siege engine would easily destroy them. Sir Thomas liked nothing better than to watch the masons, builders, carpenters and labouring peasants at work, creating something he was sure would last for a thousand years. And even when Sir Thomas was away, either fighting abroad or seeing to his lands even further north, the work did not stop. Constable de Scabious saw to that. The creak of ropes, the shouts of carters bringing stone from the quarries and the sound of timbers being hewn and dragged, were unceasing. De Scabious was a hard taskmaster and Sir Thomas, although listening with apparent concern to complaints, was more than happy that he should be so. It was an added bonus that the constable could be trusted to be reasonably honest since, a few years before, Thomas had caught him dressing up in women's clothes ready to escape from Hartslove after one of the de Granvilles' enemies had momentarily seized control of the castle. The memory still made Sir Thomas smile and de Scabious himself lived in fear that Sir Thomas would reveal his secret.

It was due to de Scabious's efforts that much of the work was now complete. Only the servants' lodgings remained unfinished. Sir Thomas was particularly proud of his plumbing arrangements. Through skilful use of well, reservoir and pipe, water was available to all three storeys of the family's new living quarters.

William and Ellie were just now making use of one of these barrels of water right outside the great hall. They were the last of Sir Thomas's abundant household to arrive at supper that evening and they were in luck. Grace was over. The visiting knights, their retinues and Sir

Thomas's own household already sat at trestles laid out across the room on which plentiful dishes of meat and fish had been placed. The fireplace was empty of logs today since it was too warm for a blaze. The noise was deafening, augmented by the growls and scufflings of countless dogs drooling in anticipation of the feast. Gryffed, William's deerhound, had taken up residence in the huge hearth with a stolen leg of lamb and shook his great brindled head at anybody who came near him.

On the wooden dais at the far end of the hall, Sir Thomas sat with Gavin at his left hand and nobody at his right. Since Lady de Granville had died, at first out of deference to Sir Thomas's evident grief and then just out of habit, the chair had been left empty. The servants soon busied themselves investing the empty chair with some spiritual and ghostly significance. Their story-telling had succeeded so well that now nobody would sit in it even if invited. Sir Thomas, who had no time for this kind of nonsense, had once given the order for the chair to be removed. But the fearful servants bade him politely but firmly to move it himself. Somehow, when it came to the point, Sir Thomas never quite managed it. 'I'm too busy,' he said. The empty chair remained.

Gavin was relieved. Always nervous of a young stepmother producing rival sons to challenge for his father's estates, the empty chair meant security. As long as the chair was there, Gavin could sleep easy. There were women in the castle, of course. Gavin himself had recently begun to notice that some of them were quite pretty. But, apart from Old Nurse – whose proper name both she and they had long forgotten – and Ellie, of course, the women were all servants. Sir Thomas welcomed visitors but he seemed uninterested in finding a third Lady de Granville. Just for good measure, however, whenever Gavin got the opportunity, he repeated the servants' stories, ostensibly scoffing at their credulity, but always making sure to end up with an enigmatic, 'But I do just wonder.' The strategy seemed to work. Half the country now knew about Lady de Granville's chair, and women who might have set their cap at Sir Thomas shivered and set their sights elsewhere.

This evening, Gavin was completely relaxed. The company at Hartslove was preparing to leave on campaign. At such times the shouting always grew wilder and wilder until, on the night before departure, it was insupportable. Departure was, however, a week off, so Sir Thomas could still just about hear what his older son was saying. With only a little exaggeration, Gavin recounted how William had not liked being told that he looked like a flea on a dragon as he was riding Sir Percy's great destrier in at the castle gate and that he had leapt off and punched Gavin on the nose.

'I thought he needed cooling down, sir, so I put him in the horse-trough; you know, the one next to the mounting block,' Gavin was saying, leaning back and enjoying his father's reaction. 'But he came out hot as a roast on the spit. When he stood on the mounting block with water dripping from his ears, I swear smoke was pouring out of his nostrils.'

Sir Thomas threw back his great grey head and laughed. Then, seeing William and Eleanor making their way over the rushes, bid his younger son welcome.

'Horse-trough cold, William?' he asked and, turning to Ellie, wagged his finger in mock reproof. 'Is that you, Eleanor, with a filthy face? What shall we do with you, and who on earth will ever marry you looking like that?'

William's face darkened again, but Ellie slid into her seat and joined in the fun.

Sir Thomas speared half a duck and looked at his mutinous younger son in a contemplative manner. 'Where is your sense of humour, William?' he asked. 'Maybe it is time you went off to learn some manners. Perhaps your uncle the bishop would drum some discipline into you. You may make a worthy knight one day but you will have to learn to control that temper.'

The chaplain, who was sitting near by, felt it appropriate to join in. 'You should ask God's help to conquer your bad habit,' he echoed sententiously as he wiped the grease from his chin with his sleeve and picked up a goblet full of wine.

'Yes, Father, indeed, Father, quite, Father,' said William, not making it exactly clear which 'Father' he was addressing. Then, turning to the chaplain and transforming his face into a picture of innocence, he asked, 'Do you yourself find that helps?'

The chaplain stopped chewing and looked at William with disapproval.

'Oh, do send him away, sir,' said Gavin, pretending to cuff William who was now seated next to him and pulling at a leg of mutton. 'We might as well discover if Will really does have it in him to be a knight.'

'If I go away, can I take a Great Horse with me?' asked William, ignoring both Gavin and the fact that his mouth was full. This was too good an opportunity to miss.

Sir Thomas was not a sentimental man. But he stopped chewing and, looking at his younger son, his mouth full of mutton, his eyes full of pleading, his head full of complaints and his heart full of longings, was suddenly reminded of himself at William's age. Why, in all heaven, shouldn't the boy have a Great Horse? William could ride and ride well. All the grooms said so. Indeed, Keeper John was very complimentary. And the little courser he was so fond of – Sacramenta, was that her name? – anyway, she was nice enough and had taught him a great deal, but William could probably manage something bigger and bolder. Sir Thomas made a decision.

'Hmmm. You want a Great Horse? I agree. A Great Horse it is. But,' and Sir Thomas was suddenly not sentimental at all, 'Great Horses are expensive. Pick your groom carefully. A good groom makes a good horse. And you'll only have one Great Horse until you are at least sixteen. If anything happens to it, you will be back with coursers, even for tournaments. Can't be fairer than that. Now, Percy,' he dismissed William and called to his most loyal friend, the man whose horse had been the unwitting cause of the earlier fracas, 'what's the news from Normandy, and any news from the east?'

'Bad, Thomas, both bad,' replied Sir Percy, stretching his legs. 'They say that King Henry is reconciled to Richard but only through his mother. Sons and fathers! Honestly. And wives and husbands are no better. Queen Eleanor is not exactly loyal, if I dare say so. She likes nothing better than to foment rebellion against Henry. I expect this is why the king has summoned us to Normandy. There must be something brewing. As for the east, I hear rumours of some new Muslim chap – Salad, I think they call him. Something like that, anyway. I tell you, Thomas, there's crusading talk in the air.'

Sir Thomas pushed his plate away. 'Come here next to me, Percy, and tell me all.'

Gavin obediently slid away from Sir Thomas and he,

Eleanor and William formed a little group at the end of the table.

'So,' said Gavin. 'A Great Horse for a small boy.'

'Shut up, Gavin,' said Ellie.

Gavin glanced at her. She need not worry. He did not want to continue squabbling. With more campaigning coming up, he wanted to part on good terms with his only brother. You never knew when your sins might catch up with you. 'Keeper John has been away bringing some young horses back from pasturing the other side of the river,' he said conversationally. 'Shall I come and help pick one out?'

William was not to be wooed so easily. 'No thanks. I'll manage.'

'There is a full brother to Montlouis among them, I think.'

'No thanks.'

'Fine.' Gavin gave up. 'I'll look forward to knocking you off in the jousting lists, then. Father mentioned our uncle the bishop. Perhaps you are really to become a priest.'

With that, Gavin got up to leave. William hardly noticed. Already, in his mind's eye, he was choosing a big bay stallion with a star and white stockings. The bay would carry him to victory in everything they undertook. It would be the best Great Horse in the world.

Eleanor watched him. She was glad for William about the horse. She knew how much he had looked forward to the day he would be released from the clutches of Old Nurse and sent off to begin his adult life. But when she tried to say so, she found it suddenly necessary to go over to the hearth and remove ticks from Gryffed's ears as if her life depended on it.

3

Dawn had broken and the daylight was bright as William left the safety of the castle walls and, accompanied by Hal, a young groom with an open, freckled face and Sir Walter de Strop, the old knight allocated to look after both of Sir Thomas's sons when they rode in the forest, he set off for the stud where his father's horses were kept and managed by Keeper John. William and Hal were the same age, and there was no young groom William trusted more. Sir Walter was an old grouch, but William was not going to complain this morning. Already he was going over in his mind exactly what he would say to Keeper John.

A great household like the de Granvilles' needed all kinds of different horses: sumpter horses for carrying packs, palfreys for ladies and clerics, baggage horses, cart and plough horses and speedy coursers for hunting. But the destriers, or Great Horses, were the pinnacle of equine perfection, used only for war and tournaments. Keeper John was in charge of a huge horse empire both over at the de Granville stud and back in the stables at Hartslove. He was, in many ways, Sir Thomas's most useful and important retainer.

William had spent many hours with Keeper John, as

had Eleanor. After the death of Lady de Granville, it had been mainly to Keeper John that he and Ellie looked for consolation. The children had soon learnt to outwit Old Nurse and vanish when her back was turned. She had never been too concerned. Sir Thomas had told her to 'bring them up, you know, in the appropriate manner,' but the 'appropriate manner' had never been clearly defined. So, although Old Nurse suspected that she was supposed to teach the children to read, when the children told her their father preferred them to ride, she felt this might well be true. It did not seem wise to ask and, anyway, she knew that Keeper John would look after them well enough. If the truth be told, Old Nurse was not really much of a reader herself. She was happiest supervising the kitchens and the laundry, not only because this gave ample excuse for frequent trips to the wine cellar, but also because it showed she was high up in the castle pecking order. Even Constable de Scabious was frightened of her and she liked to keep it that way.

William himself cared nothing for reading and writing. Today, the morning was perfect. Once the sounds of the castle were left behind, he could hear only the gentle chattering of Hal and Sir Walter amid the creaking of leather and the jangling of steel. Occasionally a lark sang its sweet song overhead, and William felt like singing, too. He settled himself deeper into the saddle. They would pass by the new monastery and William decided that he would ask for prayers to be offered up that he would choose his new horse wisely. The opportunity to tell the monks what he was going to do and make the young ones envious was too tempting to miss.

At the edge of the forest, a broad track opened out in

front of him. The middle was pitted with ruts where horses had pulled heavy carts in the wet, but three weeks of dry weather had made the turf at the edges springy and inviting. William's chestnut courser, Sacramenta, took the opportunity to snatch the reins, shy at nothing at all and break into a canter. William laughed for the sheer joy of being alive and urged the mare on.

Choosing her path with delicate agility, Sacramenta sprang forwards and was soon racing like an orange streak through the dappling shadows and out again into the open. Sir Walter and Hal were left far behind, and all William could hear was the hiss of the wind and the muffled thud of Sacramenta's hoofs. She stretched out and William leant forwards to take his weight off her back, enjoying the lashing his face got from her mane. As they pulled up to ford the river, William patted her neck. She twitched her ears as she acknowledged his caress. William ran his hand down her flank. It was only then that his conscience was smitten. From today Sacramenta would take second place to his Great Horse. He looked round to make sure Hal and Sir Walter were nowhere within sight, then lay quickly down on her neck and whispered, 'Dear Sacramenta, I'll always love you, you know.' Guiding her into the water, he let her drink while the others caught up.

The monks had just finished chanting as the party of riders approached. The foundations of the monastery were taking shape but there was as yet no roof. As the haunting strains of their prayer died away, the abbot, a thin man with a lined face, looked at his visitors with anxiety. When he saw the party comprised a boy, a groom and an old man, he visibly relaxed.

'Greetings, my friends,' he said, raising his hands in welcome.

'Greetings, Father,' said William, trying not to sound as excited as he felt. 'Pray for me. I am off to choose a Great Horse. Maybe in time we will go together to the Holy Land. Who knows.'

The abbot smiled at William's lofty tone. 'Indeed, my son.'

'Are you really going on crusade?' Another monk approached, wiping his hands on his white habit. The abbot frowned in disapproval. It was not done for junior monks to break the monastic silence. The young monk stroked Sacramenta's nose, and she gently took hold of his wide sleeve with her teeth.

'Brother Ranulf,' said the abbot, 'Silence.'

Brother Ranulf bit his lip and moved away, gently extricating his habit from Sacramenta's mouth. A small green stain was added to the multitude of others.

'I am to be sent away to learn the codes of chivalry first,' said William, nodding at Brother Ranulf, despite the abbot clicking his tongue. 'And I am to take a Great Horse with me. It will be my first.'

'And it will be very fine, I'm sure,' said the abbot, pushing Ranulf in the direction of the makeshift altar on which Mass was about to be celebrated. He turned back to William. 'Now, young sir, you go about your business and we will go about ours. God bless you and your choice.'

After another hour's riding, during which William listened politely to Sir Walter telling him exactly what to look for in his new mount, they arrived at the extensive wooden buildings and fields of the de Granville stud.

About 200 horses were separated into paddocks. Blacks, bays, iron greys and roans, the de Granville horses came in all colours, shapes and sizes. Mares with foals at foot stood contentedly in the sunshine, idly swishing away the flies with their tails. They showed no interest in the approaching cavalcade. Not so their foals, who took the opportunity to hightail round their enclosure, bucking and squealing in their excitement. Grooms scurried about their duties, carrying water, cleaning or mending saddlery and stacking sacks of grain. Cow hides were hanging in a lean-to shed, waiting to be turned into harness. The clang of the farrier's hammer ricocheted back from the hills and sparks flew from his anvil.

Keeper John waited for his visitors at the door of a huge barn. He was not surprised to see William, whose plaintive longings for a Great Horse were well known. As he watched William's easy way with Sacramenta, how they understood each other's slightest movement, he thought, as he had many times before, that if William was not destined for knighthood, he would make an excellent horse-breaker. That mare had not been easy to train. She was nervous and flighty. A bad foaling had made her no good for future breeding and only useful as a courser, a nifty horse for riding. There were plenty who thought she should be destroyed. But William had managed to make something of her. Sacramenta was now as good a mare as you could find. Even out hunting she would stand and wait when required. Couldn't get much better than that.

'Well, Master William. What brings you out here so early in the day?' Keeper John called cheerfully. 'Don't tell me Sir Thomas has relented and you are come for your Great Horse at last?'

William swung himself out of the saddle, and Sacramenta rubbed her head on his arm to get rid of an itch.

'You will never believe it, but that's about it, Keeper John,' said William, trying to look nonchalant but not succeeding. 'I am to go as a squire to my uncle the bishop and I am to take a Great Horse with me. My father sent me to choose, knowing that with your help, and of course, with Sir Walter's advice, I'd choose well.'

Keeper John whistled. 'Right, then. You'll not be wanting to wait. Give Sacramenta to young Hal and let's see what we can do. Actually, you're in luck. I have brought all the new warhorses inside today. They'll go out again at evening but they get too fat out on that pasture.'

In the cool, sweet-smelling barn, twenty large horses were tethered. Each was being curried by a groom and the scrape of the brush was interspersed with sneezes. It was the most comfortable and comforting sight in the world.

William sighed with pleasure.

'Keeper John, I think I want a bay horse,' he said. 'With good, strong bones and a wise head. Perhaps one broken to saddle last year, which has had some experience already. I need one that I can rely on and I want to be sensible.'

They walked together through the barn, past a dozen tails and rumps. Keeper John came to a halt behind an imposing iron-grey stallion. He said something to the groom, who moved to allow William and Keeper John to approach the horse's head.

'Now,' Keeper John said, 'this young destrier is not the colour you want and he is no beauty. But look at his

23

sensible eyes and deep chest. He is five years old and a decent, courageous horse. We bought him last year from Spain along with three others. I've ridden him myself out hunting. He's a little slow, perhaps, but that is not necessarily a bad thing.'

William inspected the horse but his face all the while said 'no'.

They moved on.

'Now here's a bay. That's the colour you want and he might suit you better,' said John.

Two intelligent ears pricked as the horse turned and shifted in his stall. As large as Gavin's Montlouis, he was a magnificent animal, his summer coat glowing with health. A groom was just finishing brushing out his tail. With four white socks and a white stripe, he was the horse William had been dreaming about.

'Oh, John,' William said. 'What's his name?'

'We call him Dargent,' said the keeper. 'He came in the same lot as the grey. He is three and was quite a handful when he arrived. But he's better now, eh, Peter?' he asked of the groom.

'Yes, sir. He is the best horse we've got.'

'Perhaps he is,' laughed Keeper John. 'Anyway, I have had him out with the hounds and the hawks. I am not saying he was perfect. He's strong and wilful. But his heart is in the right place, even though he has nearly had me off once or twice.'

William's eyes shone. 'Can I try him?'

'Get him ready, Peter,' commanded Keeper John. 'If Master William likes him, he may take him to the castle today.'

It was as William turned to leave the barn that he caught sight of the tops of two ears in the stall at the

24

end. They looked so like Sacramenta's ears that for a moment he thought that Hal must have led her inside to give her some shade.

'What's in there?' he asked.

'Oh,' said Keeper John, 'a fine little courser. Three years old. Actually, he is your Sacramenta's last foal. He had a bad beginning, poor fellow, and is proving difficult to train. Pity he is so small. He was bred to be a Great Horse, but can't quite make the size.'

The bay horse was being backed out of his stall, but something made William hesitate. He patted it, then more out of curiosity than anything else, walked quickly back to see Sacramenta's foal.

The stallion was liver-chestnut, almost red, the unusual colour unbroken except for a small white star between his eyes. His mane and tail, being exactly the same colour as his coat, seemed to flow out from his body, and his slender legs reminded William of a fallow deer. The horse's eyes were luminous and reflective, his muzzle slightly darker than the rest of him. Larger than Sacramenta but considerably smaller than the bay now waiting for William to mount, he looked at the boy without blinking.

'Hello, horse,' said William and, putting out his hand to touch the silken neck, was suddenly lost for words.

4

'Master William, the chestnut is a fine animal, but this is silly,' said Keeper John. 'You came for a Great Horse and you told me you wanted to be sensible. If I send you back with a courser, your father will think that you are a fool and that I have gone mad.'

It was afternoon. Hal and Sir Walter had resigned themselves to a long wait. Sir Walter had given up arguing: William really was an impossible boy.

He had ridden the bay, which had performed splendidly. Out in open country, he had tried some mock battle tactics, held a lance, galloped with an unsheathed sword and even jumped a stream or two. The bay did all that was asked and more, even though William did look – what was the phrase Gavin had used? – a bit like a flea on a dragon. But never mind that. The boy would grow into him. Then just as all seemed settled, William took a notion to ride Sacramenta's foal.

The elegant chestnut horse was brought out. He was clearly far too small for a destrier, but William insisted. The boy mounted, even though Keeper John had warned him that the horse was far from safe. And so it proved. Within moments William was on the floor. Then, of course, he had to remount. And there they had all been for an hour or more while William battled to stay on this red stallion who seemed intent on breaking all the boy's bones. Keeper John and Sir Walter advised remaining in the paddock. But William, puce in the face, was having none of that. So, opening the gate, he had remounted for a fifth or sixth time and set the horse's face towards the horizon.

What happened next, Sir Walter could not quite say. But, when William had urged the horse on, instead of plunging about, he had suddenly begun to move forwards. William asked for a canter. The horse hesitated, then, suddenly, lowered his head and obeyed. For the next twenty minutes or so William and the horse were as one. Seldom had so graceful a sight been seen at the de Granville stud. At the gallop, the horse seemed to float. When William jumped the paddock rails, all the grooms in the place stopped work to look. By the time he pulled the horse up, both Sir Walter and Keeper John, their hearts sinking, could see what had happened. The boy had fallen for a stallion that was, in every way, completely unsuitable.

So here they were, arguing. Both the bay and the chestnut were back in their stalls and William was standing, immovable, in the barn doorway.

'Keeper John, I know. But I'll explain to my father. He'll understand. Have you ridden that horse? You should have felt what I felt. I know I can't explain very clearly why I want it. But I do want it. Please, Keeper John. Have you never felt like this?'

The man sighed. The day should have been an easy one. He cursed the fact that he had brought the chestnut stallion down with the others. If only he had left it out of sight beyond the river it would have been sold before

William ever set eyes on it. Now the day had turned sour. William should know better than anyone that you cannot make a Great Horse out of a courser. What had got into the boy? He had been pestering his father for at least two years for a 'proper destrier like Montlouis' and now he had the opportunity to take one, he would have nothing but Sacramenta's foal.

He looked at William again. 'It won't do, Master William.'

William looked mutinous.

Keeper John tried a different line. 'The likelihood is that he will break down under the great weight of armour and equipment that you will have to carry.'

William shrugged, but his eyes looked disbelieving.

Keeper John pursed his lips. 'You won't change your mind?'

'No.'

'The horse will never be like Montlouis.'

'I don't care.'

'Very well, then.' Keeper John suddenly gave up. 'Hal, go and tell Peter to unsaddle the bay and saddle up the chestnut. Master William will be taking him home.'

He exchanged looks with Sir Walter.

'Tell your father I am not responsible for your choice,' Keeper John said as much to Sir Walter as to William. Then, suddenly softening, he added, 'Just remember, Master William, the bay will be here for another week or two if you should change your mind.'

'I won't.'

Keeper John raised his eyebrows but said nothing more.

In the late afternoon sun, the chestnut glowed like fire as William remounted for the homeward journey. The horse flicked his ears back for a moment, then blew out from his nose. Hal, leading Sacramenta, who seemed singularly uninterested in her offspring, caught his breath. Whatever else, the horse really was beautiful.

Sir Walter, complaining, got on to his grey.

'Well,' he said. 'Let's be off.'

William turned to take a last look at his friend. 'Keeper John,' he called. 'Thank you. I'm sorry to cause you trouble but there is just one more thing.'

John looked up.

'Does this horse have a name?'

'Yes,' the man answered. 'We call that horse Hosanna.'

5

It was late in the evening by the time the small party returned to Hartslove, with Hal leading Sacramenta and William, looking rather battered, astride his new mount. Both William and Hosanna were sweating profusely. Sir Walter, aching with gout, was now seriously worried. On the way back, Hosanna had occasionally behaved perfectly well and occasionally indulged in antics more befitting an unbroken yearling than a three year old with pretensions to being a warhorse. William had come off four times, which made about ten within twelve hours when you counted the falls he had taken earlier in the day. Thankfully, and rather surprisingly, the horse had not run off as William hit the forest floor, but waited to be remounted. Sir Walter had watched, shaking his head. Hal also watched with increasing dismay, his normally smooth forehead creased with doubt. It would be his job to look after this horse. If Hosanna managed to throw William, an experienced rider, what chance did Hal have?

After crossing Hartslove's drawbridge, William was tight-lipped and silent. Hal took Hosanna from him and led the three horses towards their suppers. Hosanna looked about him with interest but followed obediently, occasionally pushing Hal gently forwards with his nose.

Sacramenta swished her tail. Sir Walter, shouting for his own groom, declared that he was exhausted and asked William to get Old Nurse to organize some food to be sent to one of the smaller chambers. He could not face the great hall tonight. William nodded, then felt he should try to make amends.

'It will be all right,' he said to the old man. 'I know it will.'

Sir Walter sighed. 'Well, William,' he said. 'I am not going to pretend that I don't think you have made a mistake. I just hope you will not be too proud to go back for the bay if I turn out to be right. Remember, pride and an unwillingness to admit being wrong are the ruin of many a young knight. Anyway, we shall see, eh? Right now, I must get these boots off and lie down.'

'Thanks, sir, for coming with me.'

'I think you are a young fool. But go on, get your dinner.'

William turned away and went up the steps to where he could hear the noise of a meal in full swing. Splashing his face with water from the barrel, he hoped to escape detailed questioning this evening. By the following morning Hal would have burnished Hosanna until he gleamed, and maybe the horse would behave. If only he would float and jump, as he had eventually done at the stud, William thought his father would understand why William had to have him.

Fortunately for the boy, as he took his place at the top table, Sir Thomas was deep in conversation with Gavin and his friend, Adam Landless, an impoverished young knight who William knew only slightly. Ellie was sitting next to his mother's empty seat and Sir Percy next to her. Percy was telling Ellie some story to which she was only half listening. When she saw William, she at once tried to extricate herself but William shook his head and Ellie obediently remained where she was. Sir Thomas waved his tankard at his younger son. He looked grave.

'Your brother is off tomorrow,' he said. 'The king has asked him to escort Queen Eleanor to Normandy. It seems that despite having lost one son, King Henry is still squabbling with the others. Really, I do wish fathers and sons could manage to get along better. Anyway, never mind that for the moment. How did you do? Where is Sir Walter? Did Keeper John have something suitable?'

'Sir Walter has gone to lie down, sir,' replied William. 'I did come home with a horse. I hope you will like him, Father.'

'I am sure I will. We will see him in the morning before Gavin goes and when Sir Walter is back on his feet. Poor Walter. Getting old, I suppose – like all of us.' With that, Sir Thomas dismissed William with a kindly nod. William wolfed down his supper and vanished to his bed, leaving Ellie, rather puzzled and not a little hurt, to go to hers.

Amid the bustle of the departing knights, Hal brought Hosanna out into the castle courtyard for inspection the following morning. Compared to all the other warhorses stamping their feet and arching their necks in mock male fury, the new stallion did look very small and slight, even to William. Sir Thomas was most surprised but said nothing. Gavin, despite his best intentions, was much less reticent. Standing on one leg as his squire, a dumpy man called Humphrey, buckled on his spurs, he laughed out loud.

'Look, Humphrey!' he chortled. 'Lucky for you that you aren't William's squire. Look what you might have to ride!'

Hal had been up since dawn, currying off the sweat marks and washing Hosanna's mane and tail. The horse had stood patiently, even when Hal tipped water over his rump. The boy visibly winced at Gavin's scorn. He was glad when William came to stand beside him.

'I thought it was a destrier you were after, Will,' Gavin hooted at his brother. 'This horse is a midget.'

'Size isn't everything,' said William coldly.

'Well, it was you who said it was,' Gavin rejoined. 'It was you who said that Sacramenta was too small. What happened? Were the big horses too much for you, or has Keeper John gone blind? I mean to say, Father, this horse is, well, it's a lady's horse, don't you think?'

Sir Thomas was watching William closely.

'Well, sir?' William waited for his father to say something.

Sir Thomas cleared his throat, searching for the right words. 'Let's see how he goes. He is on the small side, it's true. But he is certainly a fine-looking beast. And good work, young Hal,' he said, turning to the groom. 'The horse is a picture. Go and saddle him up.'

Sir Thomas frowned at Gavin. Gavin looked unabashed and, still grinning broadly, turned to talk to his friends. Humphrey, copying his master, began to make jokes with the other squires.

As Hal led Hosanna away, Ellie, who had been hanging back, appeared from under Sir Thomas's arm.

'Why,' she exclaimed, 'the horse looks just like Sacramenta.'

'He's Sacramenta's foal, miss,' said Hal.

'He's beautiful.'

'I know.' Suddenly William was by her side, beaming. 'I knew you would think so, too.'

33

'You could have shown me last night,' said Eleanor plaintively.

'Sorry. I just wanted to get to bed. I thought it could wait until the morning.'

Eleanor smiled, but swallowed hard. The separation was beginning. Soon William would no longer automatically include her in his schemes. 'Of course,' she said and then, to cover her disappointment, she smiled and asked, 'What's his name?'

'Hosanna,' said William, looking at the horse with nervous pride.

'Hosanna,' repeated Eleanor. 'It's a good name.' She patted the horse who, turning his head, fixed her with his great dark eyes. 'Hosanna,' repeated Ellie again, this time addressing the horse. 'Yes, it suits you.'

Gavin's voice suddenly filled the air. 'Fancy him yourself, Ellie?' he shouted as he swung himself on to Montlouis. 'Don't you think that he's nothing but a pony? Now this is what I call a proper horse.' Gavin dug his spurs into Montlouis' side, making him leap forwards. Then he looked for William. 'See you in the jousting field, little brother,' he called. 'We'll have a quick display before we leave. Assuming the horse is up to carrying your weight,' he added, delighted with the laughter his comments provoked from the other knights. Adam Landless winked at William.

'See you out there,' William said sullenly. He ignored Adam. Landless by name and landless by birth, he said to himself. This morning he refused to lose his temper, contenting himself with kicking a loose stone into the gutter as he followed Hal and Hosanna back to the stables.

*

In front of Hartslove Castle was a long, flat plain with a view falling away into the valley. The grass was kept short by grazing sheep who had, this morning, been herded into a pen and were making a terrific noise. There was no fencing, but some rough stands constructed for an audience formed barriers on either side. Running down the middle of the jousting ground was a single removable pole running lengthways. The knights used this for practice sessions, to see if their horses were galloping straight. In rough jousting, when more than one knight was involved, it was removed and the sport was a free-for-all. Sir Thomas tried to discourage this, since so many good horses and knights were injured as a result.

Nevertheless, at Hartslove, tournaments were a common occurrence. Sir Thomas, although no longer taking part himself, was keen enough, provided order was maintained. Gavin was something of an expert, and it pleased Sir Thomas that William looked set to shine in his turn. Riding his own horse out into the field, having swept Ellie up and put her in front of him just as he used to when she was tiny, Sir Thomas was curious rather than alarmed by William's choice of horse. Later, he would summon Keeper John and hear the whole story, but now it was time for William to show just what had made him pick this little stallion above all the others he might have had.

The knights, led by Gavin, were nervous and excited on this, the morning of their departure. Their squires and grooms had packed up huge quantities of armour and equipment, and the great baggage train had already left Hartslove on its way to the coast. Squinting in the sun, Gavin could see it wending its way down the road. The shouts of the baggage masters rose above the baaing of the sheep as they bellowed for the packhorses to pick their feet up and keep moving. His own groom, a willing enough boy named Mark, had gone with the baggage train. Humphrey, who knew all about teasing since his last name was Smallbone, was holding Montlouis. Some of the knights, the adrenalin pumping through their veins, began to conduct a mock tournament with an invisible lance. There was laughter, strong and loud. William rode in among them, almost unnoticed. He was willing Hosanna to be good but sat easily in the saddle, knowing that the horse would explode at any hint of tension.

Hosanna looked the colour of sunset, the silver trappings that Hal had put on him sparkling against the deep red of his coat. William cantered the length of the field and came to a halt in front of his father.

'He's called Hosanna, sir,' he said, as the horse fretted and refused to stand still.

'Hosanna, eh?' said his father. 'Well, Hosanna, show us what you can do.'

The horse stamped a front foot and sneezed. Sir Thomas laughed.

William closed his legs lightly and Hosanna turned to his command.

'Gavin,' called Sir Thomas, suddenly anxious. 'I don't want either of you two boys injured this morning. Don't carry a lance. Just gallop towards each other and show us some manoeuvres.'

'Happy to, sir,' shouted Gavin. 'Right, then, Will. I'll go to the left.'

William reached his appointed slot and the two horses faced each other, about a hundred metres apart.

'When I drop this handkerchief,' bellowed Sir Thomas. 'Ready. Now.'

Montlouis began to canter towards Hosanna. Hosanna stood stock-still. After a few moments, men began to murmur. Ellie gripped Sir Thomas's arm. A ripple of amusement ran through the crowd. They sensed that a spectacle was about to unfold.

'Please,' breathed Will, 'Hosanna, please.' But Hosanna remained resolutely motionless. *I should have worn spurs*, thought Will desperately. *Oh, I should have worn spurs.*

Then, quite suddenly, Hosanna began to move. He moved from walk to gallop in less than the blink of an eye and then he was floating, straight as a die, towards Montlouis. William, his mouth half open, sat back as if carrying a lance at full speed. Hosanna reached the pole at the same time as Montlouis, who lumbered heavily along. With ears flat back, Hosanna gathered himself together until he seemed to reach full height, his head snaking. He performed a tiny, tight quarter-circle, which completely wrong-footed Montlouis, then floated off again to the end of the list. Gavin was left stranded, and the crowd cheered as Hosanna slowed and William cantered back to his father.

'Well, sir?' he asked, his face flushed with excitement and pride as Ellie clapped and shouted her approval.

Sir Thomas nodded. 'I'm impressed,' he said. 'But you are a funny boy, you know, even though I do think you have a bit of an eye for horseflesh.' He touched the star on Hosanna's forehead. The horse rubbed his head appreciatively against Sir Thomas's hand. Sir Thomas laughed. 'This horse has brains as well as beauty,' he said. 'Sir Walter tells me he has given you some fair tumbles. Well, let's see. The horse seems a bit rum, but he has certainly shown some mettle today and I rather like him. I have to say that in all my life I don't think I have seen such a turn of speed, although it seemed to me that it was the horse rather than you deciding when and how to move, eh?'

'Yes, sir,' William said. 'You are certainly right there. I think we have both got a lot to learn.'

Sir Thomas smiled. 'That's about the size of it,' he said. 'Now, I'm going to take this naughty Ellie back to the castle. Maybe I will have to confine her to the women's quarters.' His eyes twinkled as he settled Ellie once again on the front of his saddle. 'The abbot has been complaining about you, my girl. And,' he went on, despite Ellie's squeaking protests, 'I still want to know who will marry you, with your wild ways? I really don't know.' He winked at William and, calling for Sir Walter and Sir Percy, galloped off.

Gavin, on a puffing Montlouis, was waiting for William. 'Well,' he said. 'The Little Horse can certainly gallop and turn.'

'He can jump, too,' said William.

Gavin pulled a face half-derisive, half-appreciative. 'I dare say he can,' he said. 'Anyway, let's hope the Little Horse doesn't collapse when you get your first suit of armour.'

William grinned. 'And let's hope Montlouis doesn't get any slower or he'll only be good for dog meat,' he replied.

Gavin snorted. 'Right.' The boys rode on together as the other knights also made their way back to the castle courtyard. 'Will,' said Gavin looking straight ahead, 'Look after things while I am away. You know, Father and –' there was a short pause as Gavin flushed slightly,

'– well, and Ellie. And if I don't make it back, look after Ellie yourself. Oh yes, and don't forget to have the abbot say Mass every day for my soul.'

Will also kept his eyes looking firmly ahead. 'I promise,' he said.

'Thanks.'

To hide his embarrassment, Gavin turned and shouted to his friends, meeting his brother's eyes momentarily as he did so. Much was said in the glance. Then he punched William on the shoulder. 'Last one at the drawbridge is going to marry Old Nurse,' he yelled, and Montlouis and Hosanna sprang forwards together and thundered back to the stables.

6

For the next two years, William and Hosanna were inseparable. The boy was not sent to his uncle's to train as a squire. There was trouble in the county where the bishop had his power base, and Sir Thomas had to leave to organize the protection of his more distant castles against the still angry relations of his first wife.

With Gavin also away, Hartslove was empty of men except for Constable de Scabious and a few garrison knights who formed a protective guard. Sir Thomas left William at Hartslove for a purpose. Even though the boy was young, he was a de Granville and his presence might act as a deterrent to the family's enemies. Anybody attacking one of Sir Thomas's children would feel the full weight of Sir Thomas's anger. William felt very important as he went round talking to the workmen who were still busy with the renovations. His father had explained how the men were to be paid and when Constable de Scabious handed over the coins, William stood beside him. However by the second Christmas after Gavin's departure, the builders and masons at last finished their work, and the castle fell silent.

For William and Ellie, this was a time of untroubled bliss. The great upheavals in King Henry's huge empire, while involving Gavin, did not trouble them. And they were used to being by themselves. Ellie, to whom William had lent Sacramenta, became almost as proficient on a horse as William. Sir Walter tried to keep some semblance of discipline, teaching William and, by default, Ellie, all he knew. William took many tumbles from Hosanna but every day grew in confidence and skill. The horse was intelligent, willing and a quick learner with a spark of internal fire that made him stand out from the crowd. After his initial suspicions, Sir Walter came to have a healthy respect for the red horse, often marvelling that an animal so slight seemed so tireless.

'There is something about Hosanna,' Sir Walter was wont to say to Hal, 'something that William saw before I did.'

As for Hal, he grew more besotted with the horse each day and spent so much time making him look beautiful that Piers de Scabious laughingly took to using Hosanna's rump as a mirror.

Hosanna himself often seemed to listen as William and Ellie chattered beside him, and developed a particular habit of tucking his head over William's shoulder. He also stood patiently for hours while Ellie braided his mane and whickered gently when William, Ellie or Hal approached, reaching his soft nose into their hands in search of titbits. When William and Ellie stuffed food into their pockets and, accompanied by Hal and the ever patient Sir Walter, went out for the day with hawk and hound, Hosanna and Sacramenta made a striking pair. But while Hosanna was gentle in the stable and increasingly obedient to his rider, when performing his role as Great Horse he carried himself with strength and pride. Nobody made jokes any more about whether he

41

would manage to carry the weight of a fully armoured knight. Hosanna looked as though he could carry anything.

Old Nurse, who occasionally went and told Hosanna that it was his fault the children were grown so unruly, gave up even the pretence of teaching William and Ellie their letters. Indeed, she despaired of teaching the two children, particularly Ellie, anything at all. She spent much of her time sighing and popping into the cellar for a bit of liquid comfort and then she would sit in front of Hosanna, drinking and telling the horse stories about her childhood. Hosanna listened most politely and made Old Nurse smile by licking the salty sweat from the palms of her hands.

By the beginning of the winter of 1187, Sir Thomas returned to find that William was nearly as tall as him, and Hosanna had filled out, his muscles now taut and hard. Both horse and boy looked in the very peak of health, and when Sir Thomas saw the small performance they staged for him, he was delighted.

He also brought good news: Gavin was on his way back and was expected within the week. With the arrival of Sir Thomas, Hartslove slowly came to life again as men-at-arms, hearing of his return, rode into the castle courtyard demanding hospitality.

When Gavin returned, however, although he spent a few happy nights feasting and rejoicing, he was subdued. He had left full of warring zeal but, since he had spent most of his time away in the service of the queen, felt as if he had been treated more as an errand boy and nursemaid. It had been very frustrating. When people asked him to tell them stories of battles, he had to admit that he had barely seen a sword drawn in anger and had done little apart from ferry the royal ladies hither and thither. He was tetchy with William, curt with Ellie and downright unpleasant to Humphrey and Mark, who had much to put up with. He spent the days hunting with his friends, careless of his horses and even of himself. On the days that he took Montlouis out, he galloped at speed and the horse, always willing, came back exhausted. Mark spent many nights shivering in the stables, walking Gavin's horses round, trying to keep them calm.

It was when the first December frosts were biting into the ground that Montlouis fell heavily on an icy path and cut his knees. Gavin ordered Mark to take him home and return with another horse. A good day's sport was in prospect and he needed something swift. Mark was uncertain. Gavin had already used six different horses in as many days. He was not sure what was left in the stable.

'Is Will out on that Little Horse today?' Gavin asked suddenly.

'No, sir,' replied Mark nervously. 'Master William has gone to the stud. But he has left Hosanna since he had him out for a long time yesterday.'

'Bring Hosanna here.'

Mark looked horrified. It was not done to use somebody else's Great Horse. Humphrey, who was growing sick of Gavin's moods, intervened.

'Master Gavin,' he said, 'that horse is so very particularly Master William's horse I . . .'

'Since when does a squire give advice?' Gavin barked. 'Mark, bring Hosanna here. I would lend him Montlouis, so he can lend me that Little Horse of his. Bring Hosanna here now. I order it.'

'Sir.' Mark bowed, looked helplessly at Humphrey and, taking Montlouis' bridle, disappeared back up the road to do as he was bidden.

An hour later he returned, leading Hosanna. He felt bad because he had told Hal, of whom he was rather in awe, a lie.

'About time,' was all Gavin said as he mounted. 'Now then, horse, let's see what you're made of.' Calling to the huntsman, Gavin told him to gather up the hounds ready to move off again.

For the next four hours, Gavin rode Hosanna like a man possessed. The hounds found quickly, and a fox bolted from the forest into the open. The sound of the horn rang out as the running hounds warmed to the scent, singing as they raced forwards. The fox fled, avoiding the open country and making for thickets and ditches. Here stealing out of a spinney, there raking over fields, he kept the hounds pouring after him. Through sprawling hedges and coppice woods he fled, the frost sharp on his pads and the freezing air burning his lungs. The clamour was immense, rising to a climax whenever the hounds scented death.

Gavin's friends followed as best they could, their horses eventually tiring after a run of some ten miles. Adam Landless, who had only one horse to his name, hollered that he could go on no longer and, joined by several others, turned for home. Eventually even Humphrey could no longer keep up with his master and fell behind.

But Gavin spurred Hosanna on, urging the horse to jump whatever came in their way. There was no let up. And just when the hunted fox seemed caught and a rest possible, the wily animal slipped into an unstopped earth, disturbing another fox on whose track the hounds immediately fixed with refreshed enthusiasm. Hosanna barely hesitated. Gavin would not allow it. They were so close to the hounds that the horse had to twist and turn so as not to tread on them. Gavin swore. 'Forwards, forwards!' he yelled and Hosanna, his nostrils flared red with exertion, redoubled his efforts. On and on they went after the new quarry. Gavin felt as if he was flying.

The huntsman's halloo filled the air and the hounds were baying. The second fox began to tire. No earth for him and, at last, as he searched for a place to cross the river, he was bowled over. Hosanna was blowing hard when Gavin's spurs stopped digging into his sides. The huntsman's horse, dripping with sweat, had his nose on the ground.

Gavin leapt off and, seizing the fox from the jaws of the hounds, cried aloud and sounded his horn. An answer came back from some distance away but nobody else appeared.

'Only you and I here, sir. It was a good day,' the huntsman said, dismounting and wiping the sweat out of his eyes. Gavin threw the carcass to the hounds.

'It's early yet,' he said, preparing to remount. 'Let's go on.'

The huntsman looked regretfully at both the horses. 'I don't think so, sir. My horse is done and yours, too, and the other huntsmen are left well behind.'

'Nonsense,' said Gavin. 'If you cannot manage, I'll take the hounds on myself. This horse of William's, so he always boasts, never tires.'

'I really don't think –'

'I don't care what you think,' said Gavin. He remounted and blew his horn. The hounds gathered expectantly round him. 'We're off.'

Within ten minutes, the hounds found again. A fox slipped out of a thicket and plunged across a narrow clearing into another, larger wood. Intoxicated by the new scent, the hounds were soon back in full cry, and Gavin's spurs once again began to punish Hosanna's sides. The horse responded as best he could and raised a weary gallop. Gavin pushed him harder and harder. Through the woods they crashed, blood now pouring from Hosanna's nose. The fox made a huge circuit and eventually, just two miles from Hartslove, the hounds killed him. Gavin slid off Hosanna's back to grab the carcass. He shouted long and hard in his lonely victory. It was not until the horse gave a gasp and fell as if dead at his feet that he at last fell silent.

By the time the flat wooden cart had been sent for and Hosanna manhandled on to it, the daylight was long gone. Hal, white and silent, oversaw the dragging of the horse into a loose box instead of his normal stall. Mark was shaking and in tears. Hosanna bore little resemblance to the proud animal that had left the stable that morning. Hal cursed the fact that he had not been more questioning when Mark had come for the horse. The groom had implied that William's consent had been sought and given. If only I had pressed him harder, Hal berated himself. William would never have sent Hosanna out to Gavin without telling me. Now who was going to tell William when he arrived back from Keeper John's that his horse had been ridden into the ground?

Sir Thomas stamped his way to the stables. He was furious. 'Do what you can,' he said to Hal, after kneeling down to look at Hosanna. 'Spare no expense. I will send white wine from the cellar and see what Old Nurse knows about soothing pastes for the heart. Put cold water cloths on his legs and see if the heat and swelling will go down. Where's the farrier?'

'Here, sir.'

'Take the horse's shoes off. Right. We can do no more for tonight. Come and see me before Master William gets back, Hal. Luckily that won't be until the morning.' He patted Hal on the head, then turned on Mark. 'Stop snivelling, boy. This is a sorry business but tears won't help.' Humphrey led Mark away.

Hal knelt down to help the farrier. 'Light a fire in here, Hal,' said Sir Thomas as he turned to go and find Old Nurse. 'The horse will get very cold, and you, too. And don't despair. The horse may pull through. Hard to tell.' He smiled encouragingly, but as he turned away, his face was grim.

Gavin was standing in front of the hearth in the great hall. His face registered nothing.

'You've killed your brother's horse,' said Sir Thomas. 'I hope you are ashamed.'

Gavin muttered something about Hosanna seeming willing and having a fine day's hunting.

'Don't you dare speak as if you didn't know what I was talking about,' Sir Thomas interrupted, his eyes grey with rage. 'You have thoroughly abused a fine animal. The fact that it is Hosanna, on whom William has worked so hard, adds to your disgrace. Your brother sets a lot of store by that horse and with some justification. By your behaviour today you have proved yourself to be dishonourable. I cannot think of anything worse to say to a knight of my household. Now get out of my sight.'

Gavin raced out of the room and almost flattened Ellie as she came running through the door like a whirlwind. She grabbed his arm.

'What have you done,' she cried. 'Oh Gavin, what have you *done*? Hosanna is lying there like a corpse. His eyes don't even flicker.' Gavin wrenched himself free and pushed past her, running up the stone stairs.

'Now then,' said Sir Thomas, catching Ellie before she could go after him. 'This is a horrible business. We will do what we can, Ellie, but if the worst comes to the worst, we must all be brave for Will's sake. Come, my dear,' he said gently, as Ellie started to cry. 'Come, come. We must not cry but rather pray to the Virgin that Hosanna pulls through. Let's try to be calm and put our trust in the Lord and Old Nurse's paste.' With this, he took the girl into his arms and allowed himself to wipe away an unwanted tear of his own with her hair.

Hosanna did not die in the night but the morning brought no improvement in his condition. When William clattered happily into the courtyard just after breakfast with Sir Walter trailing along behind him, he was met by Hal, his eyes hollow.

Hal said nothing but the horse's name before William was off his courser and into the stables. Hosanna's stall was empty. William looked round wildly.

'He's in the loose box,' said Hal from the doorway.

William rushed to the horse and fell to his knees. 'How did this happen?'

'Master Gavin took him hunting yesterday.'

'What?'

'Master Gavin took him hunting yesterday. He sent Mark for him and I thought you had agreed.'

48

William never took his eyes off Hosanna. 'What were my last words to you before I left for the stud?'

'You said you were giving Hosanna a rest day.'

William knelt in silent agony. He stroked Hosanna's neck. 'Take Sacramenta. Get Keeper John. He may know some old remedies that could help.'

'Yes, sir.' Hal was glad to have something active to do. He had sat all night massaging the horse's legs, changing the cold cloths, whispering and weeping into Hosanna's ears. The horse had never moved, only groaned occasionally as small drops of blood still emerged from his nose. Hal would never have got through the night if Ellie had not sat with him. They had huddled together, the difference in rank forgotten in their misery.

She appeared now and knelt beside William in silence. Eventually she got up, stoked the fire and began to change the cloths herself. The blood seemed to have ceased flowing and it seemed to Ellie that Hosanna's breathing did not rattle quite so much. Whether this was a good or a bad sign, Ellie did not know.

For the next few days Hosanna was motionless. The three people who loved him most took it in turns to nurse him, but everybody tiptoed about with anxious looks on their faces. Keeper John provided a funnel down which they tried to push a thin mash of linseed and ale together with concoctions made by Old Nurse consisting of bread, water and white wine. Most ended up on the straw. Old Nurse knelt down and tried with a small bone spoon. In the weeks leading up to Christmas, the horse remained so gravely ill that Sir Thomas and Sir Walter talked privately about when the end should be called.

Gavin slunk about, eventually preparing to leave on

the pretext of being needed in the north. Christmas was a subdued affair and as soon as it was over, Gavin set off. As he stood waiting to mount Montlouis, Ellie came by dragging a sackful of hay to see if Hosanna could be tempted by the smell. She stopped when she saw Gavin, but was unable to think of anything to say. Gavin stared at her, seemed about to speak, but was put off by Adam Landless and two other young knights who came down the stone steps and into the courtyard. They were leaving with Gavin and were laughing and joshing among themselves, relieved to be getting away from what they thought was a ridiculous fuss over a horse. Looking round to make sure Sir Thomas was not within earshot, they began to tease Ellie.

'Have you not had enough breakfast, Miss Eleanor? Or are you turning into a horse?' they joked in a good-natured enough way. Ellie found herself surrounded.

'Go away,' she cried. 'Go away and leave us in peace.'

'Well really,' said Adam. 'I only ask because you've got straw in your hair. Hey, Gavin. You know your father is always asking who will marry this grubby girl? Isn't it supposed to be you? By the Virgin, you will have your hands full. When you have children, they'll probably be foals!'

Ellie tried to pass but Adam prevented her. 'What's the hurry?' he asked. 'Gavin, aren't you going to say goodbye to your intended, even if she is more worried about that red horse than she will ever be about you?'

The three young men thought it a great jape to pretend to be Hosanna, galloping round and round Ellie, then crashing at her feet as if dying from exhaustion. As they ran, they kicked the sack and Hosanna's hay went everywhere.

Ellie stood helplessly, praying for Gavin to intervene. But he did nothing, just turned away and fiddled with Montlouis' girth, muttering that Ellie was asking for trouble if she went around dragging sacks as if she were a servant. At last his friends got tired of their sport and, with a few parting ribald remarks, went to find their own horses. As soon as they were round the corner, Ellie plunged her hands into her pockets and eventually found what she was looking for.

'Here,' she said to Gavin, her voice shaking with fury and shame. 'Here. I don't want this dog any more. I hate you.'

Gavin stared at her. 'For goodness' sake, Ellie,' he said. 'Hosanna is just an animal. William can always get another.'

'You know nothing.' Ellie tried to keep her voice from sounding shrill and silly. 'And if you really do think that about Hosanna, I have even more reason for wanting nothing to do with you. If you won't take this dog, I'll just throw it into the gutter.'

Gavin laughed uncertainly. 'Do what you like,' he said and turned back to his horse so that Ellie could not see his face.

Ellie hesitated only for a second, then she let the wooden dog fall from her hand into the ruined hay. Without another word, she turned on her heel and ran towards Hosanna's loose box.

Gavin continued to fiddle with his saddle. Then he called loudly for Humphrey and Mark, shouting that he, for one, was off. Mark came running to help Gavin mount, leaving another groom to bring out the packhorses.

'Hurry up!' barked Gavin. Mark held his stirrup. Gavin

put one foot in, hesitated, and looked quickly on to the ground. The wooden dog was lying where Ellie had dropped it. Swearing under his breath, Gavin bent down, picked it up and put it in the pouch that hung from his belt. Then he glared at Mark, mounted Montlouis and, leaving everybody else to catch him up, galloped over the drawbridge and down the hill on to the north road.

On the fifth day after Gavin left, Hosanna opened his eyes and began to shift himself. Ellie, who had been asleep leaning on his flank, woke to find herself sliding into the straw. By the time she realized what had happened, Hosanna had hauled himself into a sitting position, his nose resting on his knees. The cloths had fallen off revealing legs made fat with swellings. Nevertheless, the horse was nibbling at the straw.

'William,' whispered Ellie, then jumped up and ran out. 'Get Master William,' she ordered a passing groom. 'Quick.' Hal was asleep in the corner and she kicked him until he woke up.

By the time William, who was snatching a few hours' sleep on the rushes in the great hall, arrived, Hosanna was chewing on a handful of peas. His eyes were dull and his coat matted, but he was halfway up. By evening he was standing and by the following week he was well enough to walk slowly and stiffly to the river. He stood for hours as the cold running water did its healing work, his head resting on William's shoulder. Little by little, his appetite returned. But all was not well. The horse remained very lame. As the days turned into weeks and the weeks into months, William was obliged to fetch Dargent, the big bay he had rejected from Keeper John's and accept that his beloved Hosanna was finished as a warhorse before he had even begun. After Hosanna had first stood up, William, Ellie and Hal had got into the habit of starting most sentences with, 'When Hosanna is better,' but after a while, this began to sound increasingly hollow, even to them. Summer came, and Hosanna was turned out among the buttercups. Every day, his legs were massaged and he followed William about. But, although he was no longer in acute pain, his once lustrous eyes were sad and his proud demeanour had vanished. It seemed impossible that he would ever again be ridden out of a walk.

Sir Thomas followed the horse's progress carefully and sympathetically. He knew as well as anybody how long a horse's wind and legs could take to heal. But, as the leaves began to turn, he was also obliged to think long and hard. Serious political matters were now afoot. The previous year there had been a terrible defeat for the Christian armies at Hattin in the Holy Land. The Christian king of Jerusalem had been taken prisoner and the prized relic of the True Cross stolen and defaced by the Muslims. Even Jerusalem, which the Christians had taken nearly a hundred years before, was back in Saracen hands. News was patchy. Nevertheless, Sir Thomas could see which way the wind was blowing. King Henry, who talked a good deal about a crusade, but was reluctant to go, could not last forever. Richard was his heir and it was said that he thought of nothing but a holy war. William was already fifteen. He was not a child any more. If the call to crusade came, it would come for him, too. A decision about Hosanna must be taken now. If the horse was never going to be up to the rigours of travel and battle, William's bond with him must be broken. The horse must go elsewhere, and William must not be allowed to visit him or hanker after him. Sir Thomas sighed as he reluctantly made up his mind. It was time to call a halt.

To help soften the blow, Sir Thomas told Ellie before he told William that if Hosanna was not improved by the following spring, he must be taken to the monks. The monks needed horses, too, and their lives were gentle and slow. Abbot Hugh was a good man. Hosanna would be well looked after. William cried out briefly when his father issued instructions and the stricken boy allowed Eleanor to take his arm as Sir Thomas warned against going to see the horse ever again once he had been left in his new home. 'It could only upset both you and Hosanna,' he said.

William, his anguish etched all over his face, tried to accept his father's decision as he knew a knight should, for he knew his father was right. He watched hopelessly as Hosanna's condition did not materially improve.

Thus it was that when the primroses appeared in the wood, with Eleanor riding Sacramenta and leading Dargent, William walked with Hosanna to the abbey. Every step of the journey was agony. William tried to choose the easiest route, the one which would cause Hosanna's legs the least effort, but every time the horse stumbled, the boy's heart seemed to crack. At the gatehouse he said a long and anguished goodbye, during which, although he tried to curb them, bitter tears were shed. Then, as Hosanna blew gently down his neck, William made himself pass the reins of his precious horse over to the monks and watched him walk stiffly away. Ellie did not interfere. She had said her goodbye earlier. This was William's time. As Hosanna was led towards the newly finished gatehouse, she touched William on the shoulder. He mounted Dargent and they turned to leave. As William looked back one last time, his voice suddenly rang out.

'His name, Abbot Hugh, I never told you his name.'

The abbot stopped. 'No more you did, my son,' he replied. 'What is it?'

'My horse.' It was almost a whisper and the abbot had to strain to catch it. 'My horse,' William said, his voice fighting to be steady, 'My horse is called Hosanna.'

7

The abbey, spring 1189

Abbot Hugh waited until William was out of sight before summoning one of the lay grooms to take Hosanna to the stables. He could not afford to give his monks yet another excuse for inattention during prayers by being absent any longer.

The abbot was a kindly man, but he had more on his mind than a sick horse. The abbey, supposedly a place of retreat from the world, was becoming so popular that sometimes the abbot felt that it was as busy and noisy as the castle. Last week, the singing of the divine office had been shockingly ragged, and Brother Ranulf had stared into space for almost the whole of Mass. Hosanna would simply add to the distractions. Nevertheless, the sight of William saying goodbye would have moved a heart harder than the abbot's.

'Take care of this horse,' he said to the groom. 'He comes from Hartslove. Sir Thomas may cease being quite so generous and protective of us if the horse comes to harm. And anyway, the animal has been ill-used and deserves good treatment.' After that, he forgot all about him, at any rate for the moment.

The groom took Hosanna towards the stables and found him a place among the motley collection of horses the abbey had already accumulated. Hosanna walked slowly and with obvious discomfort. When he reached the barn door he stopped and neighed, just once.

'That's right. Say goodbye to your friends,' said the groom, kindly enough. 'Come on now, let's be having you inside.' He twitched the rope. Obediently, Hosanna lowered his head and allowed himself to be led into the dark.

It was weeks later that Brother Ranulf, while meditating in the cloister, saw Hosanna for the first time. The horse was carrying fresh rushes for the refectory floor in panniers. A small boy with a sharp stick was in charge. Hosanna's mane and tail were long and unkempt, his coat greasy and his eyes dull. Nevertheless he caught Brother Ranulf's eye.

The monk looked round quickly to see if anybody was watching, then left the cloister and approached the boy.

'I haven't seen this horse before,' he said conversationally.

'No, Brother,' replied the boy. 'He's a broken-down warhorse. Not much good now, but maybe a great knight rode him once. He's a bit small, though. Perhaps it was a small knight. Perhaps he went on crusade. I dunno myself. But he came from the castle so he must have seen the king, mustn't he?'

Ranulf smiled. 'Very likely,' he said and stroked Hosanna's neck. The horse sighed, and Ranulf busied himself pulling knots from the tangled mane so that the boy should not see how agitated the word 'crusade' had made him.

It was universally known that Ranulf was having

doubts about his vocation. He had been just fifteen when Hugh had passed through the village in which Ranulf was born. Hugh had been travelling around, searching for a site on which to found a new monastery. Ranulf had been inspired by Hugh's sincerity in seeking to follow the teachings of Christ and had told his parents that he felt called by God to join him. Ranulf's parents were delighted. Having a monk in the family was excellent insurance for the afterlife. So, filled with enthusiasm and with his parents' blessing ringing in his ears, Ranulf had left his home, joined Hugh as he wandered from place to place, and then, once they had the support of Sir Thomas de Granville, had thrown his back into the building of a new house of prayer at Hartslove.

Before long, Hugh, now elected abbot, began to think of Ranulf as a possible successor. He might be young, but the other monks looked up to him. Whenever there was hardship, Ranulf embraced it. He was first in the abbey church in the morning and last to leave at night. In his enthusiasm, not only had Ranulf made his vows as a monk but had also become a priest, able to say Mass and hear confessions. He was, Abbot Hugh often mused, almost too perfect.

But, ten years after leaving home, lying in the dormitory waiting for the duty monk to come and touch his feet to wake him for matins, Ranulf had been seized by doubts. Each day prayers were said for the protection of the holy places in Palestine, the places particularly associated with Christ's suffering and death, and each day these prayers unsettled him more. Jerusalem, in Christian hands since its capture by the first crusaders, was by no means safe. Prayer was all very well. But surely, as a strong young man, he should be holding a sword not a candle? Christ's enemies would not succumb through prayer alone. Whenever knights or squires rode past the monastery, Brother Ranulf could not resist speaking to them.

Shortly after William had passed through, on his way to choose Hosanna, Ranulf's feelings grew so strong that he went to Hugh and begged to be allowed to be relieved of his vows and go to seek a position as a squire. Hugh refused. 'I see a great spiritual future for you, my son,' he said. 'This crusading talk is just the devil testing you.'

Prior Peter, the abbot's second in command, a dark man with a sharp tongue, had been less flattering. 'Don't be so arrogant and worldly,' he sniffed at Ranulf. Peter knew only too well how one monk leaving could provoke a torrent and that the abbey would suffer as a result. But it was no good. Ranulf soon became so consumed with the desire to leave and ride to the Holy Land that his attention during devotions continually wandered. Peter, who now made it his business to observe Ranulf very carefully, found fresh cause for complaint with each passing day.

After Ranulf met Hosanna, he became even more unsettled. As the abbey bell tolled endlessly through the hot summer, he shuffled ungraciously through the round of prayers, silent work and reading, his mind increasingly filled only with thoughts of the horse: *had Hosanna really been to the Holy Land as the boy suggested? What must it be like, to fight in Christ's service riding the sort of horse Hosanna must once have been?*

Despite several warnings from the abbot, Ranulf took to visiting the stables just before bed. He petted Hosanna. Sometimes, standing in the straw, he even sang parts of the psalter to him. The stallion seemed to like this and pricked up his ears. Ranulf watched him doing his work in the fields or at the mill. The horse was docile but with the docility born of pain.

Eventually, Ranulf began to slip out of the abbey church early or not turn up at all to perform the great round of communal prayer that was the primary duty of every Benedictine monk. He always had an excuse – a manuscript from the library was missing, the cresset lamps had run out of oil, he had to visit the *necessarium* unexpectedly, on account of eating rotten vegetables – and didn't want to disturb everybody by coming in late. But his excuses always sounded lame, even to him, and eventually Peter lost his temper. He wanted Hugh to punish this deliberate flouting of authority, not just because Ranulf appeared to put talking to a horse before praising the Lord but also because the monk told such flagrant lies.

'Patience, patience,' said the abbot, although privately he thought the prior had a point.

Matters came to a head through the sins of Brother Andrew, the almoner. He was a large greedy man, and to punish him for his excesses Hugh had put him in charge of handing out food, drink and medicines to the poor. Ranulf had once laughed when Andrew's misericord (the wooden blocks against which the monks leaned in church) had snapped off, leaving Andrew sprawling on the floor. Ever since then Brother Andrew had been looking to do Ranulf a disservice.

Since he had been given the job, as far as the abbot knew, Andrew had turned into a good almoner. There were few complaints. What the abbot did not know, however, was that Andrew was running a small racket. The poor who sought alms certainly received them. But they were also promised 'untold eternal rewards' if they gave some of the alms back to Andrew in order, as he told them, to secure 'a better chance of seeing Christ face to face'. The returned food, wine and medicines he kept in a locked box under a sack and either used them himself or, increasingly, sold them to passing traders.

'I'm stocktaking,' he would shout if anybody called for him while he was eating soft bread or putting on the tip of his tongue a tiny drop of expensive and unusual oil that a passing earl had brought back from the Holy Land. 'I suppose I am stocktaking in a sort of way,' he said gleefully to himself as he smoothed his red face with some of the balm he had got into the habit of stealing from the infirmary. 'And, anyway, at least I always say the office, unlike some others.'

It was when Brother Luke, the infirmarian, asked Andrew if he knew who might be stealing his jars of ointment that Andrew saw his chance. It was common knowledge that Ranulf was potty about some sick horse. Very likely, Andrew said to Luke, shaking his head with mock sorrow, very likely Ranulf was stealing from the infirmary to take to the stables. Luke went at once to the prior who went straight to the abbot.

'Brother Ranulf and that horse are a menace,' Peter said. 'I know the de Granvilles are our benefactors, but ever since that broken-down nag arrived, Brother Ranulf's behaviour has been even more contrary than usual. Now it seems Ranulf is taking medicine from the infirmary in an effort to turn the horse back into a great stallion on which, I suppose, he reckons to ride away and kill the infidel. In my view we should get rid of the animal. It is useless, anyway, for anything requiring a quicker pace than a walk. Have you seen it carrying the laundry? It has difficulty even doing that. And if the horse goes,

61

maybe Ranulf will get over his ridiculous obsession with crusading.'

'You mean we should destroy the horse? Kill it?' asked the abbot, frowning.

'Well, yes,' said Peter, shifting a little uncomfortably. 'I mean it is distracting Ranulf and it's not going to get any better,' he finished rather defensively.

The abbot sighed.

'The de Granvilles would be very upset. Before we do anything, I had better talk to Ranulf and see the horse for myself.' The prior could hardly disagree.

Hugh made his way to the stables but did not find Hosanna in good spirits. The horse was lying as if his legs were too weary to carry him. His great dark eyes were misty and he had not touched the sweet hay that lay well within reach.

The abbot stooped to stroke his neck. Hosanna moved his head slightly. The abbot knelt down and looked at him properly. Although the horse was clearly tired and dispirited, it still felt wrong to take his life just because a monk was using him as an excuse to behave dishonestly. Hugh looked at Hosanna for several minutes. 'We'll wait a week,' he said at last to nobody in particular. 'We'll wait a week.' Then he found Ranulf and asked about the missing medicines. Ranulf denied all knowledge but after the monk's recent open disobedience, Hugh could not be sure that he was not lying. He did not tell Ranulf that Hosanna's days, in all probability, were numbered.

Over the next week the atmosphere in the abbey was tense. Word got around about the irregularities in the infirmary and the almonery. Monks were found whispering in corners. Fingers were pointed. The lay servants gossiped in the village. All the while Hosanna lay or stood, eating little, unaware that his fate hung in the balance.

When seven days were past, Hugh made his decision. The stealing continued. The horse would have to go. Feeling despondent, he nevertheless sent word that the village butcher should come the following morning and take Hosanna away for slaughter. Hugh made the announcement at the daily meeting in the chapter house. As he expected, Ranulf went white, absented himself from prayers all afternoon and even went without dinner. Eventually, just before the singing of the last office of the day, the abbot made his way to the stables.

Ranulf was sitting with the horse's head in his lap.

'My son,' said Hugh, picking his way carefully over the drainage ditch that ran down the middle of the stalls. 'My son, what I have decided is best for all. The horse will never regain his proper strength and you can see from the way he holds himself that he is in almost continuous pain. If he is relieved of his suffering, you will no longer be tempted to lie and steal. Your mind will once more return to God, where it belongs. Pray for strength, my son. Pray for strength.'

Ranulf carefully laid Hosanna's head on the straw then leapt up, breaking the stable's afternoon stillness.

'Strength!' he cried. 'I have plenty of strength. Look at me, Father Abbot. I am as strong as an ox. Too strong for this monkish life. This horse has brought me a message, I am sure of it. The message is that I am to go to the Holy Land and fight to protect Christ's tomb and the other holy places from the Saracen infidels. I feel it, Father Abbot, I feel it as strongly as you feel your vocation is here.'

'My son, you are in error,' said the abbot gently. 'I have watched you from the moment you felt called to do the work of the Lord through prayer. Nothing has changed since we last spoke about this matter. This horse has no message. You are deluding yourself. Your vocation is here. Your voice raised in prayer is an inspiration to your brothers. God sends few like you. You must believe me when I say that here is where you are needed. The healthy spiritual life of a monastery depends on men of passion and strength. I watched you as you helped to build this monastery. I have seen you struggle with the demons that beset all those who renounce the world. It is these demons, not God, who are now trying to trick you into seeking personal acclaim in the field of war. Our great Father Benedict tells us that the way to heaven lies in abandoning any such quests for individual glory and merging with the collective glory of a community dedicated to prayer. Ranulf, my dear son, your crusade is here. There are souls to be won at home, even within this monastery. The Lord needs you to remain with me.'

'I don't see it.' Ranulf shook his head, not wanting to hear the abbot's words. 'I don't see it. I beg you. You may destroy this horse, but you cannot destroy my wish to leave.'

Hugh glanced at the horse, then looked again at the despairing monk.

'Do you remember your promise of obedience?'

'Yes.'

'Then go now,' said Hugh, 'And pray for this horse and yourself. If you believe He can, God will send an answer.'

'Will Hosanna still be here when I get back?'

'Yes.'

Ranulf abruptly left the stables, his head throbbing. He scarcely noticed where he put his feet but found himself in front of the crucifix in the abbey church. His fellow monks were filing in for compline, and the sun was just beginning to set. As Ranulf took his place and the plainchant began, he prayed furiously. 'Please Lord, if You have any mercy at all, save the horse Hosanna.'

The monks' voices began reciting the psalm, the verse and response rising first from one side, then the other until they filled the high vaulted chapel. '*Benedicamus Domino. Deo gratias.*' The familiarity soothed Ranulf. He shut his eyes and gave himself up to the music. 'Lord,' he found himself praying, although not sure where the words were coming from, 'Lord, if You save Hosanna and give him back his strength, I will remain true to You here. I will follow the abbot's instructions. If You can really cure the suffering of this horse, I promise not to use him as a means of escape. I even promise that, if it seems appropriate, I will give Hosanna back into Your service through returning him to Hartslove and to the boy who brought him here.'

'*In te, Domine, speravi.*'

'I ask this through your own suffering. Amen.'

Hugh did not attend compline. He remained leaning on the wooden partition, looking at Hosanna but not really seeing him. Out of habit, however, the words of the divine office came almost unbidden to his lips and he found himself praying over the horse. The stables were completely still, as still, the abbot found himself thinking, as the stable at Bethlehem. He prayed on, closing his eyes. As his prayer drew to an end and he opened his eyes again, the luminous rays of the setting sun were pouring through a crack in the stable wall. Though the rest of the animals were shrouded in shadow, Hosanna, still lying down, was lit up, a beam of extraordinary intensity catching the top of his head in such a way as to produce the effect of a halo. Hugh caught his breath. He felt he was seeing a vision. Without thinking, he dropped to his knees.

He was not the only one. Hidden behind the grain sacks was Brother Andrew. Hours earlier he had crept into the stable out of curiosity to take a look at the horse that so obsessed Ranulf and whose destruction, he believed, was now imminent. He had been on the point of creeping out when Ranulf had appeared. Andrew hid himself to wait until the coast was clear and then was trapped again by the abbot. Now he was paralysed with fear. This great shaft of light seemed to have deliberately picked out this horse whose fate Andrew's dishonesty was helping to seal. It was uncanny and disturbing. Andrew assured himself that he was not superstitious. But a voice in his head told him some things were obvious. To have produced such an effect, this horse must have magical powers. The light was unearthly. And surely only God could produce a halo? Unknown to the abbot, in his dark corner Andrew also fell on his knees and began to pray.

Once the light vanished, Hugh, treating the horse with new deference, got up and left. It now became possible for Andrew to climb out of his hiding place and approach Hosanna directly. He tentatively touched the horse's ears. They were warm. Andrew drew a small piece of apple out of his pocket. Hosanna took it and licked Andrew's hand, which the sweat of fear had made as salty as Old Nurse's. Suddenly Andrew found himself again on his knees.

'Lord,' he said, 'I think You have sent me a sign. Help me to give up my dishonest ways. Sin led to Your death on the cross. I see this clearly. Now this animal is also to die for my sins. What can I do to make amends?'

It did not take Andrew long to figure out the answer. From another of his voluminous pockets he brought out the flagon of oil brought from the Holy Land and rubbed the horse's legs with it. Then, finding a bowl, he made a small mash out of the peas and bread that were ready for the horses' suppers. He knelt down again. Hosanna sniffed carefully at the mash, pushed it about with his top lip, then began to eat. He ate until there was none left and, as Andrew slipped quietly back to the almonery, shook himself and got to his feet.

The following day, despite Peter raising his eyes to heaven with exasperation, Hugh sent the butcher away empty-handed. He never saw the evening vision repeated, but over the next few weeks he observed a remarkable change in the horse's condition.

'It's a miracle,' he told Ranulf.

'It's my prayers,' said Ranulf.

Andrew said nothing at all. For only he knew the truth: that he too had taken to visiting Hosanna each day and was using not only his ill-gotten gains to try to restore the horse's strength, but also, deep into the night, was looking up every reference to animal healing in the abbey library. Over the next two months, Hosanna found himself treated with all the oils, herbs, medicines and pastes Andrew had accumulated in his treasure chest. The monk spent hours making special mashes and rubbing the horse's ruined legs as tenderly as if they had been those of a baby.

The results of these ministrations were startling. By harvest time, Hosanna's coat began to shine again. Ranulf combed out his mane and tail until one day when he came out of the stable, far from being a horse a child could hold, one of the younger grooms found he had his hands full. At the time of the first frost, even Ranulf had to lead Hosanna out not in a rope halter but a bridle. He walked with the horse hour after hour to build up his strength. Eventually walking was not enough and, despite Prior Peter's disapproval, Ranulf got on and rode him. Hosanna was quiet at first. But as his spirits rose, he became a warhorse once more and one afternoon, to Ranulf's surprise, on hearing a hunting horn, Hosanna suddenly tossed his head and broke into his floating gallop. As Ranulf clung to the saddle, unable to stop and enjoying an unaccustomed sensation of fear, he knew that the horse could no longer be kept at the abbey. It was time for him to return to his proper life at Hartslove. He rubbed Hosanna down and covered him in a blanket to keep out the autumn chill, then steeled himself to tell Hugh that the horse was no longer suitable for the monks to use. The abbot, who had taken as close an interest in Ranulf's state of mind as Hosanna's physical health, put his hand on the monk's shoulder and nodded.

'Can you take him yourself?' he asked. 'Think hard, my son, before you answer.'

Ranulf looked Hugh straight in the eye. 'I have made promises to God about my life and this horse,' he said. 'And I believe that now, with your support and God's help, I can keep them both. I would like to go to the

Holy Land. But maybe my time will come in a different way. I am prepared to wait and pray.'

Hugh nodded. The following morning, as he blessed Hosanna in preparation for his journey home, he told Ranulf to enjoy the ride and to take his time walking back. Then he went into the abbey church to give thanks for the mysterious ways that are God's.

Ranulf arrived at Hartslove without incident. To put off the moment when he had to hand Hosanna over, he rode past the castle and found himself on the jousting field. William, who had dealt with the pain of parting from Hosanna by physically tiring himself into oblivion every day, was exercising Dargent. Both he and the bay were exhausted. William's face was thinner and harder than it had been in the spring and while he praised his horse, it was obvious that his heart was not in it.

This afternoon, he was particularly despondent. The year had been an eventful one. King Henry was dead and Richard crowned. The call for crusade was now loud and insistent. It could not be long before, along with his father, he would be leaving for the Holy Land. He was tussling with his conscience, for, despite his father's orders, he wanted desperately to go to the monastery to see Hosanna, or at least hear news of him, before leaving. He sighed, patted Dargent and turned for home. As he did so, something caught his eye. At first William thought the light was playing tricks. He shut his eyes and opened them again. He stopped breathing. This could not be a trick. There, at the edge of the field, a monk and a gleaming red horse were watching him. Willliam sat stock-still in the saddle for a moment, then he threw himself off Dargent and began to run.

'Hosanna?' he hardly dared believe it. 'Hosanna?'

Hosanna whinnied and, stretching out his head, broke into a trot. He did not stop until he had his nose once more in William's hands. Ranulf found it difficult to speak at first. He dismounted and could only smile and nod as William, scanning Hosanna's legs and neck and exclaiming all the while, asked him a million questions about the horse. Half listening to Ranulf and half shouting for anyone passing to fetch Ellie, fetch Hal, fetch everybody at Hartslove, William was almost beside himself.

Eventually Ranulf found the right words. 'There's been a miracle,' he said simply. 'Hosanna has been cured by a miracle.'

'I don't know what to say to you,' cried William.

'Say nothing. Just thank the Lord,' said Ranulf. 'Now I must go. But if you go to the Holy Land with Hosanna, please remember that a small part of me goes with you.' He paused to pat Hosanna's neck then turned away.

'I must give you something.' William didn't know where to look, at his horse or at the monk, nor how he would stop himself exploding with joy. He would happily have given Ranulf the whole castle.

'Hosanna has already given me something,' said Ranulf, turning back for a moment and stretching out his hand. Hosanna lowered his head so that Ranulf could touch the star between the horse's eyes. Ranulf smiled. 'If you know Hosanna, I think you will know what I mean.'

William looked steadily at the monk. 'Yes,' he said solemnly. Then his whole face softened and he began to look more like the boy Ranulf had seen riding to choose his first warhorse four years earlier. 'I know exactly.'

The two of them briefly clasped hands before Ranulf began his long walk back to the abbey. The monk's new strength and resolve were strong, but he did not want to test them to the extreme by watching William vault on to Hosanna and, yelling with excitement, ride him back over the castle drawbridge.

Miracles certainly come in unexpected forms, Ranulf thought to himself as he followed the path through the wood, the leaves crunching beneath his feet. When he reached the river he sat on the bank enjoying his temporary freedom from abbey routine. Then, hearing the bell toll in the distance, he got up and, with only the smallest hint of reluctance, went obediently to answer its call.

8

Holy Land, late summer 1187

Far away in the Holy Land, the muezzin's call bidding Muslims to prayer was being answered by a dark man and a boy, both richly dressed and mounted on high-stepping Arab horses. They were far from alone, travelling in the middle of a huge army raising a tempest of sand as it made its way through the scrubby grass and hills towards Jerusalem. In front and to either side, a tight-knit formation of fierce Saracen lords, known as emirs, formed a shield round the pair. Great columns of cavalry followed, and behind them archers, infantry and assorted foot soldiers plodded wearily, some wearing cloths covering their faces to try and keep the dust out of their eyes. Bare-chested mechanics were helping to push along heavily laden wagons, while camels spat and mules groaned, occasionally kicking in temper against their traces.

The great cavalcade stretched as far as the eye could see, the clouds surrounding them so thick that occasionally the whole column disappeared into a dirty yellow mist. But nothing could dull the noise of small boys yelling abuse at pack animals reluctant to move forwards in the heat of the day, men roaring ribald jokes or warnings of potholes ready to catch out the unwary, horses snorting, and fifty or so carts creaking under the weight of pieces of siege machinery carefully dismantled for the journey. Occasionally flashes of blue or red silk were visible or a spiked helmet glinted through the haze. But everything was soon swallowed up again. At intervals during the day, however, the chaotic clattering and yelling were reduced to a more orderly murmur as the cry '*Allah akbar*' stopped the great caravan and everybody prepared themselves for prayer.

Now, in the late summer afternoon sun, as the muezzin's cry rose once more, the boy dismounted and moved to grasp the bridle of the horse of the older man.

'Ah, Kamil ad-Din,' said the man with a smile, 'you are always there, before I even have time to look.'

The boy flushed with pleasure. 'Your Majesty, the great Sultan Saladin,' he said, 'is like a father to me. I do for you only what I would do for my own father, whose goodness Allah is now rewarding in heaven.'

'Always a good answer, too,' said the older man, and Kamil was momentarily confused, not knowing if this was a compliment or a rebuke.

After prayers, Kamil helped Saladin to remount and, as the dust and noise began to rise once again, took his customary place by the sultan's side, his horse's nose at the sultan's knee, his hand on his sword, ready to defend his master should the need arise.

On the whole Saladin was pleased with Kamil's punctilious observance of duty. In the five years since the boy, an orphan, had been brought to his notice by Baha ad-Din, a councillor whose advice Saladin particularly valued, Kamil had proven himself an asset to the sultan's court. Under instruction from both Saladin and Baha ad-Din, Kamil assiduously studied the Koran, paying scrupulous attention to the Hadith, the sayings attributed to the Prophet Mohammed to which Saladin attached particular importance. But it was not only the boy's piety that was noteworthy. Just months before this march to Jerusalem, in the heat of the momentous battle at Hattin during which the Christians had been routed, Kamil had proven himself a valuable soldier, too. Fearlessly plunging into the thick of the enemy, recklessly pulling out of his silk tunic the arrows that threatened to overcome him, it was young Kamil who had cut his way through to the golden tent that housed the great Christian icon, part of the wooden cross on which their God was supposed to have been crucified. That had been the deciding factor of the battle. Once the cross, being the supreme object of their faith, had been seized, the Christians cast themselves down in despair. Even the cries of King Guy of Jerusalem, as he liked to style himself, and all the Christian princes could not rally them. A Saracen victory had been assured.

Kamil, like a young lion with its prey, had dragged the cross through the ranks of the dead and dying, glorifying Allah's name in a victory salute. He had brought it to Saladin and prostrated himself. Certainly, that day the boy had earned his place at the sultan's right hand and justified the time spent on his education.

It was only afterwards that Saladin allowed a small worry to creep into his mind. Had Kamil shown too much bloodlust to be pleasing to Allah? In the aftermath of the battle, when the Christian nobility had been brought to Saladin for disposal as he saw fit, Kamil had protested as Saladin offered King Guy iced water. When Saladin had himself risen to behead Prince Arnak of Karak, Kamil seemed disappointed not to be asked to do the job instead. Kamil had also argued against sparing the life of the Countess of Tiberias and her children on the grounds that they did not deserve to live. Even the wholesale slaughter of the knights most hated by Saladin and his armies, those grand men who called themselves Templars and Hospitallers, had not seemed to appease the boy. Saladin was happy to shed blood if the time and cause were right, but he was also mindful that strength and mercy went together.

When Saladin had reminded Kamil of this, and repeated the words of the Koran that backed up his belief, Kamil had been silent, and not with the silence of agreement – he remained dissatisfied. Indeed, the fact that King Guy was to go to prison rather than be beheaded seemed to inflame him further.

Now the sultan glanced at Kamil as he rode along, proud and upright, as fine a figure of Saracen youth as could be found in the east. Maybe he was worrying unnecessarily. The memory of Kamil's real father, cut down in front of his son's nine-year-old eyes by a Christian raiding party while, unarmed, he tried to protect his wife and child, would still be strong. With Allah's help, that memory must, in time, become less sharp and Kamil would mellow.

Meanwhile, Saladin needed to decide how best to take Jerusalem. The eternal city must be delivered into Saracen hands and the great al-Aqsa mosque and the Dome of the Rock, from whence Mohammed had risen into heaven, restored to the one true faith. As the walls of Jerusalem became visible on the horizon, Saladin put thoughts of Kamil out of his mind and, calling Baha ad-Din, began to plan the assault.

Jerusalem was strongly defended and the Christians inside it were determined to hold out against their enemies. For five days Saladin rode round looking for a weak point. Eventually, moving the whole army to the north, he ordered the reconstruction of the siege engines and, as soon as they were ready, commanded that the battering of the defences should begin. For days and nights the Saracens hurled at and over the walls anything that came to hand – from great stones and burning bushes, to snakes, dead animals and 'Greek fire', a deadly mixture of sulphur, naphtha and quicklime that could not be quenched with water.

Finally, the Christians, trapped without hope of reinforcements, worn down and increasingly fearful of the sappers busy undermining the walls, sent out messengers outlining terms of surrender. But Saladin, although he wished to save his own men from unnecessary death, could not accept them. When the Christians had taken Jerusalem nearly a hundred years earlier, they had indulged in an orgy of slaughter, killing Muslims of every age and sex. If Saladin allowed the Christians to surrender and simply walk out of Jerusalem untouched, he would face a mutiny. The prevailing mood in his army was that blood must be shed for blood.

Saladin searched for a compromise. The cycle of bloodshed troubled him. Eventually he declared that if the Christians would not set fire to the city and also pay a ransom for every man, woman and child, they could leave unharmed. Kamil was disgusted. Nevertheless, the sultan prevailed and by morning all was set. Over the course of the next day, the Christians began to file out through the gates and trudge slowly over the hills, down through the valley and on to the plain, heading westwards for the sea.

Kamil was furious. He did not join in the great rejoicing when the Saracens at last gained access and dislodged the Christian cross from the great cupola of the Dome of the Rock. He was not there to hear Saladin order the cleansing of the holy places and the redecoration of the al-Aqsa mosque with gold and precious stones. Instead, from outside the city walls, he watched the sorry procession of Christians march into the hills. Then, in the evening, dressed only in an unremarkable cotton tunic, Kamil slipped on to his horse. He rode slowly and quietly as he followed the stragglers. They never noticed him behind them.

As he rode, Kamil felt no pity, even for the struggling women. Five years before, he had had a real family. His father, who had been born a few miles to the north of Saladin's own birthplace of Tikrit in Mesopotamia, had been an emir and a true follower of the Koran. He had married Kamil's mother while in Saladin's service in Egypt and brought her home to where he farmed productive land by the Tigris river. Wheat and barley, grapes, figs and melons grew in abundance and, as a child, Kamil had run about barefoot with his cousins, spoilt by what seemed to him multitudes of smiling aunts and uncles. The Christians had been a thorn in the side of the Muslims ever since Kamil could remember, and his father was often away on military business for the sultan. But the boy had felt no personal threat. In those days, he could not hate Christians – not in the same way that he hated spiders, for instance – for he had never seen one. Moreover, when his father left to fight them, he had his mother to himself and, as a treat, when lessons were over, she would pile food on to his dish and let him sit on her lap while she told him stories.

All that changed the winter of his ninth birthday. His father had come home and told his mother to pack up some things. Saladin wanted his trusted emirs constantly by his side so that they could debate finer theological points long into the night. In the spring, so Kamil's father said, they were all to travel to Saladin's camp in Syria. It was time, too, so his uncles and aunts told him, for Kamil to meet the man he would serve as an adult. Kamil quite agreed. Since he was so young, his mother was coming, too. What could be better?

Kamil had been so excited that he had been allowed to ride instead of going in the covered wagon with all their possessions and his mother. His father put him in charge of the six horses he was taking as a present for the sultan. Three were mares with foals, and their antics suited Kamil's mood. He could still remember what colour they were.

The journey had been delightful. They crossed into Syria and were just thirty miles short of their final destination. The place at which they stopped had remained vivid in Kamil's mind's eye. It had been very much in the open, sheltered only by a few trees, but the foals had been tired, and Kamil, too. His father very reluctantly made a fire. Looking back, Kamil supposed he had hoped to reach the safety of Saladin's camp before sleeping.

It all seemed to happen very quickly. As his father was packing up the next morning, a group of Christian knights had approached, their eyes on the horses. They had been smiling at first. One, who had some Arabic, offered Kamil a ride. Kamil had smiled back, despite being alarmed by the large, tear-shaped birthmark running down the side of the knight's face. His father gestured for Kamil to come to his side. The knight was affronted. He stopped smiling and instead demanded that Kamil's father hand over the six spare horses. Kamil's father refused, and angry words were exchanged. Then, one of the Muslim horse-boys spat. It was all the excuse the knights needed. They drew their swords and, before Kamil could move, they charged. One cut his father down, his unarmed father, his peace-loving father; a man only trying to hold on to what was his. His blood poured into the dust as he fell, enfolding Kamil in his arms in a desperate effort to save his son.

By the time the men had finished, only Kamil and his mother were left alive. She had been in the wagon and had hidden under some bolts of cloth. When the shouting died away, she emerged and a terrible sight greeted her. Her husband was lying face down, her son trapped underneath him. Both were motionless. The horse-boys had been run through a dozen times. All the animals were gone. She began to scream, and it was only then that Kamil moved. He pulled himself out and crawled towards her. When his mother eventually looked up, she saw her son, covered in his father's blood, holding out his arms.

Kamil remembered all these things. The memories stabbed at him. The wailings of the Christian mothers reminded him of how his own mother had rocked him until both of them could wail no more. When he saw the women carrying pathetic-looking bundles, he saw his own mother gathering what she could out of the wagon before they began to walk. The women limping reminded him how, still far from their farm, Kamil's mother had succumbed to fever and, despite Kamil's prayers, died, leaving Kamil alone. He had never made it back home. Picked up by a caravan of traders, he had asked them to take him back into Syria and to Saladin. They had obliged, and when Kamil told his story to the sultan, he had been embraced and given a home at the sultan's side. He had been in Saladin's household ever since, and had, as part of his education, been taught Norman French, the Christian's language. The boy was quick, and Saladin thought he might make a good spy.

But now, as the sultan took Jerusalem and achieved his heart's desire, Kamil was intent on his own business. In the years since his father's death, he had never stopped looking for the knight with the tear-shaped mark and now, riding among these refugee Christians, he felt certain he would find him. As darkness fell, many of the women simply collapsed on to the ground, dazed with the loss of the Holy City. Others, mindful of the evening chill, busied themselves trying to construct makeshift tents.

Kamil let his horse loose and moved about with ease among the desolate people, his dagger hidden in the folds of his clothes. His presence went unremarked and dogs that barked at him were told to be quiet. Patiently, he worked his way around the groups.

In the end, he found what he was looking for quite easily. By the light of the moon, the knight was kneeling down with his wife and son to pray. Kamil, who had waited for this moment and rehearsed it a million times, felt his breath leave his body. His hands trembled and a black roar filled his head. At last. There he was, the man who had deprived Kamil of his family, kneeling to pray with his own. The boy gazed, with fascinated horror, at the Christian mirror image of what might have been himself. He, too, could now be praying with his mother and father. Instead, he prayed with a sultan who did not approve of revenge.

The knight and his lady knelt side by side with their son behind them. They had moved slightly apart from the rest of their group and were almost hidden from public view by blankets they had draped over two stunted trees. They would be easy pickings. But now that the moment had come, Kamil found himself unable to move fast. He wanted to stare and stare at his father's murderer. In his dreams, this was not the feeling he had. In his dreams, he simply imagined different ways of killing him. Yet, faced with the man in the flesh, killing him did not seem enough. It seemed too easy. Kamil wanted to grab the knight by the throat and tell him how his mother had suffered, tell him what it was like to wake sweating every night, imagining that he was drowning in his father's blood and suffocating under his father's mangled body. He wanted to make him suffer.

The family bent their heads and intoned the Our Father. Soon they would be finished. Kamil rubbed his thumb on the sharp edge of his dagger, hoping that the pain would bring him to his senses. He must act quickly or the moment would be lost. The feel of his own blood dripping on to his fingers steadied him as he looked at the father. Yet, in the end, something made him slip forwards and cut the boy's throat instead. It was done so quickly and deftly that the victim made no sound. Then Kamil was gone.

As he found his horse, leapt on and galloped away, his breathing was shallow, almost a gasp, and his mind was filled with confusion. Never had he thought that he could meet his father's killer and leave him alive. Nor had he imagined that the knight might have a son. Now that the knight was no longer in front of him, Kamil could not work out why he had acted as he did. Certainly, the father would suffer, for his son's murder would be an appalling mystery and that, surely, would haunt him all the days of his life. But to leave the knight alive? Kamil pulled his horse up short. Maybe killing the son had been a mistake. He dropped his reins and put hands over his face, raking his fingers down over his cheeks. What would his own father have said about his son's evening's work? Kamil did not know. He tried to pray. He tried to think. But he could do neither. In the end, he drove his heels into his horse's side and, tears streaming down his face, threw his dagger into a ditch.

Saladin was waiting for him when he returned to Jerusalem. The sultan had been worried. Kamil was not usually absent from his side for so long, particularly at important moments. The retaking of the holy places was not a time suddenly to go missing. Baha ad-Din had looked uncomfortable when Saladin had asked if he knew where the boy was, and Saladin had a feeling of foreboding. As soon as Kamil entered his tent, the sultan saw a new look in his ward's eye that he did not like.

'We have missed you, Kamil,' he said, keeping his voice very even – dangerously even, thought Baha ad-Din, who was standing behind the sultan and knew his master well. 'What has kept you away from prayers this evening, the first in the city that has caused us so much blood and heartache?'

Kamil was silent. Saladin's voice became quieter still. 'Kamil, I asked you a question.'

Baha ad-Din coughed. 'You must answer,' he said. 'Remember the debt of gratitude you owe to the sultan, who has looked to your welfare all these years.'

Kamil threw up his head, fighting to clear his mind. 'I have been taking revenge,' he said. 'In the name of Allah, of His Prophet, of the sultan and my father, I have exacted a due penalty for the cruelty done to me by the infidel race that has polluted our land.'

Saladin looked at him for some moments, considering. 'I will not ask the details,' he said eventually, much to the relief of Baha ad-Din. 'But do not leave me again without permission.'

Kamil shrugged and opened his mouth to speak. Saladin raised his hand. 'I said, I will not ask for the details,' he repeated in a tone that brooked no argument. 'But I say this. Do not take revenge in my name, or in the name of Allah or Mohammed, His Prophet. The revenge you have taken is your personal responsibility. You must live with it. And die with it. The correct interpretation of the Koran is that you cannot worship Allah in blood. Whatever the provocation, try to remember this always.'

Kamil bowed but his face was expressionless, and when Saladin invited him to pray he mouthed the words, wishing they could reach his heart.

For the next two years, Kamil kept his own counsel and Saladin watched him. In matters of war, Kamil did not put a foot wrong, but when Saladin tried to speak to him about personal matters, he found the boy's eyes troubled and his lips silent. Baha ad-Din cautioned the sultan about pressing Kamil to talk, saying that he must be allowed to find his own path to peace of mind. The sultan listened to the old man, nodded, and reluctantly, with many misgivings, decided to bide his time.

9

Hartslove, 1190

As the sultan waited and watched Kamil, William, now reunited with Hosanna and happier than ever, was sitting in the great hall with his father, Ellie, Old Nurse and the castle servants. A huge fire was burning, and the women were settled round it, sewing on to surcoats the crosses that all crusaders wore. William, Gavin and their father would be taking the surcoats with them to the Holy Land when the de Granvilles accompanied King Richard there in July. The hall still smelt of Christmas and the rushes on the floor were thick with berries fallen from the holly branches hung on the walls. Will threw bones for his wolfhound as he watched Old Nurse pack up rough pilgrims' tunics, 'For when you get to Jerusalem and want to pray rather than fight'. He was paying little attention to Sir Thomas, who was trying to speak to him very seriously about the burden, both spiritual and physical, that accepting the sign of the cross entailed.

Ellie's face was mutinous, for women, as Sir Thomas made very clear, were not included. She stabbed her needle viciously into the silk of Gavin's surcoat, then cursed as she pricked her finger, and red droplets formed fuzzy patterns in the daffodil yellow. But William, although apparently only half-listening, thrilled to his father's words. The cross meant that the pope had given his blessing to fight God's war, and that if they died, which William was sure they wouldn't, they would all go to heaven.

'We are pilgrim soldiers now,' said Sir Thomas. 'We are not just going to fight, but to pray as well. This is a very special calling. We will take our staffs as well as our swords – Ellie, don't say "God's teeth", it is not ladylike – now where was I? Oh yes. When the killing is over, we will all do penance for it and then we will see what every decent Christian longs to see: the True Cross, Calvary, the Via Dolorosa – all the places associated with Christ's life and death.' He sniffed. 'Your mother and I talked of going once, when we were old. Now I am old and she's dead. That's my cross, I suppose.' Then he smiled. 'Well, at least I have my two sons, and, you, of course, Ellie dear. I shall be going to the Holy City in the company of my sons. What more could a man ask, eh?'

But William was no longer listening at all. He was bored with watching the sewing and, now that his father had finished, wanted to get back out to the stables. Since Hosanna's return from the monastery, Sir Thomas and Sir Walter set tasks to test his fitness. The horse was back performing neat turns at speed, graceful reverses and thundering charges as if he had never been ill. The horse could jump, too, and, much to Sir Thomas's alarm, he and William could be seen flying over hedges, ditches and walls. Nothing, it seemed, was beyond them. Now William wanted to check with Hal that the new saddlery he had ordered was going to be ready on time.

The following day, instead of hunting, he suggested to Ellie that they should go over to the monastery and take the monks a present. Ellie jumped at the chance. William had given her Sacramenta to ride and although she could not boast quite the skill that William exhibited, she could certainly ride better than many of the Hartslove knights. The two of them chattered away as they set off down the familiar route, with Sir Walter lagging behind, leading a packhorse laden with hares, cheese and wine. Ellie had made a ring by twisting together some of the hairs of Hosanna's tail. Although she knew the abbot would disapprove, she thought she would give it to Brother Ranulf for his part in Hosanna's recovery.

'Please don't talk all the time about the crusade, Will,' she begged as they hugged their cloaks round them and the horses' breath billowed in the freezing air. 'I know it is wrong to say so, but I'm sick of it already. You all put on your special "crusade faces" and then smile at me in that annoying way men have, as if you all have some special knowledge which, because I am a girl, I am too stupid to understand.'

'What nonsense, we don't put on any such faces,' said William, asking Hosanna to go from walk to canter and back to walk. 'Look, Ellie, this is just the manoeuvre Father says is important in a battle.'

Ellie gave up.

'I'll race you,' she said.

'Aren't you a bit old for that, Ellie. I mean –' and here William did his favourite trick of imitating Constable de Scabious's thin treble – 'You're going to be fifteen this year and should be more ladylike!'

Ellie pulled Sacramenta up, snapped off a hazel switch from the side of the track and smacked William smartly across the back with it.

'You see!' exclaimed William, 'Women can't be trusted.' And with that, he urged Hosanna into a gallop, rejoicing to hear the horse's hoofs crunching through the frozen grass and puddles.

Ellie leant forwards and Sacramenta rose to the challenge. 'Go on, girl, get your nose in front,' Ellie muttered. 'That would teach him.'

But of course Sacramenta didn't, for fast as she was, she was no match for Hosanna, and Ellie had to be content with galloping up to the monastery gatehouse some way behind, holding her breath with slight anxiety as Sacramenta slithered over the ice that had formed in sheets where the going was rough.

William was already off Hosanna, and a bevy of monks, happily disobeying the abbot, were crowded round him. Ellie pulled up and looked back. Sir Walter was nowhere to be seen. Brother Andrew, who, despite the rigours of monastic life, would soon rival Old Nurse for size, immediately broke away from the rest.

'Miss Ellie,' he said. 'I have something to show you.'

He disappeared for a moment, then returned with two huge books. Ellie dismounted. Brother Andrew was always showing her books. They were filled with pictures and words, which the monk told her were about medicines. Although nervous that William would think she was becoming girlish, Ellie was fascinated. She was envious of the ease with which Brother Andrew talked about great doctors of the past, how he could tell her what Aristotle thought and how he believed that so many diseases would eventually be cured. It was heady stuff, and when Brother Andrew returned, Ellie gazed at the words he showed her and longed to be able to read them herself. Today, he was telling her that they had just finished copying a book by the famous doctor Galen.

'This is something really special,' he said. 'Galen lived

not so long after Christ, and what he didn't know about medicine is hardly worth knowing. I've made some very special ointments, with his teaching in mind. Ointments that can cure anything. This book has taken us about two years to copy, but it is the future, Miss Eleanor, mark my words.'

'Is that a list of the medicines?' asked Ellie, peering at the words and pointing to the margin.

'Dear me, no!' said Brother Andrew. 'Those are the names of flowers and herbs, and here, look, are the pictures to match. And there is a decorated letter E. E is what your name begins with. '

'Is it?' said Ellie, smiling at Brother Andrew's enthusiasm. 'It's beautiful. Did Doctor Galen paint the letters, too?'

'No, no,' said Brother Andrew. 'One of our monks thought to illustrate our copy himself. He's clever with his brush. Now, I have another book to show you. This one is most unusual.'

He put down his book of medicines and, with difficulty, because the parchment was stiff, opened another. This one was full of pictures of animals. One, in particular, caught Ellie's eye.

'What on earth is that?' she exclaimed. She could tell the animal must be large because the man painted next door to it was tiny.

Brother Andrew was very excited. 'Yes, exactly,' he said. 'What *is* that? Well, Miss Eleanor, it is what they call an "elephant". Look, here is one of those Es again. E for elephant. This chronicle is written by a man whose name we don't know. He claims that this creature, whose name appears to be Abu L'Abbas, was given to the great emperor Charlemagne by Caliph Harun of Egypt – that's a country on the edge of the world. It can carry anything, and can charge as fast as a horse. If you notice, its back legs seem to have knees that bend like ours. Isn't that curious? If we turn the page we'll see – ah! Here comes Sir Walter. I'd better put this book down inside. We don't want it ruined.'

Sir Walter, looking rather peeved, came to a halt beside Ellie. She tried not to look cross, but could not help gazing longingly after Brother Andrew. What extraordinary things you could learn from books and what a surprise Brother Andrew would have if, one day, when he was showing Ellie a page, she could read the words to him instead of him reading them to her. Ellie's heart gave a small flutter. But now she turned to Sir Walter.

'The horse bearing gifts is rather slower than the others,' said the old knight pointedly.

Ellie gave a small, apologetic grimace. Sir Walter patted her shoulder.

'Never mind,' he said. 'Crusading fever is infectious.'

Ellie frowned and began to unpack the panniers. 'You are very patient with us, Sir Walter,' she said politely.

But Sir Walter was busy greeting the almoner, who was back, rubbing his chubby red hands together.

'Here,' said Ellie. 'No books, Brother Andrew, but six hares and six flagons of wine to go with them. Sir Thomas sends his regards and hopes you are remembering to pray for him daily.'

'As if we would forget,' said Brother Andrew, his eyes lighting up in anticipation of a feast.

At that moment, Brother Ranulf and the abbot appeared and Brother Andrew tried to look more monkishly gloomy. He winked at Ellie as she handed over the last of the presents. She smiled, then left him and walked over to where the abbot was standing, his hands clasped tightly together in front of him. Even though he was always very pleasant to her, she could almost feel his disapproval that a woman should come near his monks. She kept her eyes modestly down as she approached, congratulated him on the quality of the new bell recently installed, and then, on the pretext of asking Brother Ranulf something about Hosanna, managed to prise him from the abbot's side for just enough time shyly to hand over the ring.

'It's for you, from Hosanna,' she explained. 'Before he goes to the Holy Land.'

Brother Ranulf was thrilled. 'Thank you,' he said, quickly slipping the ring into his pocket. 'I shall treasure that.'

'Now,' called Sir Walter, who could feel the cold seeping into his bones. 'It is time we were off. Come on, you two.'

Ellie and William said their goodbyes and mounted their horses. Three monks helped Sir Walter on to his.

'Pray for us!' shouted William as the packhorse, freed from his burdens, set off at a resolute trot.

'God bless you all,' called the abbot. 'May you get safely to Jerusalem,' and he sighed.

As Hosanna disappeared into the trees, the almoner approached the abbot. 'You know, Father Abbot,' he said conversationally, 'that girl, Miss Eleanor, is really very bright. Would it not be the Lord's work to teach her to read? When she marries and has children, she could teach them in their turn.'

The abbot was too old and wise to snap. He let a moment elapse, then said, 'Now, Brother Andrew. Look into your heart and tell me whether women are anything but trouble or not.'

Brother Andrew looked into his heart and found that the abbot was right. 'Yes,' he said. 'I suppose they are.'

The abbot nodded. 'Then that is your answer,' he said and called his monks to order.

'Oh well,' said Brother Andrew to himself as he helped the abbot chivvy the monks into the cloister, 'thank God I was born a man.'

When William and Ellie got back to Hartslove, the groom removing the panniers found that they were not quite empty. At the bottom of one was a tiny, sealed box wrapped in parchment. Puzzled, Ellie unwrapped it. On the parchment was a beautifully decorated letter E, and on the box some other letters and words.

'What is it?' asked William, leaning over her shoulder.

'It is special ointment,' said Ellie, taking a wild guess. 'It's for horses – or people – close to death.'

William looked disbelieving.

'How do you know?' he asked. 'You can't read.'

'I can, a bit,' retorted Ellie. Then she added loftily, 'Ointments like these are something only women know about. I am afraid you wouldn't understand.' With that, she opened her eyes very wide and gave him an innocent smile.

William stared hard at Ellie, but she said nothing more, just raised her eyebrows and sailed up the steps leading to the great hall. For one, tiny moment, a fleeting memory of his mother passed through the boy's mind.

Hartslove was alive with people assembling for the crusade. When William followed Ellie into the hall, it was to find that Gavin had returned from Richard's court.

91

After leaving Hartslove in disgrace just over two years earlier, he had conducted himself with commendable bravery in the north before being summoned to help the new king stamp his own authority on a kingdom he knew almost nothing about. Gavin was thinner and his face had lost its boyish roundness. He looked like a knight a father could be proud of.

Sir Thomas stood with Old Nurse to watch how the two brothers greeted each other.

'Gavin!' said William, taken by surprise.

'William,' said Gavin.

They shook hands. Then Gavin, shuffling slightly, asked to see Hosanna, and the brothers went down to the stables together. Sir Thomas did not know what was said, but an hour later, both boys had come into the great hall looking a little easier in each other's company. Sir Thomas and Old Nurse exchanged glances. William was growing up, too.

At dinner that evening, Sir Thomas was again struck by his sons' deep voices, and marvelled at how Ellie, despite occasional lapses, was blossoming from a grubby urchin into a young lady.

'I have almost reached my allotted years on this earth,' he said to Sir Percy as he chewed on a leg of lamb and watched Ellie push back her hair to reveal a face of distinctive if rather unconventional beauty.

Sir Percy nodded. 'Very likely, Thomas,' he said. 'But you can be proud of your children. And that Ellie, well, orphaned she may have been, but she has lacked for nothing.'

Sir Thomas sighed. At the back of his mind was a growing certainty that he would not return from the crusade.

'I shan't see my grandchildren,' he confided as dinner drew to an end. 'But in time, Ellie will make a fine mother for them.'

After dinner, Gavin found himself standing in front of the fire with Ellie at his feet. She was playing with William's dog. Like his father, he too had been struck by her unconscious new elegance and, even though he had given her few thoughts when he was away, now he found himself suddenly in awe of her. In all his travels, no other girl had this effect on him. As a boy, Gavin had always enjoyed teasing Ellie. But now, an experienced knight, he found himself unable to think of anything appropriate to say. As Ellie murmured to the dog, Gavin felt increasingly frustrated.

He coughed. Ellie took no notice. Gavin gave up. Even though he had been back only a short time, he could already see that she was going to find it harder than William to forgive his treatment of Hosanna. He stared down, not knowing how to put matters right between them. For half an hour, he watched her play with the dog and did nothing at all. Eventually Ellie got up and, after exchanging a joke with William, slipped away.

Gavin gave one of the logs a vicious kick and sent sparks up the chimney. *Women!* he thought to himself, and decided to avoid Ellie if he could.

Ellie herself walked slowly up the steps to the women's quarters. After a frantic whispered chat with Will during dinner, she was quite prepared to forgive Gavin over Hosanna and even forget about her humiliation on the morning Gavin had left for the north. But the truth was she found herself unable to treat him as she once had. Something was different. Instead of Gavin just being an ordinary part of Hartslove life, she found his presence disturbing. This was nothing to do with Hosanna. Ellie did not know what it *was* to do with. As Old Nurse brushed her hair and helped her with her nightgown, she was irritable. She needed somebody to talk to, and somehow William did not seem the right person. She briefly contemplated confiding in Old Nurse but dismissed the thought. Old Nurse was far too old to understand the feelings of a girl of fourteen. 'When she was fourteen, if, indeed, she ever was,' Ellie muttered to herself, 'it must have been in the Dark Ages.'

The following morning, running back from the stables, Ellie ran slap bang into Gavin in the courtyard.

'Heavens, Ellie!' he said as they disentangled themselves. Ellie said nothing, but, to her acute embarrassment and fury, she knew she was blushing.

Gavin stood aside to let her pass, but, as she did so, his resolution to avoid contact with her melted away. He touched her arm.

'Ellie,' he said awkwardly, not quite knowing what words were going to emerge, but feeling that anything was better than nothing. 'I know you would prefer to end up with Will rather than me, but I'm the oldest, so we'll both have to make the best of it – unless a Saracen arrow meets its target, that is.'

Ellie could not think of a suitable reply, so they stared at each other for a bit before Gavin stepped aside and was gone. After that Ellie was in even more of a muddle than before.

There were several things still to do before the de Granvilles left for the Holy Land. William, now nearly seventeen, must be made a knight – 'dubbed to knighthood' as he rather pompously told Hal. Then, Gavin and Ellie must be betrothed. They should really be married and a son conceived before Gavin went on crusade, but Sir Thomas somehow could not bear to think of Ellie facing all that with only Old Nurse for company.

'The de Granville inheritance is in God's hands,' he told himself. 'God looks after crusaders and will surely keep at least one of my boys safe.'

It was decided that William's dubbing to knighthood would take place in July at Vezelay in France, where the king had arranged for all the crusaders to meet, so that all the nobles from his huge empire, together with the king of France and his men, could set off together. This meant that Ellie could not witness it and she was very disappointed. However, being dubbed to knighthood by the king himself was too powerful an opportunity to pass by just to please a girl.

Gavin and Ellie's betrothal was a simple affair conducted at Hartslove with the minimum of fuss. Everybody found it uncomfortable. Old Nurse cried, and Gavin and Ellie gabbled their responses. After the traditional feasting and dancing were over, William found himself filled with unfamiliar emotions that would not let him sleep. Until he saw them standing side by side and making their promises, he had never really thought seriously about Gavin and Ellie having a future together. It had always been a bit of a joke. Now that it was no longer a joke, William found he did not like it. After they all retired to bed, he tossed and turned, the picture of Ellie dancing with Gavin playing itself over and over in his mind. He found himself oddly affronted that she had not looked more unhappy. It was a relief, the next morning, to put Ellie out of his mind as he surveyed the crusading preparations.

Saddlers, fodder merchants, silversmiths, armourers,

wheelwrights, farriers and all manner of men and women were beginning to arrive and encamp in the castle courtyard. Over the next few weeks, so many turned up that they spilled outside the great curtain wall, creating a small, busy village. Carts, both open and closed, together with horses of all shapes, sizes, colours and temperaments jostled for room in the Hartslove stables or were tethered in the jousting field. Grooms and squires set up home in pavilions and tents, attracting the usual crowd of entertainers, petty thieves and those seeing the chance to make a quick shilling by offering every kind of service from laundry to tooth-pulling. The parish priest began performing a quick trade in confessions.

The clang of hammer on anvil echoed for miles. When the weather allowed, the noise was of trees being felled as thousands upon thousands of arrows were made and tipped with steel. Crossbows were strung together for the arbalesters. Swords, spears, lances, mallets and clubs formed huge ugly piles, and horse equipment, from saddles, stirrups and bits for bridles, to ropes and silken blankets, was strewn over every inch of the spring grass. Everybody got under everybody else's feet until by the beginning of Lent, Sir Thomas, losing patience, ordered the knights to take their squires and grooms and go hunting or hawking. Whatever they did, he begged them to be sure to stay out all day.

'Take advantage of the spring sunshine,' he told them. 'Help yourself to Hartslove's game. Just GET OUT!'

In all this commotion Old Nurse was in her element. She organized thousands of meals, boxed the ears of those she found asleep in places she did not think fit and made sure, in her own way, that life for Sir Thomas, despite the takeover of his home, was still tolerable. The knights, old, young, ragged and rich, teased her, to which she responded with a steely glare and a fine line in oaths. She knew all about knights. They were supposed to be full of honour and glory. Why, then, did so many things mysteriously disappear whenever they came to call, and who was it who had peed all over Sir Thomas's finest tapestry, made, with many tears and mistakes, by his late wife? Bad enough that King Richard was charging an extra tax, the Saladin tithe, to pay for this war. She was not having the knights make a pauper of Sir Thomas as well as the monstrous Saladin whom Old Nurse cursed daily in her prayers. She never seemed to sleep, and many was the knight who had his own rest disturbed by Old Nurse feeling under his blanket to see if anything had been secreted away. Nobody was too grand not to feel the sharp end of her tongue or her prying fingers. Sir Thomas, in a quiet moment, made sure that she knew of his appreciation by handing over a pouch of gold and one of his late wife's rings. He said nothing, but they understood each other very well.

Finally, in mid May, just when it seemed Hartslove could stand no more, and the crusading rhetoric from the priests was at its most fanciful, Sir Thomas declared that they were off.

The night before departure, Ellie and William snatched a moment or two together. Ellie, try as she did to hide it, was distraught at the thought of everybody leaving. This made William very uncomfortable and he determined that their goodbyes would not be prolonged. He felt much too keyed up to be of any comfort to somebody being left behind. They arranged to meet after dinner in Hosanna's stable.

When Ellie arrived, William was already there, Hosanna's head over his shoulder. Ellie greeted the horse before she turned to William, hoping to keep control of her voice.

'So,' she said, 'this is the moment everybody has been waiting for.'

William stroked Hosanna's nose with a hay stalk, which the horse tried to catch. Both William and Ellie laughed, but their laughter was not sincere. Ellie's soon turned into a sob, which she tried to hide by blowing her nose.

'It's dusty in here,' she said rather lamely.

There was an awkward silence, which William broke first.

'Take care of Sacramenta,' he said.

Ellie nodded. Hosanna moved back into his stable, and William and Ellie found themselves looking straight at each other. They stood in silence for a moment or two before William's heart melted. He took a deep breath and succumbed to an increasing and overwhelming desire to put his arms round her. He buried his face in her hair as they clung to each other as they had when they were children.

'I'll be back.' William's voice was muffled. 'You'll see, Ellie. After the king has ridden into Jerusalem, I'll ride Hosanna back over the Hartslove drawbridge.'

Then he fled so that she should not see that his face was flaming as red as Hosanna's coat.

When Ellie eventually left Hosanna's stable, her cheeks were streaked with tears. She did not see Gavin standing by the door until he caught her arm. They had spoken little since their betrothal, for Gavin had been busy and Ellie had not sought him out. This evening, he had followed William into the stables and, while William and Ellie had been with Hosanna, had been sitting with Montlouis, trying to get his own thoughts in order.

Ellie suddenly felt quite weak.

Gavin stared at her. He swallowed before he spoke.

'Can I give you back this little dog?' he asked, producing, to Ellie's surprise, the wooden toy that she had dropped in the gutter when Gavin had left Hartslove in disgrace. 'I would like you to have it again.'

Ellie, wishing her nose were not running, took it.

'I didn't know you'd picked it up,' she whispered. 'I'll keep it in my pocket. Take care of . . .'

'Yes, I'll take care of my father and Will,' Gavin interrupted. 'And I'll do my best for Hosanna, too. Now, I'd better go and find Sir Percy. Father wants to make sure he has everything he needs. Try to keep Old Nurse from emptying the cellar while we are away. Whoever returns from this adventure will be in need of a drink.'

Ellie smiled wanly and, clutching the wooden dog, watched him turn and disappear.

Early the following morning, the whole panoply of knights, grooms, soldiers, mechanics, farriers, cooks, laundresses and baggage-masters required to keep the war machine going gathered together on the tournament field for Abbot Hugh to bless. Brother Ranulf, clutching the ring made of Hosanna's hair, prayed hard for the gleaming red stallion who seemed to him to embody the noble essence of the crusade. Brother Andrew came, too, and slipped Hosanna a sweet cake fortified with mead as a farewell offering. Hosanna wrinkled his lips and made Brother Andrew laugh out loud.

The men of God began to chant as they left to walk

back to the monastery, but their voices were drowned out by the cries of the knights, each of whom wanted to make a very public vow to do his duty by God, the king and Sir Thomas. Then, for the men of war, the time for prayer was over. They called for their horses and were impatient to get going.

Humphrey brought Montlouis for Gavin while Hal held Hosanna. The two boys had decided to ride their warhorses rather than, as was more usual, have them led to the coast by a groom. On this momentous occasion, it seemed more fitting to go off in style. Humphrey was still awkward with William, feeling he had never quite been forgiven for his part in causing Hosanna's injuries. Yet Humphrey was a good squire in his way, careful in his work. William tried to be extra polite, but he was glad to have Hal, on whom he could utterly rely. It was Sir Thomas who suggested the boy combine the two roles of squire and groom. 'I think Hal will manage very well,' he told William. 'And who knows what might be in store afterwards if both jobs are properly done.' Hal was delighted and rushed off to tell his mother, who was standing at the front of the huge crowd gathered to wave the crusaders off.

Both horses were excited as Gavin and William tried to mount. The two brothers laughed. Their feelings of the night before were forgotten. They were filled with strength.

'Humphrey! Do make Montlouis stand still,' cried Gavin, as he hauled himself into the saddle.

'This is what it's all about,' William told Hosanna as the horse rubbed his head on William's back as if to tell him to hurry up. William hopped about and finally managed to climb on. 'Next stop, Jerusalem,' he grinned as Hal fussed over his stirrups and girth.

The baggage train was about twice the size of any that had left Hartslove in the past. The quartermasters rushed about with tally sticks that never tallied. The farriers scratched their heads as they counted odd numbers of iron shoes. Hal had personally loaded everything William and Hosanna needed. In God's war, and with Sir Thomas to please, everything must be just so. Hal looked over at the spare horses that the de Granvilles were taking for their own use. Dargent was among the five that William had been given – two warhorses and three coursers. Keeper John had laughed as, several days before they left, he handed over to William and Hal two smart greys and a black. 'Not long ago you were begging for one warhorse,' he had remarked. 'Now you've two and these three others to back them up. Times have changed.'

Gavin also had five horses. His other warhorse was a full brother to Montlouis called Montalan. Sir Thomas had two old and faithful greys, Philo and Phoebus. When Keeper John suggested he might like a younger horse, Sir Thomas had smiled wryly. 'I'll not be going quite as hell for leather as my boys,' he said. 'These two old fellows will suit me fine.'

The Hartslove stud was almost empty now. As the horses thronged together in the May sunshine, Hal looked at them with wonder and some consternation. 'Do you think that horses have souls?' he asked as he rode Dargent up beside William. 'And do they, like us, go straight to heaven if they die on crusade?' In view of the numbers that were likely to perish, the answer seemed important.

William, trying to get used to the feel on his legs of a new pair of quilted, chain-mail-lined chausses, was not sure. He certainly believed whole-heartedly in God, although, despite what the monks said, he saw Him as a

101

judge rather than a father. What is more, he certainly believed that the crusade must be a blessed undertaking, since the pope himself had said so. But when the pope tried to say that despite the fact that God created them, animals had no souls, William could not believe him.

'I think every living thing that performs bravely will end up in heaven,' he said to Hal, his voice sounding surer than he really felt. 'Now, can you tell if I have got this leg armour the right way round? And are you certain you packed that coif thing that goes under my helmet? Old Nurse washed it, I think.'

Hal reassured William that he had forgotten nothing. Then both boys turned and went back to say a last goodbye to Old Nurse, Keeper John and Ellie.

Ellie was trying to smile as she was briefly lifted off her feet by Sir Thomas before he mounted Phoebus.

'Good luck!' and, 'Please come home again,' she whispered into his ear and wished she could have caught his tears and put them in a casket.

She steeled herself to remain smiling for William and Gavin, as they trotted up. She patted Montlouis and touched the star between Hosanna's eyes. Then, before anybody had a chance to say a word, she fled, running back over the drawbridge and climbing up on to the castle roof. From there she watched for over two hours as the huge cavalcade gathered itself into some kind of marching order, and headed down towards the road to the coast. She could see the great de Granville banner, with its hart and river emblem, flapping in the breeze and hear the thud of 10,000 hoofs. The clanking of 1,000 iron-clad wagon wheels was deafening. Then, when all that was left was dust, she sat listening to a silence broken only by the rantings of Old Nurse as she began the massive task of clearing up.

10

Journey to the Holy Land, July 1190 to July 1191

The Hartslove crusaders met the king at Vezelay and William was dubbed to knighthood along with several others. Glowing from their ritual baths and dressed in tunics traced through with gold and silver thread, the new knights heard Mass and asked for God's blessing. Sir Thomas was thrilled that William was the first to receive his sword from the king. William bowed as Richard commanded him to honour God and spoke of the fine service provided by the de Granville family. The king made particular mention of Gavin and hoped that William appreciated the fine example he set. William's face went a little white, but he nodded. Sir Thomas thought he would burst with pride. Finally, William received his spurs.

He remembered little of the feasting and celebrations that followed. He was too overcome to take in the gorgeous pavilions and the embroidered pennants or even to appreciate fully the jewelled headband that his father gave him for Hosanna. He did recall his father helping him put on his first full suit of armour, and how they both swore and cursed because Ellie's small, strong fingers would have made securing the buckles so much easier.

At the tournament that followed, King Richard was particularly struck by Hosanna.

'A fine horse,' he said to William. 'A bit small, but he seems to have something about him that makes up for that.' The king went to Hosanna's head. 'It is strange that this white star is the only white on his whole body,' he remarked, and put his hand up to touch it. Hosanna lowered his head, and the king laughed before moving on.

'Something else to tell Ellie,' said Gavin, suddenly at William's side.

William said nothing.

A week later, they were on the move again, this time heading for Marseilles, a month's ride away, where a fleet was waiting to transport them to Acre, a coastal city in Muslim hands, and one that would have to be taken before any attempt could be made on Jerusalem. The de Granvilles were to travel in the king's ship.

In Marseilles, William was given the job of supervising the loading of the horses through the great trapdoors in the stern and he enjoyed it, even though the job was not easy. Some horses, unused to sea travel, took fright at the sound of the water below. Others refused to pass into the black hold where the animals already loaded stood in a line, divided by stall rails, each with a manger, a bed of esparto grass, ropes and a sling to help keep them upright. In the smaller ships, which took twenty horses, there was just enough room to breathe, but no room at all if a horse began to plunge about. The bigger, sixty-horse ships into which the sumpter horses were packed were steadier, but the journey for all the horses was always a considerable trial. William tried to put animals reputed to be steady next to ones that seemed rather less certain. Of their own mounts, only Montlouis had shown signs of reluctance to embark, but with a rock-like Hosanna by his side, eventually even he was persuaded to take his place in the hold, sweating but not openly panicking.

The de Granvilles' warhorses were all together in a twenty-horse ship and Hal organized their feeding and watering. He also took charge of Mark and found himself operating as an unofficial nanny to the less confident boys who were away from home for the first time. When the fleet was ready, the king's standard was hoisted and they crept out of the harbour.

The voyage was a living hell. Out in the open sea, everybody was sick and Philo, unable to drink, collapsed and died of dehydration and misery.

'If only Keeper John were here, I am sure he would know what to do,' said Hal, when William came down to the hold to find him cradling the horse's head in his lap. The groom was almost beside himself.

'I don't think so,' said William, sickened and horrified by the suffering the animals were enduring, even when the weather was relatively calm. The hold was dank and gloomy and stank of excrement and death. 'There is nothing to do, but hope the journey is not too long.'

'At least you have got other horses.' From further down the hold, a voice could be heard. It was Gavin's friend, Adam Landless. 'My horse died this morning, and he was my only one.'

William told Hal to give Adam one of the Hartslove coursers. A knight without a horse was useless.

The days began to merge together, and a succession of storms blew up that lasted for a fortnight without letting up. All the lanterns, swinging wildly, flickered and went out. In the dark, the only sound to be heard above the roar of the wind and waves was that of horses screaming and men groaning. One groom, driven mad, hauled himself out of the hold and, opening his arms to the lashing rain, threw himself overboard.

The de Granvilles huddled together just below deck, trying to stop themselves being hurled about as the ship soared and dipped like a demented bird. It was impossible to get in or out of the hold without risking life and limb. When the storms blew themselves out, the ship's master decreed that the horse carcasses should be pitched out into the open sea through a trapdoor that had remained unsealed for this purpose. William volunteered to go down to the hold to supervise.

'William,' Sir Thomas said, unable to move through seasickness, 'say a prayer as Philo goes out.' Tears were streaming down his face.

But William never said his prayer. Down in the hold, it was all he could do to point and issue ropes to drag the corpses out. The smell was overwhelming. The grooms who had remained in the hold seemed oblivious. It was just as well. The dead horses were unceremoniously hauled up a ramp and pushed out of a small opening as fast as possible. They were already bloated. As they floated into the wake, the oarsmen and the knights turned their heads away. Of the fifteen horses left, at least three others looked as if they would not last much longer.

The next few days were sunny, and it was possible to go up on deck. Gavin and William walked together. Scudding forwards with the help of a strong prevailing wind, the king's fleet made quite a spectacle. With its mixture of huge dromonds and smaller, slim-waisted galleys, oars pumping and sails flapping, the ships cut through the water and made good time. On the prow of each ship a great spur threatened any vessel that dared to issue a challenge.

Hosanna remained undisturbed, and as the weeks went past, Montlouis and the other horses became more used to the swell. The grooms commented on how steady Hosanna was and the sailors latched on to him as a mascot. As they rested from their oars, they would come down and talk to Hal. They enjoyed hearing about Hosanna's miraculous recovery at the abbey and took to touching the star on his head for luck.

At the end of September, the fleet sailed into port for a rendezvous in Sicily. The knights hung their shields over the sides of the ships and fixed standards and pennants to spearheads to announce their arrival. Sir Thomas and Gavin stood with the king as the oarsmen made a great froth and the sailors whooped and cheered.

'I have family business here,' Richard said. 'And anyway, this island can provide us with a safe harbour and a rest.' Sir Thomas, who had grown weak during the journey, thanked God.

The halt turned out to be a long one. The crusaders spent the winter on the island, recuperating and restocking their supplies while King Richard dealt with prickly matters of state. Blood was shed as relations between the Sicilians and the crusaders, who were not overly polite in their treatment of the native people, grew increasingly bitter. Sir Thomas turned diplomat and his new role meant that he failed to notice that Gavin, frustrated and bored, was taking up with new friends. He and Adam Landless now spent time gambling and drinking in the camp outside Messina. Adam was determined to win enough money to buy another horse. He won one first from a knight called Roger de Soucy, but Roger soon won the horse back. Gavin accused him of cheating. It was only because the king decreed that men caught fighting would be executed that the matter did not come to blows.

William, who watched Gavin from a distance, did not tell his father what was going on. He simply spent less and less time in his brother's company. Instead, he spent more with the horses, riding all over the island. After so many weeks standing still, they revelled in the chance to stretch their legs and gallop in the sun.

News from the Holy Land began to trickle through to Messina. King Guy of Jerusalem, released by Saladin, was already besieging Acre. His actions were considered heroic. But as the crusaders prepared to celebrate the Christmas feast in Sicily, other news also filtered through. While Richard ate off gold plate and consumed fine wine, Guy and his men were so beset by famine that they were forced to eat their horses, heads, intestines and all.

'Does the king not hear what we hear?' William asked his father. 'Why are we not setting sail at once?'

'Patience, William, patience,' said Sir Thomas. 'The king will do everything in his own time.' William looked at his father. Although showered with gifts by Richard for his services, Sir Thomas had begun to look as old as he often joked he felt. He was still cheerful and merry with his sons, but William noticed his face was lined with worry.

In the event, it was three days before Good Friday when, with a fleet of 200 ships, Richard ordered the crusaders to prepare to set off again. William, while hating making the horses go back into the hold, was exultant.

This time, however, Gavin was not with them.

'I have decided that I will travel with my friends,' he said. 'And my horses will come with me.'

'But Montlouis travels so well next to Hosanna,' said William.

A look of uncertainty crossed Gavin's face.

'You surely don't need that little horse to lend courage to the great Montlouis,' came the voice of Adam Landless from behind them. 'Why not travel with me? After all, you may remember that I won your other horse – Montalan is he called? – at cards last night, so Montlouis will be among friends.'

William turned on Gavin, his face furious.

'You idiot!' he said, and walked off, shouting for another knight to bring his horse forwards.

Three days away from the Sicilian coast, a huge storm, bigger than anything the crusading army had felt before, blew up in the night. Down below the deck of the king's ship, Hal held on to Hosanna for dear life as the ship rose, hesitated for one dreadful second then, with a terrible heave, plunged down into a wall of water that threatened to drown them all. The noise was appalling. Through the keening wind and the rain beating like a thousand drums Hal could hear the sailors cursing and crying as the oars were torn from their rollocks and the stores came loose from their moorings. Some of the other grooms were on their knees or even just lying face down in the filthy straw, praying to the Virgin. William appeared in the chaos, abandoning his place on the deck above. He did not try to shout above the creaking and howling, but fought his way over to Hal and, after an almighty struggle to fix Hosanna's slings, both of them buried their faces in his mane.

All night the sea roared but the next morning an almost surreal calm had descended, as if the storm had been nothing but a bad dream. But it had not been a bad dream. Richard's fleet was scattered and Gavin's ship had disappeared. All around the king's galley, amid a floating forest of smashed wood, corpses of men and horses in terrible attitudes of violent death floated past. William stood, white-faced, with his father, dreading to see his brother's face or Montlouis' familiar head in among the flotsam. Sir Thomas urged everybody to pray rather than stare. But many, like William, were beyond prayer. The whole venture, which had begun so proudly, seemed to be turning sour, from the months of inactivity in Sicily to the pointless deaths of so many before they had even reached the Holy Land.

'Surely God should protect us on our journey,' William said to Sir Thomas.

'God works in His own ways,' his father replied, his face greyer than ever.

There was nothing to do but push forwards to Cyprus, the next planned stop, an island that Richard was determined to take under his control since it was close enough to the coast of Palestine to be crucial to the crusaders' efforts.

William and Sir Thomas spoke little as Richard's ship pressed on. Sir Thomas could not even bring himself to condemn his eldest son's decision to travel separately since he did not know if he was alive or dead.

After three weeks' further sailing, during which Richard's ship stopped at many islands in search of news, what remained of his fleet reached Limassol. Almost immediately, just outside the harbour, William spotted Gavin's shield hung over the side of a very battered ship that had once been painted blue. Surely they would not hang the shield of a drowned knight? They had not. As they sailed nearer, Sir Thomas and William could see Gavin and Adam among a group of men sitting on deck, playing dice.

William, careless of his dignity in his relief, called out Gavin's name again and again. But his brother barely nodded. As William got close enough to board, he could see his brother's hands were shaking and his face was hard and closed.

Gavin had had a terrible journey. At least twenty of the men who had mustered at Hartslove, including Humphrey and Mark, men who had followed him and changed ships, were drowned in front of his eyes. Montalan had also gone when, the hail and wind having rotted the caulk that secured it, the great trapdoor in the ship's side blew open and all the horses tethered beside it had been swept off their feet. Montlouis had only been saved by a load of barrels that had slid across the hold, dividing it in two. Every time he shut his eyes, Gavin could still hear Humphrey's pleas for help, help that Gavin was unable to give. And he could still see Montalan swimming past, his eyes wide, his nostrils flared, searching; searching for land he would never reach. Gavin conveyed none of this to William. He did not know how. He simply gave his brother and father a desultory wave and carried on with his game.

William, deeply hurt by Gavin's coolness, re-boarded Richard's ship. Sir Thomas patted him on the back.

'Your brother has learnt a hard lesson,' he said. 'He needs some time to deal with it.'

William pursed his lips. 'Gavin seems to learn no lessons,' he said.

'Don't speak of your brother like that,' said his father wearily. 'Come, I think the king has something for you to do.'

Richard was sitting in a small room, surrounded by a group of knights. William noticed how, just before entering, his father made himself stand up straight and smile. William felt a sudden chill.

'Father,' he said. 'Are you –'

'I'm absolutely fine,' said Sir Thomas. 'Just a little tired. Now, Will. Listen carefully to the king. This is a big moment for you and Hosanna.'

William squeezed his father's hand, then went apprehensively into the king's presence.

'Good,' said Richard, when William approached. 'I have a job, and your father says you are just the man to do it.'

Richard outlined his plan. The ruler of Cyprus, Isaac Comnenus, a disaffected member of the Greek imperial family, was posing as a friend to the crusaders, but was in fact allied with Saladin. He would have to be got rid of. Richard could not risk Cyprus offering support to Saladin's army. Under cover of darkness, the horses were to be disembarked into the shallow sea about a hundred metres offshore. They would surround the Griffons, the Cypriot army who had made camp on the beach, and by morning Richard was to be in control of the capital city. William's task was to get to the beach and lead a charge.

'Hosanna, I'm told, gives men and horses confidence,' said Richard. 'If he will disembark straight into the sea, it seems likely that the other horses and men will follow. And I hear he can jump. If he will leap over the barricades that they have erected, who knows? The others may, too.'

William's face lit up.

'Yes, sire,' he said. 'We will do our best.'

William felt no nerves waiting for the darkness to fall, though this was his first experience of battle. He and Hal discussed how best to prepare Hosanna, and what saddlery he should wear. Having got Hosanna ready, Hal was busy organizing the horses that would follow him out.

When the order came for the operation to begin, William, wearing only light armour, climbed down into the hold. Hosanna whickered gently as Hal led him out of his stall and helped William to mount. Lying almost flat along Hosanna's neck because the roof of the hold was so low, William whispered encouragement into his ears. They twitched. He felt his own heart beating fast as the gangplank was lowered and, with only a momentary hesitation, Hosanna stepped on to it. The wooden slats were steeply inclined and barely rested on the sea floor. The horse slithered momentarily, then struck boldly off into the waves. Within a few strokes, he found his feet and, snorting, made his way on to the beach.

'Sssssh,' said William.

It was a propitious start. Where Hosanna went, the other horses followed. Some of the knights had preferred to wear heavier armour and sail to the beach in flat-bottomed boats while their grooms brought their horses. William grinned. Jumping in heavy armour was extremely painful. The knights who had followed his lead and worn only a breastplate and helmet, would find themselves much more comfortable. But the task of getting the knights to the beach had been accomplished, and in silence.

Now for the next stage. When they were all assembled, at William's signal, they charged. The enemy, most of whom were dozing, were completely taken aback. Jerked into wakefulness by the pounding of horses' hoofs, they stood helpless at the sight of a flame-coloured horse and its young rider, followed by fifty other knights, flying over the upturned wagons, old doors and great piles of wood that the Griffons had thought would form an insuperable barrier. The day was won before breakfast.

As William galloped through the streets of Limassol, he hollered his victory, and when, later in the day, Richard rewarded him with a jewelled dagger, William held it up to show his peers.

Gavin, who had not been asked to take part in the adventure because, so he said by way of explanation, Montlouis could not be relied upon in water, looked on with envy. He knew why Richard had not chosen him. It was he, Gavin, who could no longer be relied upon.

The taking of the island provided rich rewards for all, including Richard, who captured Isaac's horse, which, so the knights whispered, was the swiftest in the world. Richard offered it to William, who thought his heart would burst with pride. The king laughed as William refused it, as everybody knew he would.

'I already have a horse, sire,' William said. 'I need no other.'

'Would you exchange him for this one?'

'With all respect, sire, no.'

Later, William and Sir Thomas rode together into the hills and looked over the sea. If they strained their eyes, they could see the cedar-covered mountains of Lebanon just visible over the horizon.

'That's it, William,' Sir Thomas said. 'Next stop, the

Holy Land.' They stood in silence for a while before turning to ride back to the city.

After William gave Hosanna to Hal to feed, he bumped into Gavin, Adam and several others. They were drunk.

'Here's your precious brother,' they taunted Gavin. 'Now, why not show him some real life. Does he even know what goes on in the back streets of Limassol? We think it is your brotherly duty to show him the beautiful girls of Cyprus. Hey, Will! A crusader can have a rare good time here! And to a hero like you, well, you can have your pick!'

William ignored them. As Gavin half-heartedly tried to grab him, he slid past and went to find his father, about whom he was increasingly worried. *Sometimes*, he thought, *it is as if I were the older son.* Gavin seemed barely to have noticed their father's tired face and troubled expression.

It was only a short month before all was secure and the fleet sailed on to Acre. This time Gavin travelled with William and Sir Thomas. Nothing was said, but when Hal went to collect Montlouis to put him next to Hosanna, Gavin did not object. Their arrival at Acre, a year after setting out, was an emotional moment. The Christians besieging the city were almost beside themselves with relief, and the crusaders felt that their real task was about to begin.

Walking to the horse-lines on the evening of their first day to see if his faithful Phoebus was still in one piece, even Sir Thomas had a spring in his step. 'Well, old man,' he said to his horse. 'This is the beginning of something great.'

But, two days later, William was sickly and by midday

he was delirious. For a day, he slipped in and out of consciousness as his father watched, helpless.

Sir Thomas consulted a priest who had been living outside Acre, for advice. The priest looked sadly at the old man, but could offer little hope. 'It's the fever,' he said. 'Acre is full of it. So many get it, and most do not recover. You can only pray for him – and for your king, who I hear is also ill.'

Sir Thomas sank down in despair. Surely William, having been through so much, could not die delirious, not even knowing where he was? And surely the king could not die now, just when his real work was about to start?

Already, the hideous reality of siege warfare in a hot climate was sinking in. Acre and its environs were little better than a cesspit, with polluted water, filth everywhere and mutilated corpses being thrown both in and out of the city as if they had never been living people. Sir Thomas remembered William's joy at the vision of the cedar-covered mountains. Was this the reality? Was the crusading dream nothing more than a dismal, stinking nightmare of famine, plague, flies, heat and dust? The rumours they had heard in Sicily about men eating their horses had been true. And much worse things were happening. Some men were being accused of cannibalism. Others were reduced to gibbering idiots, having eaten rats that were themselves sick from eating flyblown carrion.

Sir Thomas shuddered as William, lying in a stifling tent, launched yet again into a long complaint about Old Nurse setting him on fire. Dropping to his knees, Sir Thomas began to pray. 'If anybody should die pointlessly of illness rather than gloriously in battle, let it be me,' he begged. 'Please, Lord, if You have any mercy, spare my son. Please spare my son.'

11

Acre, 1191

For over a week it seemed as if Sir Thomas's prayers would not be answered. He never left William's side, and Gavin lurched in and out, torn between pity and horror. Eventually Sir Thomas bowed his head to the inevitable and sent Gavin to look for a priest. Gavin was glad to be doing something. As he rode out, he could see Acre's domes and minarets over the city walls. He could also hear the muezzin and whistled to drown out the sound.

Acre was still held by the Saracens, but only just. Hours were spent discussing the quickest way to make it fall. Once in Christian hands it would provide a good port for reinforcements and supplies. However, careful planning was required. More than a third of the city's perimeter was water and, on a treacherous, rocky outcrop, a tower known as the Tower of the Flies had been built to help protect the city from attack by sea. To the landward side, another tall building, nicknamed the Cursed Tower, provided cover for Saracen archers. As occasional arrows whistled through the air, despite the heat, Gavin was glad to be wearing his armour. It was commonly believed that this tower was where the silver that had been paid to Judas Iscariot, the apostle who betrayed Jesus, was forged. Gavin could well believe it.

A river flowed into the city but it was narrow and shallow – 'Good for making glass,' as some of the siege mechanics observed, 'but useless for watering two armies and a city.' The 'two armies' referred to another difficulty that the arriving Christians found themselves facing. For while the Christians under King Guy of Jerusalem had begun one siege, they found themselves, in their turn, besieged by Saladin who now had them trapped on the plain between hostile hills and a hostile city. It was deadlock.

Gavin had not been as happy to reach Acre as everybody else. He was still unable to rid himself of nightmare visions of drowning men and horses. The shortages of food, the brown water and the constant presence of death suited his mood even though these conditions were killing more people than any battle. Men and horses were visibly shrinking inside their trappings. The only thing that kept the Christians going, Gavin thought to himself as he dodged another arrow, was the thought that the plight of the Saracens holed up inside Acre must be even worse than the plight of those camped outside.

He urged Montlouis into a canter. He could not find a priest so he would find a drink instead. Putting William to the back of his mind, he looked for a friendly face. It did not take long to find one and by the time Gavin returned to Sir Thomas, he was swaying on his feet.

Sir Thomas looked at him with both sympathy and fury.

'No priest,' slurred Gavin and sank down. Sir Thomas said nothing. He watched as William grew steadily weaker, sweating and shivering in equal measure.

'Better to drown than burn,' the youth muttered again and again. That night, Sir Thomas all but gave up hope, for William began to rave about Hosanna and would not let up. Gavin, still stupid with drink, was slumped in the corner, his mouth half open. William suddenly fixed his eyes on him.

'Who are you? Why don't you tell me where Hosanna is?' he complained, sounding twelve years old again. His fingers never stopped pulling at his covers.

'I know Hosanna is dead,' he went on, his voice rising. 'I know you have killed him.' For an hour or more William repeated himself until Gavin, pricked to madness through his stupor, leapt up.

'Hosanna is not dead,' he bellowed. 'I'll go and get him so that you can see for yourself.' He lurched to his feet, disappeared into the darkness and returned shortly after, pulling the horse under the awning. Sir Thomas tried to get up but found himself too giddy. He sat down again and held on to his chair. He felt terribly thirsty but one look at the water made his stomach turn.

Hosanna, who, under the care of Hal, was still shining, seemed unfazed by the unusual situation, and when he had steadied himself, Sir Thomas leant forwards and put William's hands on his horse's head. 'What is there to lose, what is there to gain?' he muttered, then thought, *I, too, am losing my mind.* Hosanna put his nose close to William's pillow and, when the dust of the tent tickled his nose, sneezed. A thousand little droplets flew over William's face. Sir Thomas moved slowly to wipe them off.

Gavin stared at him. 'You're shaking, Father,' he said.

'It's nothing,' replied Sir Thomas. 'You've had too much to drink.' Then he sat down again. 'Take the horse away now, Gavin,' he said. 'He can do William no good here.'

Gavin took Hosanna back to Hal, then, like a homeless dog, he found a blanket and fell into a heavy sleep.

Sir Thomas was wrong. Later in the night the crisis in William's fever passed. By morning the boy was sleeping easily and the following day he propped himself up and recognized his father, sitting by his bed.

William leant forwards.

'Father?' he said and touched Sir Thomas's hand. It was cold. William, weak and pale, went rigid with shock. While he had managed to cling on to life, Sir Thomas, overcome with weakness and fatigue, had not. He was stone dead. William sank back. When he finally managed to wake his brother, Gavin howled like a wolf.

Once William was strong enough to walk, they buried Sir Thomas's body in the tunnel dug by French sappers to undermine Acre's walls. The corpse, surrounded by what brush and timber could be gathered from the plain and surrounding hills, was set alight and, as they watched the walls sink and crumble as the fire took advantage of the sappers' work, Gavin and William felt that their father would have approved. King Richard, whose own sickness had also passed, told them how much he would miss Sir Thomas and that he would be remembered as a kind and honourable man. Sickness was cruel, but their father had done his crusading duty. William and Gavin bowed when the king had finished, but his words were small consolation.

Still far from well, William was silent in his grief. He tried to pray but all he could hear was his father's voice, joking with Old Nurse or teasing Ellie in the great hall at Hartslove. Gavin, on the other hand, went wild. He blamed the Saracens and cursed them to hell. Night after night he paced the tent, muttering and swearing until his poison slowly seeped into his brother's soul, too. But in contrast with Gavin's quick, hot fury, William's hatred grew inch by inch and was cold as steel. While God might give Sir Thomas due reward in heaven, here on earth the Saracens must pay. When William could once again wield a sword, he rode Hosanna around the camp, exhorting his fellow crusaders to redouble their efforts. Then he took his turn to scale the long ladders now propped up all over the city walls for the Christians to climb and punched and stabbed any of the enemy who came within his reach. His dagger bloody, he told himself he would never look on any Saracen without remembering his father's suffering and death.

The end of the siege came suddenly. The Saracens, realizing that Acre could be defended no longer, sued for terms of surrender. After much haggling, an agreement was reached involving the exchange of captives and ransom money, and the Muslim enemy slowly began to emerge from the city. Those acting as hostages were herded to one side, a huge group numbering over 3,000. William, leading Hosanna and Dargent to drink at one of the dirty channels, stared at their thin faces. *Why*, he thought to himself with surprise, *they look quite ordinary*. But he hardened his heart and soon turned his gaze elsewhere.

Richard sent for him. Along with the Duke of Burgundy, he was to go to Saladin's camp to discuss delivery of ransom money for all the captives – a responsibility earned, Richard said, as a reward for the number of Saracens the boy had killed in the siege. The two sides met in the open. William rode behind the duke and stared at Saladin, whose eyes were dark and inscrutable. The duke was loud in his demands. Saladin was courteous as he denied them. When Richard was told, he seethed with fury. Finally, he sent William to call together his senior knights.

'Friends and fellow crusaders,' he said, 'we can go no further, saddled as we are with all these Saracen captives. Saladin refuses to pay the ransom. So we must now decide. Shall we wait while Saladin marshals yet more forces to defy us, or shall we cut our losses, execute the prisoners and move on to Jerusalem?'

There was a moment's silence before Gavin stepped forwards, his hand on the hilt of his sword. 'Kill the captives. They are nothing but dogs,' he said, loudly and clearly. 'Kill them.'

There was a short pause before Adam Landless, then the Duke of Burgundy, then one influential knight after another, all stepped forwards to agree. They began to shout, and William found himself joining in.

The following afternoon all was prepared. The prisoners were herded into an open space just outside the city walls. They thought they were going home. It was only when faced with a solid and silent battery of mounted Christian soldiers, lances poised and swords unsheathed, that they suddenly realized what was about to happen. Some dropped to their knees, some invoked Allah's name, while others began to talk fast and loudly, shaking their heads.

Gavin and Montlouis stood in the first line of soldiers. William on Hosanna was behind in the second. In the baking afternoon sun the trumpeter gave the sound, and at first slowly, then faster and faster, Richard's men, shouting the names of knights already dead, bore down on the unarmed enemy. They rode straight through them, spearing, slicing, stabbing and slashing. Wave after wave, they charged at the prisoners until not one remained alive. By the end, the horses were finding it difficult to keep their feet in the lake of blood.

But while Montlouis, urged on by Gavin, thundered towards the victims, Hosanna, for the first time in years, refused to move forwards at all. It did not matter what William did. As the knights beside him galloped towards the enemy, the horse remained stock-still. Hosanna seemed neither angry nor afraid, but nothing William could do would make him carry the boy into the massacre. William's sword remained unbloodied and his hands clean. Eventually, after a long struggle, William dismounted and threw Hosanna's reins to Hal in disgust. He shouted for Dargent. Hosanna, who had been such a talisman, was making a spectacle of himself. Shaking with humiliation and fury, William struck the horse with the flat of his sword. It was the first time he had ever raised his hand against him. Hosanna did not flinch but a long weal arose on his neck and drops of blood speckled the sand as Hal silently led him away.

By the time Dargent was ready, it was all over.

Afterwards, nobody spoke about either the massacre or Hosanna's behaviour. The dead bodies were dumped in a pyre and burnt. Sand was spread over the blood. It was as if nothing had ever happened.

But not for William. The weal on Hosanna's neck festered and wept. As William watched Hal try to clean it as best he could, the boy's conscience hurt him. What was he turning into? Sickened as much by his own behaviour as he had earlier been upset by Hosanna's, William could not rest.

Everybody else was happy, rejoicing at the news that the march towards Jerusalem, the event they had all been waiting for, could now begin. Having come so far, they could not afford to be squeamish. They were to go to Jaffa first, another important port, but one which the Saracens were already abandoning because they knew they could not defend it. The Christians could not wait to get going. Gradually, as Hosanna's weal began to heal and the army was once again on the move, William made a big effort to push his own confusions away. Like the king, he must concentrate on the task ahead. So he joined the queue for fresh supplies coming in from the coast and ate and drank his fill. He talked to Hal and discussed how best to keep the horses healthy. When he heard soldiers and grooms singing as they went about their work, he did his best to join in. He told himself that soon, the horror of the massacre would, like the voyage and his illness, recede.

Before the march to Jaffa began, the king commanded a great feast to be held in Sir Thomas's memory. All the Hartslove men still surviving were present and Gavin promised such rewards as were now in his gift as their new lord. He also told Adam Landless there would be a place for him in his household. But to the new friends he had made on the journey, Gavin offered nothing. Since his father's death, he could not bear the sight of them. William was relieved. Gavin needed steady companions, for his actions were growing increasingly reckless. After the feast, as the army moved away from the city, there were few forage or reconnaissance parties for which he did not volunteer. Occasionally he returned with Muslim heads attached to his saddle, something that sickened William. Displaying heads, even though this was also what the king did, was, to his mind, a mark not of heroism but of barbarism. Could God possibly approve of such things? When Gavin displayed his gruesome trophies, William, although his hatred of the Saracens was as strong as ever, avoided him. Once he asked Gavin if he would tell Ellie the sort of things crusaders did. Gavin laughed. 'Women cannot understand these things,' he said.

'But they can be ashamed,' William answered.

Gavin just shrugged his shoulders. 'Everybody has to get through this in their own way, little brother,' he said, and walked off.

Gavin soon wore his horses thin through overuse, but the army as a whole, as it marched south, looked in reasonably good shape. The journey was undertaken in strict formation, the spare horses and the baggage train protected by the sea on one side and the great column of knights and men-at-arms on the other.

Nevertheless, even with the king's genius for strategy, the route was hazardous. The knights were continually harassed by Saracen archers galloping towards them on their swift ponies, aiming great clouds of arrows with deadly accuracy, then galloping away. It was, William thought after a fifth day spent pulling the darts out of his thick undercoat, like being attacked by a swarm of bees. To save Dargent and Hosanna, he was riding one of his coursers and sat hunched in the saddle. Ringing in his ears was the king's order, repeated forcefully every day, that nobody was to break ranks unless the trumpet sounded a charge. For the moment the trumpet was silent.

Gavin, travelling near the rear of the column with a splitting headache, was goaded almost beyond endurance. The men in front of him looked like hedgehogs as the arrows stuck in their woollen jerkins. They had cursed these jerkins for being far too hot, but now they were certainly feeling the benefit. The horses had much less protection and began to fall by the score, not silently but with frantic neighs and terrible groans. Their bodies were left in the blazing sun for the jackals and vultures to dispose of. There was no other option.

At night there was some respite and early in the morning, as the Christians began to march, but before the Saracens geared themselves for attack, William sometimes looked at the landscape and marvelled at its variety. The army travelled through woods and over pleasant-looking rivers. Along the coast, the plants grew so luxuriously that it made progress difficult for the baggage animals. Truly, thought William, this could be the land of milk and honey. But then the arrows would start raining down, and it was hell again.

At the end of a fortnight, the road grew narrow between the mountains, and Richard saw that a major ambush was more and more likely. He ordered his knights to ride their warhorses – the time was coming when the Christians would have to retaliate. William asked Hal to saddle Dargent, but Hal was unwilling. Dargent had cast a shoe and was likely to go lame. William would have to ride Hosanna. Hal put as much armour on the horse as he thought he could bear, and William, his heart heavy, took his place in the column.

There was no let-up from the Saracen attacks. As the Christians approached the forest of Arsuf, despite the king constantly reiterating his order to keep marching straight ahead, tempers were frayed. The enemy edged ever closer and poured out of the hills in increasing numbers. William tried not to hear the pleas of the wounded men or the anguish of the horses left behind to face their fate alone. The order was not to break the column. They must obey the order or all would be lost.

As the thuds and cries grew ever louder, and his eyes, despite his visor, smarted with dust, William felt suffocated by the heat and kept a mailed hand on Hosanna's neck. The horse stepped out eagerly as the sun rose. The weal on his neck was well healed but had left a permanent ridge of proud flesh. William steadied him with his voice. He tried not to think of what was happening. He tried, instead, to focus on Jerusalem.

Arrows were now glancing off Hosanna's shoulders every minute and William wildly swept them away. Suddenly, a terrible, unbidden thought made him shiver. If Richard ordered a charge now, would Hosanna obey? The horse seemed willing enough, his ears pricked forwards. Surely he would. But if he did, did that mean that the king had been wrong in ordering the massacre of the prisoners at Acre, and that Hosanna had somehow felt it?

William wished he could talk everything through with Ellie. Then he shuddered and ducked to avoid a crossbow bolt. It missed William but hit the next horse, which sank to the ground, its leg shattered. The knight shouted in his distress. *Oh God*, thought William. No. How could he wish that anybody he loved should see what the crusade was really about? As he rode on through the filthy, choking air, William realized that he did not know what he would say about any of it if he ever got home again.

Then a voice broke through the uproar. It was Gavin's. 'This is intolerable!' he shouted as he pulled another dart from Montlouis' neck.

The Saracen war cry of '*Allah akbar*' was all around them. It echoed inside the steel of William's helmet. Behind him, a rattling grunt signalled the end of another horse, caught by an arrow straight through the throat. Blood spattered all over William's back but he dared not look round.

Then he heard Gavin again, almost screaming. 'Tell the king!' he yelled. 'Tell the king we can bear this no longer! We will be remembered as cowards if we don't retaliate before we are all dead. We are losing our horses one after another. Come on, my friends, let's charge!' William, ignoring the order to face forwards, spun Hosanna round.

'Gavin! No!' he yelled. 'No!'

But Gavin paid no heed. He swung Montlouis out of the column and, raising his lance, swept headlong towards the Saracen horde. Seeing Gavin break formation, other men, also driven to distraction by the mayhem around them, turned to attack. The king realized that he was powerless to control his scattering troops and took the only decision he could.

'Sound the charge!' he yelled at the trumpeter, and with shouts of 'God and Jerusalem!' all the Christians were suddenly galloping after Gavin and towards their tormentors.

Gavin reached the enemy first. He lost his lance at once and set about with his sword. The Saracens were taken aback by his lunatic bravery and seemed nonplussed until a dark boy on a high-stepping Arab stallion unsheathed his sword and matched Gavin, strike for strike.

Kamil had been waiting for such an opportunity. His horse teased Montlouis like a ballet dancer teasing an elephant and, never changing his expression, Kamil evaded Gavin's sword with ease. Only the arrival of the entire Christian army, with Hosanna in the thick of it, saved Gavin from certain death. The impetus swept Kamil away, and Gavin found himself among the group of Hospitaller knights who had reached the Saracens after him.

As for Kamil, just for a moment, in the melee, he found himself galloping by the side of a remarkably beautiful flame-coloured horse. As Hosanna swung away, Kamil watched him. Then, knowing that the knights' charge spelt defeat for the Saracens in this particular battle, Kamil headed back to the hills, but not before he had made a mental note to look for the red horse again.

Once the Christian charge got under way, the Saracen forces scattered, leaving thousands of dead and dying from both sides in their wake. King Richard, after giving his men a severe lecture about not breaking the rules he had set down, commended many knights for their bravery. When he had been reprimanded for his disregard for orders, even Gavin's precipitate charge was forgiven, although the king was clearly displeased. It had been Richard's intention to draw the Saracens to a place where they could have been surrounded. As it was, the king himself, riding the fleet horse he had taken from the ruler of Cyprus, had been forced to pursue the

Saracens, leaving his own men vulnerable. It was small consolation that many of the enemy were caught, and disappointing that Saladin was not among them. As for the Christians, they too lost many men, including Adam Landless.

Gavin bit his lip. As he rode back through the scenes of devastation at the king's side, he looked with distaste at the soldiers who had returned to the battlefield and were loading themselves with plunder from the fallen. It was, needless to say, customary. Nevertheless, it was not something Richard encouraged, and when Gavin saw Adam's looted body he was, notwithstanding the king's presence, violently sick. Richard was not sympathetic.

Only ten miles away, in the Saracen camp, Saladin was striding around his tent angry and worried. Baha ad-Din was standing by the flap, looking out and listening to messengers. Wounded soldiers were streaming past.

'Kamil had no business to get close enough to the Christians for them to charge,' said Saladin, his voice furious. 'Hundreds of men have been killed. And for what?'

Baha ad-Din did not have time to reply before Kamil himself was galloping towards him. Saladin left his tent and stood, his hands on his sword, as the boy leapt off his horse and stood silently before him. He did not receive his customary smile of greeting. Instead, Saladin's eyes were cold.

'Your bloodlust has caused us to suffer what the Christians will call a defeat,' he said curtly.

'The boy did what he thought Allah would want.' Baha ad-Din was hot in Kamil's defence.

130

'Kamil did what Kamil wanted. Is that not so, Kamil?' Saladin was not to be pacified so easily.

'The Christians seemed an easy target,' Kamil replied. 'We killed many before they turned to attack.'

'That is not the point,' said Saladin. 'Their King Richard seldom makes a mistake. When he charges, we are always likely to lose hundreds of men. We also have a clear chain of command when it comes to provoking a battle, as you well know, Kamil. You are not yet part of that chain. Please remember that. I should punish you. This time I will not. But next time you will not be so lucky.'

Kamil left Saladin's presence and sat in sullen silence in the outer tent. Saladin's eternal lectures were beginning to make him more than impatient. The sultan was always so careful in his strategies and the results were so slow. In Kamil's estimation, he showed far too much tolerance and far too little thirst for vengeance. Maybe that was because Saladin's family had not been cut down in cold blood. Feelings of resentment and frustration filled Kamil's soul. Everybody thought Saladin was a hero. Well, maybe he was not such a hero after all. How could anybody who really hated Christians care so much for rules and chains of command when opportunities for slaughter presented themselves?

After pacifying Saladin, Baha ad-Din found Kamil and sat down beside him.

He noted the boy's expression, and chose his words deliberately.

'Be careful, Kamil,' he said, keeping his voice gentle. 'I know your heart is warm and turns to Allah. But you must not let your wish to do Allah's work allow you to forget that you are a boy in the service of the sultan.

When the sultan wishes to punish he is not merciful. I repeat, be careful.' Kamil did not reply and after a few moments, Baha ad-Din left him to his thoughts.

A tall man with sly eyes and a short black beard was also watching Kamil. After Baha ad-Din had gone, he came to sit beside him and began talking in a low voice.

12

Jaffa, early September 1191

Richard, meanwhile, gathered up his forces again, and in three days his army reached Jaffa. There, the knights experienced a side of crusading life they had not encountered before. Although the town itself had been destroyed by the Saracens, the orchards and suburban gardens had been left. The trees were heavy with fruit, and flowers filled the air with rich and exotic scents. Richard ordered camp to be struck in an olive grove. This surely was the Promised Land. The sun was still hot, but, without their armour on, it was not unbearable.

Along with the other soldiers, William, Gavin and Hal gorged themselves on figs, grapes and pomegranates and flavoured their tasteless dried beef with lemon juice. Before leaving the battle site at Arsuf, many men had cut slabs of flesh from the dead horses to supplement the biscuits and hard bread they were all heartily sick of. They had brought sackfuls of it with them, which they now proceeded to roast.

But although the smell of fresh meat sometimes made William's mouth water, his stomach revolted at the sight. 'Never, never will I let that happen to you,' he promised Hosanna, now tethered in a field, where the September grazing was thick and juicy. 'I will bury you if I have to, but I will never, ever, eat you.'

Hosanna, stamping his feet to get rid of the flies and occasionally neighing to Montlouis, gently pushed the boy to one side to get to a more attractive piece of grass. Then, in his old accustomed way, he stood with his head over William's shoulder.

William stroked his nose. 'At least we are still alive,' he murmured and the horse stopped chewing for a moment as if in agreement.

With so much fresh food and water, everybody, from the common soldiers to the most aristocratic knights, felt refreshed and reinvigorated. Prayers were said for the dead. Horses were mourned as well as eaten. William, although he missed his father desperately, began once again to feel that the crusade was, if not splendid, at least a righteous endeavour. He practised battle tactics on Hosanna, pretending to storm the gates of Jerusalem single-handed. How sharp and agile the horse was! He could pull up from a full gallop in seconds, whipping round and galloping back the other way or in any direction William chose. His floating gait was William's for the asking and the horse went backwards and sideways at the slightest touch of rein and leg. He was both proud and obedient, a perfect combination. Sometimes William got so carried away with Hosanna that he forgot where he was and turned round to shout to Ellie to watch. When he realized his mistake he would blush and hope nobody noticed.

Richard alone seemed troubled. He had many things on his mind. First of all, he knew that some of his knights had already set sail back to Acre – only two days' voyage if the winds were good – intent on bringing down wine and women to add fresh delights to the festive atmosphere. These would be a bad distraction. But worse than this, Richard could no longer ignore something that had been obvious, at least to him, since they had arrived at Acre and the geography of the Holy Land became clearer. Jerusalem, the object of such veneration, the reason so many knights had set out, was an impossible target for a crusading army with no regular reinforcements. Even if the Christians managed to take it, and even with Cyprus in friendly hands, how on earth could a city so far inland be supplied and defended?

As his knights relaxed, Richard spent many sleepless nights wondering if it might be possible to convince the men he was leading to forget about the holy places and settle instead for the coastal towns until a bigger force and, perhaps, more settlers who could help the army, could be summoned from France and England. The king could see no easy way to persuade them. Jerusalem was the beacon that kept his men going through the heat, dust, horror and discomfort. To remove the one goal they all had in common would be dangerous and might precipitate a revolt.

The king wrestled with this problem alone. One night he walked out in the early hours and found himself standing beside Hosanna, whose behaviour over the Saracen prisoners the king knew about and found disconcerting. He spent hours looking at the horse, whose coat had a ghost-like sheen in the moonlight. Richard found him a peaceful companion. As Hosanna had once listened to Old Nurse, he now seemed to listen to the king, his dark eyes full of something Richard could not quite describe. It was not, he decided, wisdom. It was more like looking into your own soul. He told Hosanna as much, and Hosanna bent his head to scratch it on Richard's arm, rubbing his white star against the king's breast. 'If only human beings were as forgiving as you seem to be,' Richard said as he finally bid the horse goodnight.

The king never told William of this conversation. But whenever he found himself riding alongside the red horse, the king had the uncanny feeling that somehow their destinies were intertwined. 'Superstitious nonsense,' he told himself. Nevertheless, he too began to touch Hosanna's star for luck, just as the sailors had on the voyage out.

Every day brought new frustrations for Richard. Much to his fury, and to William's dismay, Gavin, who Richard hoped would forget his wild ways and turn into the useful adviser he had once been, was one of those knights who sailed back to Acre in search of amusement. He returned not only with a woman on each arm, but something very curious.

'Will, look what I came by!' he said to his brother, kicking open the flap of the tent the morning after he got back. The women giggled. 'No, not you,' Gavin squeezed their arms, then told them to wait outside. He dropped a roll of parchment into William's hands.

William unrolled it, then looked up at Gavin. 'What is it?' he asked.

'It's a letter, or so they tell me,' said Gavin. 'There was a pouch of documents that arrived for the king. Other people had also managed to get things to the ship that brought it over. Apparently this is for you. Look! This, so they say, is your name. And just guess who it is from.'

'I can't guess,' said William. 'I don't know anybody who can write. Oh, except Brother Andrew, Brother

136

Ranulf and Old Nurse – and I am sure she has forgotten how. Anyway, nobody I know would send a letter all the way out here.'

Gavin jumped up. 'You are wrong,' he cried. 'Quite wrong.'

He leant down. 'The letter,' he said, 'is from Ellie. There. Little Ellie has learnt to write and she has written not to me but to you. Well, what do you think of that?'

William was dumbfounded. 'Ellie? How do you know?'

'I got somebody to read it to me.'

'You read my letter?' William was outraged.

'Well, you can't read it, can you,' Gavin retorted. 'So would you like to hear what it says? It's not long. One of the girls here can read. I'll call her in.'

Before William could say anything, Gavin pulled one of his highly painted women into the tent.

The woman, winking at Gavin, took the letter from William and began to read.

'"Dear William",' she said in a heavy accent, clearing her throat. '"It is a long time since you left. I have decided to learn to read and write. Brother Ranulf helps me. I hope you are being a fine crusader and have killed many infidels. I imagine you in Jerusalem with Hosanna laying on a bed of golden straw. We hear news of great victories. Not much has happened here but I am sorry to say that Sir Walter has died. We buried him a week ago. Constable de Scabious is fussing about as usual. I don't trust him. The roof has been leaking. Sacramenta is well and Old Nurse is as fat as ever. She was drunk last week and fell in the fish pond. Please come home soon. I love you very much and dream about you every night" –'

William looked up, horrified.

Gavin roared with laughter. 'I got Marcella to make

that bit up,' he crowed. He pretended to spank her. 'Now, Marcella, be a good girl and tell Will what it really says.'

The woman grinned. 'It says, "Please send love to Sir Thomas and to Gavin. Your affectionate sister, Eleanor".'

William snatched the letter back. Gavin leered at him.

'"Your affectionate sister Eleanor",' he squeaked in an attempt to imitate Ellie's voice. '"Your affectionate sister, Eleanor". Affectionate *sister*, I *don't* think.'

William, his cheeks ablaze, leapt up and tried to push both Gavin and Marcella out of his tent.

'Get out, get out!' he cried. 'Ellie does not even know our father is dead. Get out.'

'Keep your hair on,' Gavin was still laughing, but a little more uncertainly now. 'She'll know soon enough.'

'Get out, get out before I punch you!' William shouted wildly. 'How dare you allow one of those women to read Ellie's letter and pronounce our father's name! How dare you?'

Gavin sighed with mock remorse. 'Marcella, we are not wanted here,' he said. 'Come on, let's go and find somewhere where we can talk in a rather more civilized manner.'

And with that, Gavin span the woman round and caused her to shriek with delight as he pushed his hand into the fold of her clothes.

William threw himself back on his bed and stared at the marks on the page. It seemed extraordinary that Ellie had made them. He traced the letters slowly with his finger, trying to remember which word must be which. Ellie said not much had changed. But it obviously had. For a start, Sir Walter was dead. Then, after years of both of them avoiding doing either, Ellie was now good at reading and writing. He tried to imagine her sitting with Brother Ranulf, struggling with the alphabet. He wondered if she had gone to the abbey or whether Ranulf came to the castle. But soon all he could see in his mind's eye was the green of English pastures, the chestnut trees outside the home he loved and Ellie's face, alight with fun as she told him of her latest ruse for teasing the monks. A terrible feeling of homesickness overcame him and, securing the tent flap so that Gavin and his women could not easily re-enter, William, clutching the first letter he had ever received in his life, dropped on to his knees and wept.

13

Hartslove, 1191

Actually, Ellie had lied, not about Sacramenta being well or Old Nurse being as fat as ever, but about nothing having happened at Hartslove since the crusaders had vanished down the road on that May morning, now more than a year before. Crusaders' castles were supposed to be under the special protection of God while their lords were away, but it was beginning to be Ellie's experience that God did not always do His job very well. It was not Sir Thomas's fault. His complete faith in the immunity from harm of a crusader's domestic property had allowed him to leave Sir Walter de Strop and Constable de Scabious in charge without a moment's hesitation. Non-crusading knights exploited the lightly defended castles of their crusading brethren on pain of hell. And as for servants who took advantage of their master's absence in the Holy Land, well, the devil had special tortures lined up for them. So Sir Thomas never dreamt that his long-standing constable might prove an uncomfortable guardian for Ellie and Old Nurse. At first, Ellie could not quite put her finger on why Constable de Scabious was making her uncomfortable. He was punctiliously polite and almost greasily pleasant. Nevertheless, by the time William actually read the letter in which Ellie said she did not trust de Scabious, she not only mistrusted the constable but was frightened of him as well.

It all started after they had buried Sir Walter, just before the first, dismal Christmas the crusaders were away. She found the constable looking at her in a way that he would never have dared had Sir Thomas been around.

Ellie was right to be nervous. Constable de Scabious had always harboured ambitions. While Sir Walter had taken Sir Thomas's place, these ambitions had been kept in check. But now that Sir Walter was dead and, so de Scabious calculated, Sir Thomas himself was almost certain to take the constable's shameful, cowardly secret to a foreign grave, the time seemed ripe to allow those ambitions to flourish a little. His flirtation with women's clothing would not be revealed. He could concentrate on his future. After all, so he reasoned to himself, it was only luck that had made the de Granvilles powerful castellans and the de Scabiouses their servants. If the de Scabiouses had chosen to ride next to the Conqueror at the Battle of Hastings, they might have ended up masters of Hartslove, with de Granvilles as lowly serfs. But the de Scabiouses were too humble for that kind of sword-wielding bravado. They had stayed with the baggage train as the Conqueror fought for his life, thus allowing others the opportunity to go for glory. With true generosity of spirit, the de Scabiouses confined themselves to dealing with more mundane matters. Now it was only fair that they should get their just rewards for not pushing themselves forwards. Moreover it should not be overlooked (although it always seemed to be, which was another injustice) that crouching between two pack animals was just as dangerous as engaging the enemy. Why, one of Sir Piers's ancestors had had his leg broken by a kicking mule, and very nasty it had been, too.

So, the constable reasoned as, on the Twelfth Night, he gave the orders for the Christmas holly branches to be taken out of the great hall and burnt, should Gavin de Granville marry Ellie and end up master of even more valuable land while he, the faithful steward, had to make do with a common woman who would not even bring so much as a fish pond as her dowry? No. He would make Eleanor his. The man was not deluded enough to imagine that Ellie would choose to break her betrothal to Gavin and give herself willingly to a man growing grey and heavy in middle age. The way to secure his prize was to compromise her in some way so that she felt lucky to find anybody to marry her at all. And if Gavin did return, well, he was not going to want to marry a girl with a reputation.

De Scabious took to watching Ellie and noticed that she often rode out with only one serving woman, a dumpy creature called Margery, for company and was away for three or four hours. Neither rain nor sleet seemed to put her off. Business always seemed to prevent him from following her, so de Scabious began to smile at Margery and eventually took to paying her a few compliments. The woman was delighted. Maybe the constable was looking for a wife. She took to washing her hair and rubbing her lardy face with rose water. By the time the spring flowers began to push through, de Scabious thought he had Margery just where he wanted her.

'Where do you and Miss Eleanor go when you ride out?' he asked one day, with a glutinous smile.

Margery winked conspiratorially.

'Now then, Constable,' she purred. 'That is between me and the young lady.'

'Of course,' said the constable, cheekily tweaking her arm. 'You young ladies and your secrets!' They both giggled. Then the constable seemed to become rather more serious. 'It is just that I am in charge of security and we wouldn't want anything to happen to her now, would we?'

He spanked Margery lightly on the backside as he went off and called back to her, 'You must keep Miss Eleanor's counsel if that is what she has asked, of course. My only concern is that if anything were to happen to her, well, the penalties for you would be . . . Still, I am sure you know what you are about.' Then he vanished.

A day or two later, the constable came into the courtyard just as Ellie and Margery returned. Ellie slipped away before he could speak to her, but Margery fluttered her eyelashes, inviting him to help her. De Scabious went forwards and was nearly flattened as, like a sack of potatoes, Margery slid from the horse and into his arms. As her fat fingers twisted round his neck and her foul breath warmed his face, de Scabious struggled not to choke. But it was worth the effort. Rubbing her cheek against his, Margery disclosed that Ellie rode to a small clearing near the abbey at least four times a week and sat either in a tumbledown forester's hut or, now that the weather was better, out among the trees with Brother Ranulf, learning her letters.

'Teaching her her letters, eh!' exclaimed the constable. 'She wouldn't learn them from Old Nurse. But maybe the monks have a better way of teaching.' He leered, and Margery leered back.

143

'Oh, no, I don't think so, sir,' she said, feigning innocence and feeling a tinge of guilt since Ellie had paid her chaperone well for her silence.

'Well, perhaps not,' said the constable. 'But what does Abbot Hugh make of it?'

'I don't believe the abbot knows,' replied the woman, trying to keep hold of the constable just as hard as he was trying to disentangle himself.

'Ah,' said the constable, as he finally released himself. 'Well, run along now. You must hide that complexion of yours from the wind, or it will be ruined.'

Margery simpered and took herself off. It was really for Ellie's own good that she had spilled her secret. After all, two such attractive women alone in the forest with a load of monks near by! *I must think of my own reputation*, she thought. *Particularly now that the nice constable has taken a shine to me*. And she hugged herself with glee.

The constable's plan was very simple. He would keep himself absolutely in the right. He quickly learnt from Margery exactly where the clearing that had become Ellie's schoolroom was situated and, on the pretext of being concerned, ordered one of the garrison soldiers to follow her, taking care he was not seen.

'We don't want Miss Eleanor to think we do not trust her, do we?' he said. 'But I would like you to report back anything you witness. The thing is, you just never know about these monks.'

Luck was with the constable. Ellie and Brother Ranulf had grown close. She never tired of hearing about all the stages involved in Hosanna's cure and he, although knowing that he was going behind his abbot's back, found Ellie such an apt pupil that he could not believe it was wrong to teach her her letters. She told him that she wanted to surprise Brother Andrew one day, by being able to read one of his books when he showed it to her. Surely, Brother Ranulf persuaded himself as he crept back into the abbey in time for choir, praying that his absence had not been noticed, this was a praiseworthy ambition, one in keeping with Christ's parable of the talents?

However, as the weeks went by, the monk and the girl began to find more to talk about than just Hosanna and the alphabet. One day, as Margery sat dozing under her fur cloak and the spying soldier shivered from his damp perch behind a bush, for the sun still had not much warmth in it, Brother Ranulf shyly showed Ellie that he kept the ring she had made for him from Hosanna's tail on a cord round his neck. This gesture unlocked Ellie's heart and, losing any kind of reserve, she began to tell Brother Ranulf openly of her mistrust of Constable de Scabious and her fears for the future.

The soldier reported this to the constable. From his hiding place, the soldier could not tell what Ellie said, but he could confirm that the girl and the monk were certainly thick as thieves. The constable tried to conceal his glee.

'Oh dear,' he said, sighing deeply. 'A ring! Fancy! Well, just keep watching and report everything, I mean *everything*, to me.'

The soldier nodded and eventually saw Ranulf help Ellie write her letter to William. After that, for some weeks, he was able to tell the constable no books were brought out. All that Ellie and the monk did was to sit together, talking, among the forget-me-nots and blue-bells, as spring became summer.

Ellie came to rely heavily on these conversations, but

145

the soldier grew bored with watching. He yawned through the long days and dreamt of tournaments. Then, just before harvest, he struck gold.

It was a hot afternoon and, sitting with her back to an oak tree, Ellie was plaiting daisies. Brother Ranulf was sitting next to her, their knees almost touching. Some distance away, Margery was fast asleep, her mouth wide open. A curious thrush hopped about beside her, its head on one side.

Ellie stopped plaiting to watch the thrush. But she did not really see it. Her head was full of other things. 'They will come back, won't they?' she said, turning to Brother Ranulf. She had asked the monk this question a hundred times already, but this did not stop her asking again. 'I can't believe they won't,' she went on, throwing the daisies away. 'I am so frightened for William, Gavin and Sir Thomas that sometimes I can't sleep at night. Why can't the Saracens just give up their religion and become Christians? It seems so easy to me. After all, they can't want to go to hell, can they?'

Brother Ranulf tried to soothe her. 'It is difficult to understand, I know,' he said. 'But we have to hope and trust. And, of course, they have Hosanna with them.'

They were both quite still for a moment, their minds going to places that neither of them wanted to go. Eventually it was Ellie who whispered it.

'Horses hardly ever come back, Brother Ranulf. We both know that.' And she burst into tears at the horror of it all.

Brother Ranulf, unable to bear her misery and feeling pretty miserable himself, lost all his self-control and hugged her. It was, he said to himself as she clung to him, a one-off. He would never allow himself the luxury again, and when Ellie finally stopped crying, he gently pushed her away. These meetings would have to stop. But soon. Not quite yet.

The soldier, with his ringside view, was thrilled. The constable was right. You really couldn't trust these monks. When he reported back, he was given a penny and told to continue his vigil, for, if you were to accuse a monk, it was important to gather as much evidence as possible.

'Miss Eleanor's honour will be perfectly safe if you are there,' the constable said sanctimoniously. The soldier did not hear him say, 'Got 'em!' as he left the room.

In the end, it was even easier than de Scabious had dared to hope.

When the summer's sun lost its heat and the leaves began to turn, Sacramenta was startled by a deer as she cantered towards the clearing. The mare shied violently and Ellie, who had not been paying much attention, was thrown, hitting her head on a tree root. Brother Ranulf, who was waiting for Ellie and who had steeled himself to tell her that their meetings must stop, came rushing when he heard the commotion. Terrified by the sight of the girl lying as still as a corpse, he forgot all about the danger to himself and sent Margery back to the castle for help.

'I'll stay with Ellie,' he cried. 'Go on, Margery, gallop.'

The spy, secreted among the branches, remained where he was. He saw the monk pick Ellie up and carry her carefully to the blanket he had brought for them to sit on. He saw him loosen Ellie's clothing and heard him begging her to breathe. Then, the monk sat rocking her in his arms until she came round. As Ellie began to stir, Brother Ranulf bent close – very close – to hear what she was saying. He remained with his head bowed for some time.

When Margery returned, she had the constable, several knights and a cart in tow. De Scabious said nothing to Brother Ranulf, simply lifted Ellie on to a pallet and headed straight back to Hartslove. The monk was distraught. As Ellie was carried off, he went back to the abbey and, flinging himself on to his knees in his cell, begged God to forgive him and to restore Ellie back to full health.

For once, God did as He was asked, and Ellie, under the ministrations of Old Nurse, was declared out of danger before the week was out. Old Nurse, who asked no questions when Ellie was carried upstairs by de Scabious, would let nobody near her charge and, when Ellie was eventually fit to talk, Old Nurse at first tried to make light of the whole affair.

'I don't know what you have been doing, my girl,' she said, bustling about with an armful of linen, 'But Constable de Scabious is putting it about that one of the monks took advantage of you when you were unconscious. He says your betrothal to Gavin is history. Now I have not looked after you all these years without knowing something about you. I don't believe anything that de Scabious says. And as for all this other nonsense about the monk having a ring next to his heart and you being spotted embracing in the forest, well, it is just idle gossip with no foundation.'

Ellie, lying in bed, took some time to understand what Old Nurse was saying. Then she suddenly sat up, flung the pad off the bump on her head and exploded. 'That good-for-nothing fat, warty woman! She was supposed just to accompany me. But she has been spying on me!'

Old Nurse stopped in her tracks, came over to Ellie's bed and sat down heavily, her ruddy face suddenly a nasty shade of green. 'Miss Ellie,' she said. 'Miss Ellie. What are you saying? Tell me these rumours are not true.'

Ellie defended herself. 'Of course they are not true, Old Nurse. Well, at least, Brother Ranulf has got a ring. But it is from Hosanna, not from me. And what if he did hug me? He's like a brother!'

Old Nurse looked at Ellie. 'But he is a brother of a different sort, Ellie. What on earth were you thinking of?'

'Oh, Old Nurse,' Ellie began to speak very fast. 'I wanted to learn to read to impress Brother Andrew.'

Old Nurse looked disbelieving. She had never seen Ellie inclined to read. But, apart from clicking her tongue, she said nothing and let Ellie continue.

'Brother Ranulf said he would teach me, but it would have to be in the forest because he thought Abbot Hugh would not agree. So I have been learning. I have written a letter to William,' the girl cried wildly. 'And we talked sometimes about Hosanna, and once I cried and Brother Ranulf hugged me. That's all, I swear it. I swear it on my mother's grave.'

'They say he behaved inappropriately when you came off Sacramenta,' said Old Nurse, frowning now.

'I'm sure he only did what was right.'

'Can you remember?'

'No, of course I can't remember,' Eleanor was almost beside herself. 'But I just know he wouldn't.'

'Others say differently,' said Old Nurse slowly. 'Others say that Brother Ranulf has been looking for an excuse to be sent away from the abbey so that he can go on crusade, and that you have provided one.'

Ellie opened her mouth to deny it, then shut it again. 'Oh, Old Nurse,' she whispered. 'I don't believe that.'

Old Nurse wiped her nose on her apron. 'Ellie, my sweet, it does not matter much what you believe. It is what others believe that counts. Why did you not tell me, or take me with you when you went into the wood?'

'You are too fat to ride,' said Ellie dully. 'And I knew you would disapprove. I was supposed to have lessons from you, remember?'

Old Nurse sighed. 'Well,' she said, 'we must make the best of it. I shall keep my ears open, and Ellie, please don't hide anything from me now. Come, let's get you dressed. But if I were you, I would stay up here until the whole thing blows over.'

But it did not blow over. Constable de Scabious saw to that. All through the autumn, there were meetings with the abbot, and, in the servants' quarters, except when Old Nurse appeared, gossip was rife. It was generally agreed that the marriage arranged between Gavin and Ellie could not, in all propriety, now take place. Gavin, if he returned, would be a holy crusader. Ellie was little better than a – well, nobody quite liked to say.

Margery, convinced that she was making herself indispensable to the constable, embellished her story with great enthusiasm. 'I saw what I saw,' she said, tapping her nasal warts with a finger covered in dough as she kneaded the bread. 'And I really couldn't say more. But you couldn't credit it, could you? A well-bred young girl and a monk. Innocent? Believe that and you will believe that men will one day go to the moon.'

On All Souls' Day, Brother Ranulf was publicly flogged by his fellow monks and sent to live by himself in a small hermitage outside the abbey walls. He was frantic for news about Ellie, but knew that if he asked, further opprobrium would be heaped on both their heads. His only hope was that one or more of the de Granvilles would return home and soon. He knew they would believe him. He would swear his and Ellie's innocence on Hosanna's name.

Ellie's fate seemed rather worse. The abbot and Constable de Scabious saw her together. Standing in front of the fire in the great hall, Ellie refused to 'confess' to the abbot since, she declared, she had nothing to confess. Abbot Hugh was inclined to try and diminish the whole affair. *If only*, he thought, *so many people did not know about it*. He felt sorry for the girl. But he also knew that an abbot trying to cover up for a monk was, in these times of reform, just not possible. Even as Ellie protested her innocence, the abbot knew that the sad truth was that both Ellie and Brother Ranulf were seriously compromised in the eyes of both the neighbourhood and the Church.

'Miss Eleanor,' he said at last, 'I do not know what to do. Maybe you are still pure, maybe not. But as most people now think that you have been alone with a man, and a monk at that, one thing I do know is that you can no longer marry Gavin de Granville. This means you will be fair game for knights on the prowl. You have lands, my dear girl. And,' he paused, wondering how best to say what he felt he had to say, 'We hear of great losses in the east. It may be that Gavin will never return. Perhaps, in view of what has happened, the best thing would be for you to enter a nunnery. That way at least your lands will be in good hands, for the Lady Abbess will take charge of them. And, child, you could even end up an abbess yourself – a good way to make up to God for all that has happened.'

Ellie was aghast. 'I don't want to be a nun,' she said, trying to keep her voice steady.

The abbot looked at her. 'Many people do things they don't want to do,' he said gently. 'Brother Ranulf is living alone in a hermitage. Do you think that is what he wanted?'

Ellie's eyes filled with tears. But she would not give in. 'I don't want to be a nun,' she repeated.

'My dear, I think you have no choice.'

Constable de Scabious, standing by the wall, his face full of mock consternation, cleared his throat. Here was his opportunity. 'Maybe I could venture to offer a solution?' he asked in what he thought of as his nicest voice.

Ellie and the abbot turned to look at him. 'I am Sir Thomas's right-hand man,' the constable said. 'Miss Eleanor was under my protection, so it is only right that I should take responsibility. If Miss Eleanor would do me the honour,' he left a dramatic moment of silence, 'I am prepared to marry her. The damage to my reputation would, of course, be significant. But her dowry lands would probably help me get over my natural reluctance to link myself to somebody with a tainted past. And, of course, if Master Gavin cannot marry her himself – which he clearly cannot – I expect he would prefer her lands to go to friend rather than foe. If you don't mind me saying so, abbot, if Miss Eleanor's lands go to the Church, they will be lost to everybody.'

Ellie almost laughed. Had the constable gone mad?

'I would rather die than marry you,' she said. 'You must know that.'

The constable looked hurt. 'Well, my dear,' he said. 'If Sir Thomas and his sons don't come back, and you know as well as I do that they are very likely already dead, you would be marrying me anyway,' he said. 'Sir Thomas left me in control here, and the deed could be done in a trice. But, let's be reasonable. After you have lain in the arms of a monk, even if Gavin does return, he will certainly not want to marry you. Plenty more young girls for him to choose from. My intentions are kind. I thought I might spare you that shame and also give you an escape route from the nunnery.'

Ellie looked at the abbot, real fear in her eyes. But he offered no comfort.

'My dear, it is quite a good offer,' he said. 'Constable Piers de Scabious is not a bad man and nobody will dare impugn your reputation once you are betrothed to him.'

'I can't,' said Ellie, her voice rising. How, oh how, had her reading and writing lessons come to this? She began to edge out of the room.

The last thing she heard as she reached the door was the constable. 'I don't think, Miss Eleanor, that you have much choice,' he was saying and his smile was triumphant. Even before he had finished, Ellie had fled upstairs and barred her door.

14

Between Lydda and Ramle, late September 1191

Except with Gavin, forage duty was never popular. But since the king had taken his turn – and had very nearly been captured by Saladin's troops when, after six hours in the boiling sun, he had dismounted and sat underneath a shady tamarisk bush for a rest – the knights had no excuse not to volunteer. They had left the orchards of Jaffa behind them and were now camped between Lydda and Ramle, marching through inhospitable territory. Richard had not yet found a way of telling anybody that Jerusalem was an impossible target, and so it was still towards this goal that the Christian forces were making their way.

William and Gavin set off just after dawn on a food-finding mission with a group led by a knight with a fearsome reputation, Reginald de Courtois. There were four of them out in front: Reginald, the Count of Dreux, William and Gavin. Following them rather more slowly were three wagons' drawn by mules and six sumpter horses with panniers to fill. Ten other knights protected this group. They had all started together, but now the four knights in the vanguard were nearly ten miles from the main body of the army, with the wagons nearly two miles behind them. Hosanna was jogging next to

Montlouis – the horses went well together. Gavin, for once, seemed in high good humour. His women had been dispatched back to Acre, but this did not stop him from teasing William unmercifully, asking if, once they returned to Acre themselves, he would like to meet Marcella and take some lessons from her. William was sulking. Reginald occasionally growled at Gavin to keep his voice down.

Even in late September, the sun's glare was soon uncomfortable for armed men, and it was with relief that shortly after ten o'clock Reginald spotted what he was looking for: a patch of green in the brown scrub. About a mile away, there seemed to be a small settlement surrounded by wells. It did not look protected. Indeed, as the knights drew closer they could make out figures, mainly women carrying water, and almost naked children playing in the dirt.

'There will be no slaughter of these people unless they resist,' said Reginald. 'We will simply secure the place, then wait for the wagons. They should not be too long behind us. Is that understood?'

The count, William and Gavin murmured their assent and gathered together in close formation. Gavin was now quiet. Between them and the settlement rose some small, stony hillocks on which Reginald kept a close eye. It was not until it was too late that they heard the thunder of hoofs not from in front but from behind. Out of nowhere, or so it seemed, a small band of Saracens rushed across the plain, brandishing their weapons and shattering the peace of the morning with their cries.

In an instant, everything changed. The Christian knights, with the ease of long practice, formed a star, their horses' tails in the centre. They held their lances

155

directly in front of them. William heard Gavin's breathing become shallow.

'God protect us,' Gavin muttered.

'God protect us,' William repeated trying to keep his voice low and steady. Underneath him, Hosanna pawed the ground. 'Help me, Hosanna,' the boy whispered and the horse's ears pricked back as if to catch the words.

There were about fifteen Saracens, most mounted on small, agile ponies that were easy to leap on and off. At their head rode Kamil on his Arab. Compared to the Saracens' mounts, the Great Horses of the knights looked large and cumbersome. Hosanna, so much smaller and more elegant than the others, immediately caught Kamil's attention. Ah! That horse again. He would have that horse. Shouting instructions to his men to kill the knights but be sure to spare the red horse, Kamil waited until his soldiers had disabled the knights' lances then rushed in to challenge Reginald in single combat.

Reginald could do nothing else but break the formation. He shouted for each knight to defend himself as he sent his horse forwards, his sword raised. But despite his superior height and weight, he could not manoeuvre quickly enough to outflank his younger, slighter enemy. Kamil, using his wits as well as his weapons, presented the knight with an opening, but only if he leant down. Then, before Reginald could regain his balance, Kamil slipped round and pushed him from his horse. Another Saracen immediately moved in for the kill.

The Count of Dreux, meanwhile, was being attacked on all sides. He killed four of Kamil's men before going down shouting, 'God and the Holy Sepulchre!' Blood poured from a hundred wounds. Gavin and William, engaged in struggles of their own, pushed Montlouis and

Hosanna close together, nose to tail, so that horses and knights could protect each other.

Kamil shouted to his men to break them apart. Then, when Gavin was fully engaged on the side away from Hosanna, Kamil rode up behind William and raised his sword. Gavin sensed rather than saw what was about to happen and thrust his spurs into Montlouis' left flank. As he had been trained to do, the horse leapt sideways, pushing Hosanna out of the way and causing Kamil's blow to miss William's neck and fall instead directly on to Gavin's right arm. Gavin's sword dropped out of his hand as Kamil, spitting with vengeance, pulled his horse round and plunged his own sword directly into Montlouis' heart. The horse sighed, shuddered, then sank to the ground, his eyes wide. Gavin fell directly underneath him.

William pulled Hosanna up and leapt off as best he could, cursing his unwieldy armour. Tearing off his mailed gloves he tugged and pulled at Gavin in an effort to pull him free as Montlouis finally rolled over and was still. Gavin cried out as Montlouis' blood flowed into the sand. But there was no time for mourning. Two Saracen men rushed at William, their swords poised.

'Stop!' Kamil shouted before the first death blow sliced down. 'Stop! This skirmish is over. Go and see to our wounded. This Christian is mine.'

His men obeyed and Kamil dismounted. He walked over to catch a snorting, blowing Hosanna, grabbed the reins and vaulted easily into the saddle. Then he rode over to William. Standing above the brothers, his sword above his head, Kamil was a terrifying sight.

'Are you prepared for death?' he cried in Arabic.

Neither Gavin nor William could understand him, but it was plain what he meant. Gavin, in considerable pain, gave a small groan. William, still kneeling, said nothing. He kept his eyes glued to Hosanna's hoofs.

'If you beg for your life I will spare you,' said Kamil, suddenly switching to the Norman French he had learned as a young boy. 'I'm told Christians will always beg.'

Addressed in his own language, William looked up slowly. 'We will not beg,' he said. He wanted to touch Hosanna's nose, now so close above him, but he could not let go of Gavin.

Kamil glanced down, preparing to strike. But as he did so Hosanna bent his head, covering William's with his own. To kill William, Kamil would have to pull Hosanna away. Something – perhaps it was because the horse's gesture seemed so like a caress – prevented Kamil from twitching the reins. Before he had really thought, he found himself lowering his sword. The Saracen soldiers looked surprised. Was their bloodthirsty master becoming soft? Kamil noticed their expressions, but instead of their faces he saw, in his mind's eye, the face of the knight with the teardrop birthmark, the knight he had allowed to live, and who still haunted his dreams. Yet still, and Kamil groaned inwardly, he could not bring himself to pick up his sword. The Christian kneeling before him was hardly a knight. He was just a boy of about Kamil's own age. Venting his frustration, Kamil kicked Hosanna hard in the ribs. The horse grunted but wheeled round obediently.

'Let these men go,' Kamil ordered, speaking in Arabic again and glaring so hard that his own men shrank from him. 'There is no need for us to shed their blood when their deaths will be worse for being slow. They will die in the desert. Come, collect up the spare horses and let's be gone.'

Kamil was about to ride off when he turned back.

'This horse,' he said to William, again in French, 'what is its name?'

William stood up slowly. It was not until he was standing straight that he trusted himself to speak.

'Who are you?' he asked. 'How do you know our language?'

Kamil looked down. 'When you want to kill vermin, you learn how they behave,' he said. 'Many of us speak your language.'

'Is that how you think of us, as vermin?'

'Yes.'

William was silent for a moment and then looked at Kamil again. 'It is curious,' he said simply. 'Because that is exactly how we think of you.'

Kamil gave a bitter laugh.

'Well then,' he said, 'we understand each other perfectly.' Hosanna was restive, and Kamil had difficulty keeping him still. 'Stand!' he ordered. Hosanna obeyed.

William watched in agony.

'You see,' said Kamil. 'The horse also understands me perfectly. Now answer my question. I want to know if my new horse has a name.'

'The horse –' William said slowly and in utter despair, 'my horse. My horse is called Hosanna.'

Kamil, showing not a glimmer of pity, nodded and spat into the sand. Then he folded his legs round Hosanna's sides and galloped off. Soon he and his men were out of sight.

William stood quite still for a few moments, then knelt down, took his brother in his arms and began to shake uncontrollably.

*

Three days later, William and Gavin were picked up by another foraging party. They were almost unrecognizable. William had carried Gavin as best he could, trying to find his way back to the camp. Their tongues were black. Gavin's wounded arm was completely useless. When William could finally speak again, he uttered only one word, 'Hosanna,' and turned his face to the wall. Hal, overwhelmed with grief, could be comforted by no one, not even by Dargent, although he did his best.

15

Saladin's camp, east of Jerusalem, autumn 1191

Kamil was very pleased with his new horse. He found the chestnut stallion responsive and quick. He was also braver than Kamil's customary Arab. On the way back to Saladin's camp, he leapt over water-filled dykes without hesitation and even, when a snake crossed their path, stood still while Kamil killed it with a spear. By the time Kamil dismounted, he was sure that he had never had a horse quite like him. The only trouble was the horse's name which, because the word was so inextricably linked to Christian worship, Kamil refused to use. It did not matter.

'I shall call you Red Horse,' said Kamil, as he led Hosanna to his new quarters.

Hosanna found himself in the lap of luxury. He was stationed slightly away from the other horses, shaded from the sun by a silk awning. Kamil's previous horse was sent to the horse-lines, and Hosanna had his undivided attention. Nothing was too much trouble. Kamil felt in his bones that he had stumbled on something very valuable. He had not had the horse three days before he ordered a special bridle made of soft and supple oiled camel skin. After a cursory look at the jewelled headband Sir Thomas had given William when he was dubbed to knighthood, Kamil threw it away. Then he ordered special brushes, and took care to groom Hosanna himself. He frowned when he found the remains of the weal on Hosanna's neck and wondered how it had got there. It was the horse's only blemish apart from a few lumps on his legs. Kamil didn't mind. He thought the scars gave the horse character.

Not that the horse needed any more character. Hosanna charmed his new owner with his intelligence. He did not have to be held if Kamil mounted or dismounted. But within seconds of Kamil leaping on, he could go like the wind. He bent his head willingly to Kamil's commands, stepping neatly in any direction the boy chose. One afternoon, to much applause, Kamil taught Hosanna to rear and to do a half-turn at the canter. Saladin came to look, and was pleased to see that Kamil had found something to do other than sit and look mutinous.

Kamil found Hosanna no pushover. The horse had lost none of his spirit and once or twice he dumped Kamil unceremoniously in the sand. It said something for the red horse that Kamil took this in good part. Far from punishing him, Kamil soon learnt to respect as well as love him. As the days grew colder, he sometimes found Hosanna looking steadfastly into the distance, his dark eyes inscrutable. At times like this, Kamil would pet him and make much of him. But although Hosanna seemed happy enough rubbing his head against Kamil's soothing hands, he continued to gaze at something Kamil could not see himself.

'I think you were fond of that boy, Red Horse,' Kamil said one day as he brought Hosanna a piece of sweet bread and a thicker blanket. It was November and the winter rains threatened. 'And I think he was nice to you. But you must forget him. You are a Saracen horse now. It's not too bad a life, don't you agree?' And Hosanna stopped looking into the distance and blew down Kamil's neck instead.

The rains came. Life was no longer comfortable. Kamil had a tent constructed for Hosanna and complained to the tent-maker when it leaked. He employed a small boy to clean the wet mud and sand from Hosanna's legs after he had been exercised and always made sure the horse's grain ration had not been touched by rats. On days when it hailed, Kamil did not take Hosanna out. Seeing to the horse's welfare kept him from thinking too much and Kamil was grateful for that.

Things were not going well for the Saracens. Saladin, like Richard, was becoming more and more troubled by the progress of the crusade. In the sultan's estimation, despite occasional minor victories for his own men, the Christians had been too successful. If they decided to take Jerusalem, Saladin wondered if he could stop them. The emirs inside the Holy City had an unholy fear of Richard. Furthermore, the Saracen army, unused to being in the field for so long, was becoming restive. The men wanted to go home. Baha ad-Din had heard rumours relayed from the bazaar at Acre that more Christians were going to arrive, and Saladin no longer held any ports from which to launch sea attacks. Now that Richard was in the Holy Land, the Christians had become bold. Everything pointed towards making a truce. But a truce with Richard? Would this king, who everybody now called Lionheart, be willing to make a deal with a Muslim? And indeed, could Saladin, without losing face, make a deal with a man who had ordered the merciless slaughter of over 3,000 Saracen prisoners at Acre?

At the beginning of December, the sultan called in Baha ad-Din and also sent for Kamil. The boy seemed calmer now. Maybe training that red horse had something to do with it. If there were troubled times ahead, relations between himself and his ward, strained in a way Saladin could not understand ever since the Saracens had retaken Jerusalem, must be put back on their old footing. When Kamil arrived and made his bow, Saladin took his hands.

'Ah, Kamil, you are cold. Come, I have a fire. When I have time, I must come and take a close look at your new friend. My emirs think it is very funny that you call him Red Horse instead of using whatever name the Christians gave him,' he said. 'And I hear he is smart as well as beautiful.'

Kamil responded with a smile. 'He is a good horse,' he said and took his old place by the sultan's side.

Baha ad-Din was pleased. Maybe, at eighteen, Kamil was growing up. But he was soon to be disappointed. When Saladin brought up the question of a truce and outlined his reasons, Kamil's mood blackened.

'We cannot make peace after all they have done,' he said. 'How can we make peace with people who do not think of us as human beings?'

'What they think of us is not the point,' said Saladin drily. 'I am telling you, as my most trusted friends, that we cannot beat them.'

'If you would allow us to visit their camp at night we could,' responded Kamil, clenching his fists. 'There are other ways to beat them than open warfare.'

'And they are the wrong ways,' replied Saladin,

watching the boy closely. 'We all have certain rules of combat, the Christians as well as us. They broke them by massacring our unarmed captives. We cannot descend to that level. If we break the rules of combat, anarchy takes over. We are not barbarians, for all the nonsense the Christians put about.'

Kamil was silent as Baha ad-Din and Saladin spoke of how a truce might be achieved and what its terms might be. Then he exploded.

'This is utter betrayal,' he said. 'Truce means that the Christians keep the coast. Without the coast, how can we make Jerusalem safe? In reality, truce means handing back our holy places to them eventually. It would be . . .' he stopped, looked furiously at Saladin and then went on, 'it would be treachery.'

The sultan half got up and reached for his sword. For a moment Baha ad-Din thought he was going to kill Kamil. Then he sat down again.

'Killing all the Christians is impossible, Kamil,' he said. 'And anyway, it is not the way of Allah. My son, think hard. Show some foresight. Come, I depend on you. You may well be called to take over from me one day. Even a sultan cannot live forever. But I must see that you have a head as well as a heart.'

Kamil looked stunned. 'Take over from you?'

'Yes,' said Saladin evenly. 'Now. Let us pray and when we have prayed we will talk some more.'

Kamil prostrated himself and prayed hard. Maybe Saladin was right, but he did not feel it in his heart. In his heart, all he felt was fury at himself for his failure properly to avenge his father, and a deep hatred of the Christians in his land. After prayers, Kamil left the sultan, but not before Saladin had ordered him most particularly to stay close at all times. Kamil bowed. The sultan's will was his command. Saladin smiled but said nothing more.

Over the next few weeks, Kamil again found himself several times in conversation with the man with the black beard, the one who had been so friendly after the Christian cavalry charge during which he had first spotted the red horse. The man had such an open, intelligent face and kind smile that Kamil was disposed to like him. He himself did not look out for the man, but more and more often they seemed to find themselves buying herbs and vegetables from the same woman at the market or taking shelter from the weather in the same cave. Once, when Kamil was returning to the camp on Hosanna, the man gave him a beautiful saddle-cloth, 'In praise,' so he said, 'of a beautiful red horse.' Kamil began to think of him as a friend.

The man's name was Abdul Raq. He spoke well of the sultan and extolled the glories of the Muslim people. But he was no sycophant and Kamil found that he had interesting views that he liked to listen to. Little by little Kamil began to confide his own hopes. He told him about Saladin's plans for a truce and how uncomfortable this made him feel. Raq never condemned the sultan, even sympathized and agreed with some of the things Kamil revealed that the sultan had said. But after a while he openly wondered what the sultan had in mind in the longer term.

One day, just before the Christian New Year, the two met as Kamil stormed out, bitter and furious, from the sultan's tent. Truce now seemed inevitable.

'You seem upset, my friend,' said Raq. 'Let's walk a little until you cool off.'

As they walked, Kamil grew more and more careless of his words.

'Saladin has got it wrong,' he said at last. 'Where is a true leader? Where can we find one who knows that the only way we can extol Allah is to kill all the Christians who are polluting our soil. They have land of their own where they can worship in their own way. Why do they come here? Jerusalem is not their city, even though the prophet Jesus died there. If we make a truce, we will never be rid of them.'

Abdul Raq was silent for a moment or two.

'There is a leader,' he said eventually, keeping his voice low and not looking at Kamil, 'who would think you very wise.'

'I wish I could meet him,' cried Kamil before he could stop himself.

Abdul Raq turned to look at him.

'It could be arranged,' he said quietly.

Kamil felt he was on the brink of something momentous. He looked at Raq. How far could he really trust this man?

Raq made a motion with his hands. 'You must make up your own mind,' he said. 'I shall say nothing. We know too much about each other now, you and I.'

Kamil took a deep breath. 'Then arrange it,' he said and, turning on his heel to hide his anxiety, he went to find his horse.

Two weeks later, Kamil found himself riding fast through the desert very early in the morning. He was accompanied by an unknown man to whom he had been introduced by Raq. Everything seemed to have happened so quickly that Kamil had had no time to be nervous. And now, Hosanna felt so fit and keen that even in the bitter cold, it was still a pleasure to be out. The dark did not seem threatening to Kamil. It felt like a friend. Raq had approached him the day before and introduced the man who was now acting as guide. The guide had whispered that Kamil should be mounted and ready by midnight. He would come and find him. The man had done exactly that, and they had set off without exchanging another word.

The rain made the ground into sludge. But it soon ceased to fall and, as the pair rode up off the plain heading north, the going became lighter. Kamil was amazed at the ability of the horses to find their feet in the dark, but neither stumbled. He leant forwards and ran his hand down Hosanna's neck. Hosanna, concentrating on keeping his feet, did not acknowledge his caress.

They sped on through all the hours of darkness and all the following day and night. They rested only for two or three hours at a time. When dawn broke on the third day, they had reached the bottom of a group of small mountains, the peak of the highest glimmering with a light scattering of snow. Kamil felt no sense of exhaustion and nor did Hosanna. As they began to push up, following a gorge cut by a river, the red horse scrambled and climbed with no apparent effort. The guide's horse was struggling now, but Hosanna, right up behind it, was tireless.

All day they followed the river, until at last, as darkness fell, they began to climb more steeply. Further and further up they went, the air growing thin. The sides of the gorge closed in on them, until Kamil felt almost claustrophobic, and for the first time, he began to wonder what he was doing. If the sultan found out where he was, it would mean certain death. But, when the gorge opened out again, and the guide intimated that they would camp for the night where a tumbling stream offered water for the horses, Kamil reassured himself.

The sultan will not find out, he reasoned, watching the other man, almost out of nothing, conjure up a fire. Kamil took the food and drink that he was offered. *The sultan and Baha ad-Din think I have gone to consult the imam in Jerusalem to see about strengthening my knowledge of the Koran*, he thought as he shared his bread with Hosanna. *They will never know the truth*. Nevertheless, Kamil did not sleep well.

They rose again at dawn and were away twenty minutes later. Above their heads, eagles circled. The guide was anxious to push on. The going was very steep now, and the rocks offered an uncertain foothold. Kamil could not disguise his relief when the guide pulled up.

'We have arrived,' he said, indicating that Kamil should go in front of him through a great gash in the side of the gorge.

Kamil went through the gash, scrambled up a little more, then found himself riding along a ledge. To his right, the drop was well over sixty metres and sheer. He caught his breath and put his hand on Hosanna's mane to stop himself feeling dizzy. The horse flicked back his ears and stepped carefully over the fallen debris that lay in his way. The ledge seemed to lead nowhere, but there was no turning back and the guide was pushing him on. Kamil felt suddenly sick. Was this a trick? However just before the end of the ledge, completely invisible until you were right beside it, was another gap in the rock face. Kamil turned and found himself riding through spiky grass again as the path opened into a small hidden plateau between two peaks. He drew in his breath sharply. It was stunningly beautiful, with the sun's rays just beginning to push against the brooding shadows cast by the rocks.

In front of him some rough buildings had been constructed with roofs made of straw and mud. They were very simple. From a hole in the roof of one, smoke rose. About fifty men were standing outside, apparently ready to greet him. All were heavily armed.

Kamil dismounted. He let Hosanna go but hoped the horse would stay near him. He was disappointed when a small boy came and led him away.

The men said nothing. They were dressed in long blue tunics with daggers strapped to their arms and sword belts round their hips. Their beards were dyed a curious shade of red. As Kamil approached they parted, and the boy found himself in front of a small, rather round man, sitting on a chair cracking walnuts.

He looked up and his smile sent his whole face into creases. 'Greetings, my friend,' he said, spitting out some shell. 'I am Rashid ed-Din Sinan. But I am better known as the Old Man of the Mountain. My friend Abdul Raq tells me you wanted to see me.'

Kamil swallowed hard. He suddenly felt weak.

Sinan looked at him kindly. 'Come, sit,' he said, and one of his men ran off to get another chair. 'Catch your breath. May I offer tea?'

Kamil nodded. 'Tea for our visitor,' said Sinan, and immediately a table was brought. Cups and sweets were laid out.

Sinan allowed Kamil to take his time, making pleasant conversation about the weather and complimenting Kamil on his horse. Kamil began to relax. Gently, Sinan brought the conversation round to the crusade and Saladin's desire for a truce.

'What a good man the sultan is,' he said, rather to Kamil's surprise. 'But how misguided. Allah needs strong men these days, for strong deeds must be done.' Sinan sighed.

Kamil was quick to agree. 'With a truce, we will never get rid of the Christians,' he said. 'Surely that cannot be the will of Allah?'

Sinan paused to consider. 'It is my view that it is not,' he said. There was silence.

'Kamil,' said Sinan at last. 'There are important and difficult things to be done. Things that are right are often not easy. Are you prepared for such things?'

Kamil nodded slowly. But Sinan was not ready to confide in him just yet. The Old Man paid careful attention as he asked the boy questions about the Koran. Soon he abandoned questions and began to weave a web of ideas. He talked for a long time. Kamil was spellbound by his voice and by the apparent truth of his words. He nodded his head many times.

'If we are to create a perfect world as Allah commands,' Sinan said at last, 'we must be prepared to show perfect obedience. Are you prepared?'

Kamil nodded again.

'Let me show you,' said Sinan. He got up and took Kamil back through the gash in the mountainside. In single file they walked to the end of the ledge and looked down at the drop to the rocks below. Kamil began to breathe more quickly.

'Look up!' Sinan commanded. Kamil, his head reeling, did as he was told. Above him, on a rocky outcrop, two men stood on guard duty. Sinan clapped his hands and the men stood to attention.

The Old Man of the Mountain spoke only three words.

Then the two men, without hesitation, walked to the end of the ridge and, making not even the smallest of sounds, jumped. The only scream was Kamil's. Sinan put out his arm and steadied him as the bodies of the men shattered on the rocks below. Kamil was covered in sweat.

Sinan, apparently unmoved, waited for a moment or two. Then he spoke in a calm and even voice. 'Never betray your feelings,' he said. 'That is the first rule.'

He stood patiently as Kamil pulled himself together.

Sinan went on, 'These men you see here would do anything, not for me but for Allah. I asked them to die for Allah and they have. Could you do the same?'

Kamil could scarcely take in what had just happened. But, mesmerized by the Old Man's voice, by his power and by his unassailable logic, he nodded slowly. 'I hope I could,' he whispered.

'My boy,' said Sinan. 'Death is what some men do best. But yours is a different path. Allah expects something else from men of your quality. He will give you the strength to do whatever is asked of you just as He gave those men the strength to do what was asked of them. To every man his unique moment of glory.'

Kamil was silent. He could not trust his voice.

'Now,' said Sinan, guiding him back along the path and through the gash. 'Let us talk of other things. Tell me a little about yourself.'

They returned to the table as if nothing had happened. Kamil sat down trying to hide his shaking legs. With gentle probing from Sinan, he told him of his father's death and of the vengeance he had failed to take, killing the son, but leaving the knight alive. He did not mention, however, how he had come by the red horse, or his failure to kill William. Something stopped him. As Kamil spoke, the Old Man nodded and smiled, for all the world like a benign elderly grandfather. When he had finished, Sinan showed him where he could rest before his return journey and settled the boy down with his own hands.

'Was your father Muhyi ad-Din?' he asked as he stood in the doorway of one of the huts. 'The learned scholar?'

'Yes,' said Kamil. 'Did you know him?'

Sinan nodded. 'He was a fine man,' he said softly. 'Now sleep.'

To his surprise, Kamil fell asleep almost at once. The reference to his father had filled him with relief and confidence. For the first night in many months, he slept without dreaming.

A few hours later he was woken by a man bearing hot, spiced tea. He drank it, then straightened his clothes and went out. Hosanna was already saddled and waiting for him. Sinan was holding the horse's rein and stroking him. Though he tried to pretend it was something to do with just waking up, the sight made Kamil shiver. There was something about the way the Old Man was touching Hosanna that made him feel uneasy.

'It has been good that we met,' Sinan said, handing the reins to Kamil. 'When we are ready, you will get a message telling you what to do. Remember, it is for Allah that we act, not for ourselves. The crusaders have defiled our land long enough. Men like your father deserve more than you killing one small boy and Saladin making a truce. He would expect great things of you and your chance to perform great things will come soon. Meanwhile, keep close to the sultan and try to guide him along the right paths.'

Kamil nodded. He dismissed his feeling of foreboding. Instead he was filled with gratitude. This was the leader he had been looking for. He thanked the Old Man for his hospitality. Sinan accepted his thanks and patted him on the arm. 'Now,' he said, 'The guide will take you back. Take care on your journey. We will meet again.'

Kamil swung himself on to Hosanna and smiled. 'Until then,' he said softly and chided Hosanna for his impatience as he followed the guide out on to the ledge once more.

16

After his return to Saladin's camp, it did not take long for the call to come. While he was waiting, Kamil was especially attentive to Saladin. He did not let his hostility to the idea of a truce completely vanish lest the sultan suspect something was up, but he was polite, and smiled at the sultan when their eyes met. Saladin noted aloud that the boy's temper had improved since his visit to Jerusalem. Kamil seemed to be offering constructive suggestions instead of harsh criticism. He said as much to Baha ad-Din in Kamil's hearing.

'Young boys do grow up,' was Baha ad-Din's only response, but he too was pleased by Kamil's behaviour. Riding out with him was a pleasure again. 'Perhaps the imam at Jerusalem and the horse between them have made him see sense.' The sultan seemed to nod, and all three shared breakfast.

Abdul Raq now spoke to Kamil only occasionally and never asked about the meeting with the Old Man. When they did meet, Kamil told him briefly what the sultan was thinking, but did not hang around for pleasantries. Two weeks after his visit to the mountains, however, Raq found Kamil in the red horse's tent. The sky was dark, but the rain was holding off. The red horse kept his distance as Raq slithered through the tent flap, but Kamil chose not to notice.

Raq smiled. 'Well,' he said, 'I am here both to admire your horse and to tell you that the time has come. Are you ready?'

Kamil nodded, his heart thumping. He stood up and gave Hosanna an apple.

Raq watched but his expression never changed. 'The sultan is to be assassinated,' he said.

Kamil gasped.

'Don't worry,' Raq said. 'You are not to perform the deed yourself. You are simply to provide the opportunity. You are to ask the sultan if he would like to try your horse, and if you can go out together the day after tomorrow, early in the morning. Suggest that it might be nice if it was just be the two of you, since you have something to say to him in private. You will indicate that you wish to apologize for your previous opposition to his plans. The assassins will find an opportunity.'

'Is that all?'

Raq looked at the boy curiously. 'Not quite. The assassins will be waiting behind the rocks about two miles from this camp. You and the sultan will swap horses and you will encourage the sultan to gallop round the rocks to test the red horse's speed. There will be an ambush.' Raq paused. 'In order that you are not suspected of treachery, the red horse will also be killed. Everybody knows how fond you are of the animal and will never imagine you could be party to anything that would involve his death.'

Kamil stood absolutely still. What little colour there was left in his face drained away. Raq got up. 'Do you understand?' he asked.

176

Kamil swallowed. 'This order comes from the Old Man?'

'Directly,' said Raq. 'He said that this challenge would be a true test of your faith in Allah and of your respect for your father.'

'Yes,' whispered Kamil. 'Yes, I see.'

'We will not speak again until it is over,' said Raq and he slunk off.

Kamil left the red horse's tent. He could not look at him. In his mind, Kamil replayed his meeting with Sinan over and over again. He could hear him talking, explaining why such sacrifices were the only way and why they should be seen as a true test of Kamil's love for Allah. Kamil steeled himself. He must do as he had promised. But his heart felt like lead. He got a groom to feed and brush Hosanna, saying that he did not feel well.

The next day, Kamil approached the sultan as if in a dream, extolled the virtues of his horse and asked if they could ride out together, 'Just like in the old days.'

'Come and try my red horse,' he said, trying to keep in his mind's eye the vision of his father lying in his own blood while the knight with the mark like a teardrop shouted in victory. 'He truly is a wonder. You would enjoy him. And I have something I would like to discuss with you.'

Saladin smiled. 'It will be a great pleasure, Kamil,' he said and agreed to meet the boy early the following morning.

It was Saladin himself who told his bodyguards to remain in the camp. 'I shall be safe with Kamil,' he told them as the winter sun tried its best to give out some heat. 'And the crusading knights are some distance away. It is good to go out alone sometimes.'

Kamil could scarcely believe that the plan was going without a hitch. He should have rejoiced, but he could hardly breathe.

The guards were not happy. But they nodded as Saladin and Kamil mounted their horses and rode off. Hosanna, bright gold in the morning light, his mane and tail like spun silk, strode out well. After half a mile or so, the two men swapped horses. Kamil tried to smile as he handed Hosanna over. Oh! But the horse was so beautiful!

Hosanna carried the sultan with ease and executed the manoeuvres asked of him with spirit and joy. He even reared on command and made Saladin laugh.

Finally, unable to bear the tension a moment longer, Kamil urged the sultan to gallop round the rocks.

'You have not tried him at full speed,' he cried, his voice hard and loud. Saladin nodded, then paused. If he was alarmed by Kamil's white face, he did not show it.

'I have never asked you,' he said, still in a conversational tone, 'what this horse's real name is.' For a moment Kamil thought wildly that he would tell Saladin the whole tale. But he could not. When he opened his mouth, however, what came out was almost as unexpected.

'The horse?' he cried. 'Oh, the horse is called Hosanna.' Hosanna, hearing his name for the first time in almost five months, turned his head and looked directly up at Kamil's face.

At that moment, Kamil knew he could not do what was asked of him. But it was too late. Saladin was already urging Hosanna into that peculiar floating gallop that was special only to him. Kamil was paralysed with horror. Then, just as Saladin neared the rocks, he found his voice and his spurs. Digging the steel hard into the sultan's horse, Kamil shouted and raised his whip above his head in an effort to make it go faster. But his voice mocked him in the wind. Hosanna was too far away. Now Saladin was almost at the rocks. Soon he had disappeared. Kamil was crazy with horror. 'No! No!' he howled.

Then he was at the rocks himself, turning behind them. It took him a moment to understand what he saw. Standing on the ground, apparently uninjured, was Saladin. Hosanna, unharmed, was beside him. Baha ad-Din was there too, leaning down. At his feet, dead, lay Abdul Raq and one of Saladin's most trusted servants. Both bore the mark of Baha ad-Din's dagger in their hearts. Saladin said nothing. Kamil, stunned, uncomprehending and breathing heavily, dropped off his horse.

'I am ready to die, too,' were the only words he could think to say as he knelt in the sand.

Saladin looked at him. 'Kamil,' he said gently, 'do you think the one true Allah could ever demand what the Old Man demanded?'

Kamil, sobbing now, shook his head.

'I had you followed the day you went up the mountain,' the sultan went on. 'I did not tell Baha ad-Din until yesterday because I wanted to see what you would do. But let's not speak of that just now.' And sitting Kamil down, Saladin took from his horse's saddlebags his own, much-thumbed copy of the Koran. He opened it and showed Kamil how, although the great book speaks of blood and revenge, it is also full of passages relating to righteous conduct, truth and beauty, things combined in the horse Kamil had been ready to sacrifice in the name of hate.

'Sacrifices must be made in the name of honour and

love,' he said. 'Only then is the sacrificial gift worthy of the giver.' Kamil was quieter now. 'One day,' the sultan said, 'one day, Kamil, I will demand something of you and see if you have understood what I have just told you.'

Then Saladin got up, handed Hosanna over, took his own horse and rode back to his camp.

17

Richard's camp, west of Jerusalem, winter 1191

Since Hosanna had been taken by Kamil, negotiations between Richard and Saladin had been endless and unproductive. The winter rains made everybody bad-tempered, and the morale of the Christians sank as the mud rose. On leaving the orchards of Jaffa at the end of November, while Kamil was enjoying himself on Hosanna, the Christians were trying to reach Jerusalem. Having boiled all summer, now the rain never seemed to let up. Violent hailstorms tested the horses to extremes. At first, the knights and even the humbler soldiers refused to be downcast as they struggled on. At least they were on the last leg to the Holy City. However, soon the misery of travelling when every step was a struggle wore down even the most optimistic crusaders.

William hardly noticed the weather. In the two months since the loss of Hosanna, his body had easily recovered from the three days without water, but the absence of his horse was a daily grief to him. Every time emissaries came from Saladin's camp he looked in vain for Kamil. Sometimes he saw a flash of red in a Muslim raiding party, but the horse was never Hosanna. Often he felt he had remained sane only because Gavin's injuries were so grave that the surgeon had had to amputate his brother's sword arm just below the shoulder, and William must be on hand to help him. Kamil's blow had done irreparable damage in itself and Gavin's arm had filled with poison. Luckily he had been too delirious to understand fully what was going on, but the pain he felt as the surgeon, his apron splattered with blood and pus, took his saw, had been real enough. William had been there to ply his brother with drink and hold him down. Amid Gavin's cries, his own had been drowned out.

After the operation William and Hal had looked after the sick man between them. When Richard called for them to move on from Jaffa, Gavin was propped up in a wagon while William, now riding Dargent, made sure the driver chose the smoothest route. He was determined that his brother should not die. He could not bear to lose everything: his father, his brother and both their beloved horses. When Gavin looked feverish, William comforted himself by consulting the surgeon, who told him that he could find no evidence of poison in the wound and that, with careful nursing, it would heal. William did not hesitate to steal things from the stores to try and make nutritious meals. He even took to slipping some of the ointment that Brother Andrew had given to Ellie into Gavin's soup and stirring until it melted. Progress was good at first, but when Gavin fully realized what had happened to him, he seemed to suffer a mental collapse. A knight minus his sword arm was useless. A knight who had seen his squire and groom drown and his father die was an abomination. He could not get past these thoughts.

As he sat in the wagon, Gavin brooded about why God had allowed terrible things to happen. *I am being punished for my sins*, he thought to himself. *But what has Will ever done, except good?* He was haunted by the loss of Hosanna and the effect it was having on his brother. William's face looked so empty and desperate. At night, although William and Hal did their best to make him comfortable, Gavin could not rest for wondering whether, if he had behaved differently, things might have turned out better. As it was, he must live with the knowledge that the rest of his life was tainted.

At the beginning of December, when they climbed into the hills and were almost within sight of the Holy City, the wheels of the wagons became completely bogged down. As the soldiers dug and swore, Richard told the knights to pitch their tents. They would make camp and have a meeting. William, as he always did, asked Gavin to come and listen, but Gavin shook his head. What good was he to the king now? William flung on his cloak and went on his own. He stood at the back as the king confided in his knights the true extent of his fears about the geographical position of Jerusalem and the difficulties that would arise, not so much from conquering it, but from keeping it, even assuming they could get there at all in this weather.

'It is impossible to continue,' said Richard. 'I have told Saladin that both we and the Saracens are bleeding to death, that the country is utterly ruined and that enough goods and lives have been sacrificed on both sides.'

The knights began to mutter. It was true that conditions were dreadful, but to many, the prospect of abandoning Jerusalem, with its promise of physical as well as spiritual comforts, was intolerable. If they retreated now, would they ever come back here?

Soaked to the skin, William hurried back to his tent. Just before he entered, he stopped, forced a more cheerful expression on to his face, then bent down and went through the flap, shaking himself like a dog.

Gavin was slumped on a rug, leaning against some cushions. The stump of his arm was still extremely painful. He barely looked up when William came in because he found it very difficult to meet his brother's eyes.

'They say the weather will change for the better in the not too distant future,' said William brightly. 'Apparently February is awful, but the rains stop in March. The king wants our opinion about what we should do next.'

Gavin moved his head, indicating that he had nothing to say. But William went on anyway. 'He has told us that the negotiations over a truce are stuck and wants to know if we should go on to Jerusalem or just reinforce the towns we have taken and leave Jerusalem for another expedition. I am not sure what I think.' He sat down next to his brother. 'What about you?'

'It's all the same,' said Gavin.

William looked at him. 'Maybe we will get home quicker if we don't go to Jerusalem.'

Gavin looked blank.

'But God must want us to take Jerusalem,' William went on, 'or all this has been for nothing. And then it is dreadful to think of the True Cross being in the hands of our enemies.'

Gavin still said nothing. William waited a few minutes. Then he pulled himself close and forced Gavin to look at him. His face was ashen white and Gavin noticed how thin it had become.

'Gavin,' William said, all the false cheerfulness leaving

his voice. 'Gavin. Please. Please don't look away. Please speak to me. I am losing everything. I need you.'

'You don't need me,' said Gavin, trying not to sound pathetic. 'My sins have brought disaster to me and perhaps to you, too. You don't need me.'

But William, desperate, was not put off. 'I need you because you are still my elder brother,' he said. 'I need you because, in all this madness and confusion, you are what I know. At Hartslove we often fought and you nearly killed Hosanna. But we are here now and we are alive. You have lost your arm and I have lost my beautiful horse. Neither is replaceable. But we cannot just give up. We must rise to the terrible challenge that God has set us. I will have to accept that Hosanna is not coming back and you will have to use me as your right arm. Please, Gavin,' William's voice was breaking. 'Our father would expect this of us. Please help me. I can't do it on my own.'

Gavin looked at his brother's pleading face. 'Will,' he said at last, 'I can't.'

'You must,' urged William. 'Being together, helping each other, is all that will save us.'

'Don't ask me,' begged Gavin. 'I am no good for anybody.'

'Oh, how can you say that!' cried William. 'You are our father's son. You are a de Granville. We can do anything.'

Gavin looked away to disguise the trembling in his lips. What William said struck deep into his heart. Yet how could he explain to William how unworthy he felt, unworthy to be a de Granville, unworthy, really, to be alive, when better men had died?

William was sitting with his head in his hands. Gavin

185

looked at him. He could see his brother sitting just like that at Hartslove after some childish disappointment. He could hear his father and Old Nurse chiding him and Ellie laughing. What would they all think now? Memories of the day he had hunted Hosanna into the ground flooded back. Although nearly everybody else had given the horse up for dead, William had kept faith and after Hosanna's return had even told Gavin he had forgiven him. Maybe now was Gavin's opportunity to make proper amends. Maybe this was his final chance, if only he could find the strength to take it.

Gavin regained control of his face and then slowly and awkwardly put his arm over William's shoulders. William did not move for a moment, then shifted so that he could look straight into Gavin's eyes. His own were full of misery and questions. Gavin swallowed hard. But, slowly, he nodded his head.

'I will try for your sake and for the sake of everything we have left behind,' he said. 'But you will have to help me, Will. I will depend on you.' Gavin looked uncertain about what to do next, so William grasped his hand.

'You can depend on me, Gavin,' he whispered with a ghost of a smile. 'We will face whatever comes with the help of God, the king, Father and Hosanna. For them and with their help, we will get through this and get home.'

Gavin repeated the words William was saying, once in a whisper, then again more strongly. When silence fell, they sat without moving, two brothers pushed together by losses neither could cope with on their own.

Movement outside told them that something further was afoot. Hal pushed his head round the flap to say that the knights had demanded another meeting with the king.

Without a word, William helped Gavin to rise, smarten himself up and walk to the meeting place. When the king came, the knights' spokesman said that the knights disagreed and wanted at least to attempt to take Jerusalem. Both the de Granvilles nodded their heads. Richard accepted the decision but looked extremely unhappy. As he left, he saw that Gavin was at William's side.

'I'm glad to see you are recovered,' he said. 'Now, keep yourself warm and as dry as possible. This rain is almost worse than the sun. When you feel strong enough, keep close to me. If you are a true son to your father, you will help me now.'

When they set off the next morning, William got on to Phoebus, the grey stallion belonging to his father who, unlike his companion, had survived the journey. He told Hal to make Dargent ready for Gavin. The horse was well trained and William thought that if Gavin could ride for just half an hour, it would boost his confidence. Gavin looked less certain, but William insisted and eventually, gritting his teeth at the embarrassment of having to be helped to mount, and saying nothing to William about the pain his wound was causing, he got on. To his surprise, he almost immediately felt better.

'It's good to see the world from this height, instead of having to look up at everybody from the wagon,' he said, not quite managing a smile.

William was content. After half an hour, he helped Gavin dismount. Gavin looked exhausted, but it was a start. Each day he did a little more until finally, under some welcome weak winter sunshine, he managed a whole day.

*

Christmas came, and the two young men toasted each other and the king and shivered. Short of food, their clothes rotting on their bodies, the army was now camped only twelve miles from Jerusalem. Only twelve miles. But Jaffa itself was barely thirty miles from the Holy City as the crow flies and it had taken them a month to get this far. Everything was now in a terrible condition. The wood for the siege engines had disintegrated, many of the wagons were in a state of collapse and half the men were limping with foot rot. Almost every day the rain beat down, as if to punish them.

Richard convened another meeting. It was very acrimonious. Despite everything, many of Richard's men still wanted to press on, but others, including Gavin and William, could see that Richard had been right and that the weather was making the great crusade for Jerusalem completely hopeless. Richard pushed as hard as he could for at least a temporary retreat.

'Our scouts have been talking again to Saladin,' he said, 'and the points at issue between us are these: Jerusalem, the True Cross that was taken at Hattin, and the land. I have said to Saladin that Jerusalem is for us an object of worship that we could not give up in the long term even if there was only one of us left in the world. The land from here to beyond the River Jordan must, therefore, be consigned to us. I also said that the Cross, which is for them just a piece of wood of no value, is for us of enormous importance. I said that if it were returned to us, and the other conditions met, that we would be able to make peace and rest from this endless labour.'

'And did he agree?' asked one of the younger knights sounding contemptuous.

Richard tried not to show his impatience. 'Through the councillor Baha ad-Din, he sent the following message,' he replied. 'That Jerusalem is as much theirs as ours and is even more sacred to them because it is the place from which Mohammed made his ascent into heaven. It is also the place where Muslims will gather on the Day of Judgement. This is not a surprise. This is what Saladin must say.'

The young knight snorted. 'I suppose we should encourage talk about the Day of Judgement. Maybe they will all be cast down into hell.'

Richard was not amused. 'The point is that they will not renounce Jerusalem,' he said. 'They also say that the land was originally theirs and that we have only taken over bits of it because they were weak when our ancestors first arrived here. Saladin refuses to give up the Cross except in exchange for something of benefit to Islam. This is how matters lie. Yet look around you. Look at the condition of this army. I would be glad to hear your opinions.'

The knights began to talk. Gavin, noticing how tired Richard looked, got up and spoke to the company, emphasizing the reality before them, how there was more to be lost than gained from pressing on. Eventually, having made Richard promise to return in the spring with fresh siege engines, enough senior knights voted for a temporary retreat to carry the day.

The journey back to the coast was bitter. They made their way to Ascalon, a southern coastal town that Richard was determined to fortify and leave in Christian hands. But by the end of January, as they arrived, Richard noted that many men had deserted.

For Gavin, the respite at Ascalon was a godsend. The rain let up, and he and William were able to dry out. Their boots had all but collapsed, but there was time to have new ones made from the skins found in the houses of the Saracens who had fled. After resting to recover from the journey, at William's tentative suggestion, Gavin began to practise wielding a sword with his left arm. It was hard at first and Gavin was often disheartened. By the time the rains died away, however, William, who was always very gentle with his brother, found himself nearly poked in the eye and forced to defend himself properly. That day was the first time Gavin laughed without constraint.

'Life in the old dog yet!' he cried, almost with his former vigour. 'Once I put you in the horse-trough at Hartslove with one arm. I dare say I'll do it again.'

William threw back his head and whooped. 'Race you back to the tent,' he shouted. As Phoebus lurched into his best canter, William tried his best not to compare the grey's lumbering efforts to the floating gallop that had once filled him with delight.

They spent six months at Ascalon and Gavin grew confident enough to commission some new armour to protect his right shoulder. He practised with his sword until he was now almost as good at fighting with his left arm as he had been with his right. He confided to the king that he felt ready for action. The two men spent much time riding together through the orchards and out, scouting, on to the plain, and as they rode, they talked. The king had begun to admire Gavin's spirit; he was changed by his suffering. When Gavin told Richard that his recovery was all down to William, Richard said that both young men were a credit to their father's name.

Once or twice, Gavin brought up the subject of Hosanna and was surprised at Richard's sympathy. Becoming sentimental about horses was frowned upon, but the king seemed genuinely concerned. 'I would be sorry to lose the horse I gained in Cyprus,' he said. 'We will do all we can to find Hosanna, but the chances are slim.'

How the crusade would end was also the subject of many discussions. Even with better weather approaching and the army recovered in health, Richard confided in Gavin that his misgivings about taking Jerusalem had grown rather than receded. At last both agreed it was for Richard to confront his knights once again. When the king proposed abandoning Jerusalem, Gavin and some of the other knights backed him, but many were unsure. Then an unhelpful priest preached a sermon reminding the crusaders that God would not forgive a Christian king for betraying the Holy City. The king, made uneasy by the priest and booed by his men, felt trapped. Sighing deeply, he told Gavin to announce that the army would set out once more.

At first all went well. The sun was growing strong again, but the soldiers were cheerful. Gavin told William that occasionally the king even spoke of 'when we take Jerusalem' rather than his usual 'if'. But riding out with Richard on a clear morning in June, confidently controlling Dargent with one hand, Gavin cantered up into a small group of hills from which, to his surprise and awe, he could actually see the Holy City. He called the king to come and look. Richard refused. Remaining steadfastly in a dip and turning his horse away, he told Gavin he would not look on a city he had little hope of delivering. Gavin was shocked.

'But what can stop us now?' he asked.

'Do you not understand? Have you not listened to our spies?' Richard was exasperated. 'Look towards the walls. What do you see?'

Gavin squinted in the sun. 'I see black pennants flying,' he said, puzzled. 'There seem to be lots of them.'

'Do you know what they mean?'

'No, sire,' replied Gavin.

Richard made his horse walk on. Gavin cantered down the hill and caught him up. 'They mean that the Saracens have poisoned the wells and springs,' the king said. 'Wagons are bringing water in from the outside for those inside the city walls. When we arrive, unless our supply line can be established immediately, we will rescue the holy places and then die of thirst.'

There was a long pause in which all that was audible was the gentle thud of hoofs in the sand. 'How are we going to tell the men?' asked Gavin at last.

Richard raised his eyebrows. 'We have to hope that God will help us,' he said and, searching for inspiration, he prepared to give his army the news he knew it least wanted to hear.

18

The meeting did not go well. At times Gavin feared for the king's physical safety as soldiers and knights alike openly accused him of betraying the crusading ideal. Some even went so far as to argue that if the whole crusading army died attempting to take Jerusalem, their deaths would be a glorious victory, since the pope had promised they would all go straight to heaven. Richard called for silence and put forward a proposal that, he felt, allowed the Christians to retreat with honour.

'My friends,' he said, 'my friends, we must now make a very difficult decision. On the one hand, Jerusalem lies before us for the second time, apparently ready for us to take. On the other, I have it on authority that a combined fleet of ships from our friends in Italy is even now sailing into the harbour at Acre, ready to transport us all to the Nile delta.'

A confused muttering broke out. This was something new. Wasn't the Nile delta in Egypt? Why go there when Jerusalem was so close? William glanced at Gavin, but Gavin's face was impassive.

Richard allowed the muttering to become a row before raising his hand. A knight called Henry de Winchelsea shouted for quiet. The key to Jerusalem, Richard

193

explained, lay in securing Egypt to prevent Saladin being able to call on an unlimited supply of men and provisions. Taking Jerusalem now, with Saladin's army increasing every day and the borders to the south open, would invite failure.

Richard's words were greeted with silence. The soldiers looked at each other, a little of the wind taken out of their sails. Nobody seemed sure what to do. Richard began again.

'The decision about whether or not to go on and take Jerusalem now, at this moment, is a hard one and one that we must take together,' he said. 'Christ and the holy places still wait to be avenged. That fact remains. It is also true that we have all suffered a great deal to get this far. Many of you have made grievous sacrifices and just as God will not forget, neither will I, as your king, forget. But I ask again, should we risk throwing away all we have achieved up to now to storm the holy city? If we do that, we will all surely die and the city will fall back to the Saracens shortly after. Or should we make the final assault when we can be sure that our victory is secure? Should we release the holy places from Saracen pollution for a week, then watch each other die of thirst for lack of uncontaminated water or, when we take the holy places back – for we surely will – should it be forever?'

Gavin watched, fascinated, as Richard skilfully guided the thoughts of knights and soldiers the way he favoured. Once Richard was confident that doubts had been sewn about a straightforward assault, he played his final card.

'I leave the decision up to you,' he said. 'A committee of twenty must be set up, drawn from the commanders of this army. The whole army, including myself, will abide by the committee's decision. Whatever happens will be your responsibility.' With that Richard dismissed the gathering but, as he walked past him, Gavin could see that the king already knew he had won.

Back in the tent, Gavin found William in a gloomy mood. He tried not to show Gavin how much he thought about Hosanna, but now he could not help himself.

'If we don't go forwards to Jerusalem, I know that I will never see Hosanna again,' he said, his face twitching in his agitation. 'I mean, I probably won't anyway. But I am sure that the emir who took him is in Jerusalem. I just know he is.'

Gavin sat down.

'The committee meets in an hour,' he said. 'I am to be part of it. But I'm afraid we won't try for Jerusalem,' he went on, looking at William, wishing there was some way he could make things better. 'But don't give up hope just yet. The king has an interest in Hosanna. Raiding parties are still going out. It is possible that someone will see Hosanna and at least get news to you that he is well.'

William would not be comforted. 'I promised Ellie that I would ride Hosanna over the drawbridge at home,' he said. 'I promised.'

'It was a rash promise,' said Gavin gently, 'and one which Ellie will not have taken seriously. And anyway, we don't even know if we will make it home yet. Have you forgotten the journey out here?' Gavin shuddered. 'We have that to face in reverse before we trot up the road to Hartslove.'

William knew his brother was right, but desperation made him clutch at straws. 'Perhaps I could ride to Jerusalem and ask if anybody has seen Hosanna,' he said.

Gavin was determined not to give his brother false hope. 'You know that is impossible,' he said trying to think what his father would be suggesting if he was still alive. He would, Gavin was sure, have come up with something positive. 'Perhaps we should pray,' Gavin said at last, rather lamely. 'It can't do any harm.'

William gave his brother a withering look. 'Why, in the midst of all the misery of war, would God be interested in a horse?' he asked.

Gavin shrugged. 'Why should He not be? And anyway, Hosanna is not just any horse, is he?' And with that, Gavin, rather self-consciously, knelt down.

William watched him, but a growing noise outside soon made Gavin get up and look outside. Within moments he was back, his face lit up with excitement.

'Will, get ready!' he cried. 'Scouts have located a huge Saracen caravan. They say there are thousands of laden camels and mules. But also they say there are hundreds of horses, some of which they recognize as captured from us. The whole caravan is headed for Jerusalem. Saladin has obviously called for reinforcements and these are them. Richard has already dispatched 200 mounted soldiers and 100 knights to try and cut the caravan off. Quick, let's get you dressed! There is a real chance that Hosanna might be there, too.'

Before Gavin had finished speaking, William was pulling on his quilted shirt and mail surcoat. Gavin rushed out to tell Hal to saddle Phoebus as quickly as possible, then ran back to help William, who could barely do up his sword belt, his hands were shaking so much with excited hope. Swearing and cursing at his one-armed clumsiness, Gavin eventually used his teeth.

'Take care,' he said, his mouth full of leather straps. 'Keep your wits about you. And if you find Hosanna, don't lose your head.' Once William was ready, they paused for a moment, then Gavin put his arm on William's shoulder. 'Good luck,' he said. 'Oh, good luck.'

William ran to where Hal had the grey waiting. He helped William to mount, then picked up a bridle lying in a heap of rugs and cloths behind him. 'Just in case,' he murmured, and put it into one of William's saddlebags. William said nothing, but wheeled Phoebus round and galloped after the detachment whose armour he could see shimmering in the heat about half a mile away.

The scouts had been right. The caravan was a huge one. Nearly 4,000 camels and mules together with hundreds of wagons and covered carts were protected by about 200 Saracens, all armed to the teeth. But although the Saracens were watchful, the camels, despite their heavy bags, were restive.

This was clear to the attacking knights and they decided to see if it could work to their advantage. With recklessness borne of faith, frustration and sheer greed at the booty being held out under their noses, the whole Christian contingent broke every rule of engagement and galloped straight for the caravan, barking like mad dogs. The effect was startling. The camels went wild and bolted. The knights then divided and, still barking, half of them galloped round behind the lumbering animals who, confused and alarmed, swayed to a momentary halt, before turning round and fleeing back. This caused the mules to panic, and the horses, many of whom were running loose, took flight too and swept through their Saracen escort, knocking many men over in the rush. The entire herd soon disappeared into the desert.

In the ensuing chaos the knights and soldiers drew their swords and killed the enemy indiscriminately. The resistance was negligible. When the few Saracens who were left began to beg for their lives, the knights ordered the soldiers to sheath their swords and start trying to get the booty under control. As the dust cleared, the sight of the soldiers trying to round up the camels, both men and beasts whistling and spitting their disapproval, had all the knights rocking with laughter.

All except William. He ignored the main body of the caravan and followed the horses. After galloping for about a quarter of a mile, they stopped and milled about, unsure what to do next. Two stallions began to roar as William approached, but neither was Hosanna. For the next hour, William rode slowly in among the throng, who pushed and thrust against him. Whenever he saw a flash of chestnut, his heart rose, only to sink when he found himself mistaken. Eventually, he stood up in his stirrups and shouted, his voice like a sob, 'Hosanna! Hosanna! Hosanna!' There was no answering whicker; no slim, elegant head standing out from the multicoloured sea of manes and tails; no soft, inquisitive nose against his pocket. William slowly sank back into his saddle.

When he was quite sure Hosanna was not there, he returned to the caravan. Some of the horses joined him, until eventually they all followed, and William found himself at the head of the whole vast herd. Men stopped to stare at the extraordinary sight.

The horses of the dead Saracens were being gathered up by a company of archers. Ignoring the herd behind him, William kept his eyes flitting from the captured horses to the faces of the dead and injured men strewn about in the scrub. He did not care what condition the man was in, but he hoped against hope that he would find the face of the emir he often saw in his dreams. But it was no good.

Racked with disappointment, William could take no pleasure in the heaps of gold, silver, spices and food that had the rest of the raiding party dancing with delight. He helped to re-order the wagons and secure all the captured bolts of silk, stacks of chain mail, tents and cushions so that the booty could be taken back to the Christian camp. He watched as men slapped each other on the back. But he felt only devastation. He could not – would not – believe Hosanna was dead. But where was the young man who had stolen him?

Gavin and Hal were among the crowds standing waiting as the great caravan of Muslim spoils was driven towards them. It caused much rejoicing. But when they spotted William empty-handed, their faces fell. Hal turned away, leaving Gavin to help William dismount.

'I am so sorry,' he said. 'I really am sorry, Will.'

'It was a long shot, I suppose,' said William, attempting, but failing, to be cheerful.

Gavin was very matter-of-fact. He knew just what his father would do now. 'Right then,' he said. 'Go and get all this stuff off and let's see what these thousands of camels produce.'

William was grateful to Gavin for not offering false comforts. If Gavin could be strong, he must be, too. Nevertheless, as he struggled out of his armour, William allowed himself a few moments of weakness, sinking down on to his knees and angrily dashing away the tears he was embarrassed to find rolling down his cheeks. He rubbed his face with a cloth, wishing he had some spare water to splash over his head. Hosanna was gone. He would have to get used to it. He was lucky to have Phoebus and lucky to have a brother still alive. He went back to Gavin and found him sitting with some silver dishes and a chess set, taken from one of the ten wagonloads of exquisitely carved ornaments that were being unpacked.

'Not quite what we expected to take home as souvenirs,' said Gavin, setting out the pieces on the chequered board, 'but they'll do.'

And because there was nothing else for it, William sat down and Gavin taught him to play.

Just over a dozen miles away, two miles east of Jerusalem, Hosanna was standing, his eyes half-shut and his tail rhythmically brushing the flies from his flanks. Kamil was sitting with Saladin underneath a silken canopy that swayed in the light summer breeze. The rains of winter were forgotten, and Hosanna's coat was gleaming in the sun. Kamil listened carefully and sympathetically as the sultan outlined his increasing worries over the stalemate in the war. Kamil could nearly always be found close to the horse-lines. Since that terrible day behind the rocks, nobody was allowed to feed or brush Hosanna apart from himself. He could not help but worry that the Old Man's reach was very long and he would know just how to punish Kamil if he chose to do so. The horse was so fond of Kamil now that when he was loosed from his tether, he would often follow him about. Baha ad-Din joked that the horse slept in Kamil's tent at night. Kamil smiled, but the truth was not so far away. The boy often crept out to sleep next to Hosanna under the stars.

Now Saladin was telling him that the emirs who led the people in Jerusalem were nothing but a bunch of cowards. They had seen the Christian army on the horizon and were ready to give in. 'I believe we can hold out against Richard. Time and water are both on our side,' he said. 'But the difficulty is persuading those living inside the city walls to have faith.'

Before Kamil had time to answer, Hosanna suddenly raised his head, his mane rippling in the wind. He pricked his ears, then whinnied three times. Kamil looked up. 'Ho, Red Horse,' he said. 'What have you heard?' Hosanna remained staring into the desert for some time, then lowered his head and carried on picking at the fresh grass Kamil had cut for him.

Saladin was smiling. 'Kamil,' he said. 'You are like a son to me. But the red horse is truly your brother.'

Kamil laughed, then became serious again. 'He has taught me many things,' he said. 'And not all of them to do with horsemanship.'

Both men were silent. The shadow of Abdul Raq and the Old Man still hung over them. Kamil started to say something, then stopped.

'What is it?' asked Saladin gently.

'Have you noticed?' Kamil was suddenly rather shy. 'Have you noticed how the colour of blood clashes with the red horse's coat?'

Saladin considered. 'I had not noticed,' he answered. 'But what you say is true. Blood and that horse do not go together.'

Kamil tried to be flippant. 'For that reason, I am always careful now whom I kill,' he said, and to hide his confusion, busied himself pushing the grass that Hosanna had scattered into a neat pile. He still could not tell the sultan about the night he had killed the Christian boy, but his soul felt calmer and his temper less quick. On the nights he slept alongside the red horse, he slept well, the horse's presence keeping his nightmares away. Inspired by their interest in his horse, he had begun to teach some of the sons of the emirs how to train their own horses and surprised himself by finding he enjoyed it. The little boys worshipped Hosanna, and the horse patiently allowed them to fuss over him. Kamil had quite a following.

Saladin looked at the boy with love in his eyes. 'Yes,' he said. 'I notice that you are now more careful about many things.' The young man blushed and was grateful to find an excuse to lean forwards and remove a stray stalk from Hosanna's mane.

But the red horse was restless and eventually Kamil got up. As he rose he caught sight of the bedraggled remains of the vanquished caravan limping past the sentries posted at the entrance to the Saracen camp.

'Allah help us!' he exclaimed. 'What on earth has happened?' He quickly put out his hand and helped the sultan to his feet. From all over the camp, people were shouting and rushing forwards with water.

As Saladin approached, the distraught and thirsty men began noisily to disclaim any responsibility for losing the valuable cargo with which they had been entrusted. They told how the knights had barked like dogs, how the camels had gone mad and scattered the mules and horses. 'Then the horses came back,' said one soldier, still gulping water. 'They were all following a knight who appeared from nowhere. So they were gathered up, too, and taken back to the Christian camp. We were lucky to escape with our lives.'

Saladin was furious. 'Are you part of the great caravan from Egypt?' he asked. 'I particularly sent word to the emirs not to send such huge quantities of livestock and goods all at once. The Christians may be vile and uncouth but they are brave. With that prize in front of them, they will have been completely fearless. Have we lost everything?'

The men nodded, trembling with fear. 'We are all that is left.'

Saladin said nothing more, but bidding Kamil go round and gather his counsellors together, he went to his tent.

The leading emirs and the sultan talked for a week, trying to decide whether to take on Richard's army face to face and recapture some of the lost booty or to allow the Christians to proceed to Jerusalem and lay siege to it. They knew that the Christians were camped twelve miles west of the Holy City and that, if they began to move forwards, the Saracens could not stop them. Nevertheless, once the Christians were outside the city walls and busy constructing their siege engines, then the Saracens could besiege them in their turn, as had happened the year before at Acre. The Christians would be stuck.

However, the emirs knew this strategy carried its own dangers. They could not rely on the fortitude of their fellow Muslims in Jerusalem, who, by all accounts, were in favour of giving in to the Christians. The reputation of Richard the Lionheart went in front of him. If the Muslims in Jerusalem offered him the keys of the city, with the coastal towns already in Christian hands and plentiful supplies to keep their army fed, who knew how long Richard could hold out? Then, a miracle occurred.

A mounted spy galloped into Saladin's camp. 'They're leaving,' he shouted. 'They're leaving.' Saladin was disbelieving. The spy insisted.

'I have seen the so-called great Christian army,' he said. 'Before they began to pursue the caravan from Egypt, they seemed to be having some kind of meeting. They did not look happy. It seems that the great Richard is not so great after all. Just when they seemed on course for Jerusalem, they are moving away, moving away, I tell you, taking all that booty with them.'

Saladin called for his horse and at the head of 100 cavalry, he rode out. Kamil leapt on to Hosanna and was at Saladin's side. Their horses were fit, and after just over an hour's riding, they could see a huge dust storm on the horizon. The Christian army was indeed rolling away.

Saladin turned to Kamil. 'Allah is merciful,' he said. 'Should we suspect a trap?'

Kamil considered. 'The Christians must have seen that we have poisoned the wells and lost all hope,' he said. 'I suspect they are headed back for the port of Acre to regroup. They will be anxious not to lose all the booty they have just captured. Maybe, once at Acre, they will decide to go home. But I don't believe they will want to go without even setting foot in Jerusalem. Perhaps now is the right time for us to march to the port of Jaffa and organize an assault to take it back into Muslim hands. It is the least well defended and it would cut the territory they control into two. If we can take Jaffa, the Christians would no longer hold the whole coast. Also, if they change their minds and head back to Jerusalem, the loss of Jaffa would be a great inconvenience.'

'My son, you are beginning to think like a general,' said Saladin. 'Go and give the orders. Unless the Christians do something unexpected, we will make for Jaffa. Send spies to follow King Richard's army. Let us be circumspect and ready for anything.'

As soon as they returned to the Saracen camp, Kamil gave the orders and the army prepared to move. Spies flew back and forth, and the Saracen army waited to see if the decision to head for Jaffa remained the best one.

Three days later, a small detachment set out on a swift, forced march for the coast. Kamil rode Hosanna at the head of it. It was his job to reconnoitre the route and to watch out for ambushes. This was a job he loved. Hosanna felt like a tightly strung bow beneath him, and the soldiers who were following soon got used to the sight of their leader on his fiery horse, always slightly too far ahead for safety, performing what looked to them like a dance. Sometimes they muttered to each other about horses and circuses but on the whole they enjoyed the spectacle.

Kamil was in his element. Urging the soldiers on and talking strategy with his fellow emirs, he felt a new sense of purpose, one that did not depend on slaughter, but on tactics. The men, even the older ones, trusted him. He could see it. They accepted his instructions without question. Under his command, they arrived safely outside Jaffa within four days, for the going was good even for the pack animals, and they were unchallenged. Indeed, the Christians inside the city were taken completely by surprise at the sight of the Saracen soldiers and only just managed to shut the gates in time. For five days they held out, fighting like demons, before Kamil's men pushed their way through the gates and were in among them, swords and maces swinging with deadly accuracy. Kamil fought up at the front, Hosanna responsive to his every movement, shouting, cajoling and exhorting his men to greater and greater efforts. He seemed to be everywhere at once, regardless of danger. In the brief breaks he took to catch his breath, his own soldiers would come and touch the horse's star, as if the aura that seemed to keep him safe might pass on to them. Kamil did not stop them.

When the city eventually fell, Kamil found himself riding Hosanna inside Jaffa's walls, flushing the enemy out from side alleys and behind garden walls. The noise and stench of death was all around him, but he did not flinch. Directing his men to perform a city-wide sweep to locate pockets of resistance, he also ordered the preparation of enclosures into which the many captives could be herded.

In one corner of the city, a group of particularly miserable captives was huddled. They were all knights, and Kamil rode over to see that they were put with the rest. The Christian king would pay handsomely for their release, and they could be transported to Acre and go home with the other crusaders. As he rode up, he could see one of the knights arguing with his Saracen captor. The knight seemed to be begging.

'Ah, Kamil ad-Din,' the emir said as Kamil approached. 'I can't understand the language, but I think he wants his weapons back,' and he laughed.

Kamil looked at the knight. 'Yes?' he said in Norman French. It was not until the knight turned to look at him that, with a cold shock, Kamil caught sight of the teardrop birthmark that could still keep him awake at night. Hosanna halted.

'I don't want my weapons,' said the knight. 'Just that little dagger.' He was trying to keep his dignity but there was pleading as well as bitterness in his voice. 'It was my boy's,' he said. 'He was murdered as we left Jerusalem. His mother has died of fever. It is the only thing I have left that was his.'

Kamil's face registered nothing, but inside, his heart

was burning. His eyes misted over. In a moment, Saladin's teaching, the Koran, everything Kamil had learnt was consumed by flames in his head. He dismounted. Here was his chance. He could kill this man now and properly avenge his father. It would not be necessary to explain to the emir. Many things were done in war. Few were questioned.

As he let go of Hosanna's rein to reach for his sword, his hand briefly touched the ridge caused by William's blow to the horse at Acre a year before. Almost of its own accord, Kamil's hand stopped there. He did not know the cause of the scar, but he found himself smoothing over it again and again. Hosanna shifted slightly and turned his head to rub it on Kamil's shoulder.

The knight was looking curiously at Kamil. He dropped to his knees.

'I beg you,' he said, 'Kill me now. I have nothing left. I have not led a good life. Now it is time to end it. My wife and my son have gone before me. I long to see them again, and I hope, as a crusader, I will be forgiven my sins and go straight to heaven. But please, when I am buried, bury my son's dagger by my side.'

Kamil stopped smoothing Hosanna's scar. He looked down.

'Get up,' he said softly. 'Get up. You and your kind have caused untold suffering in this land. Take your son's dagger, and keep it by you always. Let it be the knife in your heart. Let it, every day, remind you of what you have lost, and if it ever takes life again, may God never forgive you. Now go home and never come back.'

Kamil took the dagger from the emir, silencing his protests with his hand. 'I know what I am doing,' he said in Arabic. The emir shrugged.

'Here,' said Kamil, and he gave the dagger to the knight.

The knight took it and slid it under his armour, so that it rested next to his skin. 'Thank you,' he said, with tears in his eyes. 'Thank you.'

Kamil did not acknowledge his thanks. He nodded to the emir, who, looking at Kamil as if he were mad, chivvied his prisoners out of their corner and pushed them towards a bigger group headed for the pen near the city gates. Kamil did not look after them. He mounted Hosanna and, pushing his thoughts down for scrutiny at a more appropriate time, carried on with the job in hand.

Only the capture of the citadel, the great tower at the heart of the city, remained to be accomplished before he would be able to report to the sultan that if the Christians were counting on Jaffa to help with their assault on Jerusalem, they could count on it no longer. Kamil dodged stray arrows and told his men that if they fought hard, this victory at Jaffa might go down in the books of history as the beginning of the end of this Christian crusade. They cheered at the thought. Then Kamil sent for some superior marksmen.

'Concentrate now on the citadel,' he told them. 'It should only take a day, at the outside, to secure it. If you can, get the Christians out dead or alive without setting fire to it. We don't want to spend weeks building it up again and we will need it for our own defence.' The marksmen nodded and left him.

Later, when darkness fell and the fighting was all but over for the day, Kamil rode out of the city and down to the shore. He was dog-tired. He dismounted, took off his helmet and looked out to sea.

Hosanna stood with his head over Kamil's shoulder. The young man leant back. The memories of the day were very sharp and Kamil now allowed them to flood over him. He could see every detail of the Christian knight's face and recall every word of their conversation. He relived it again and again. Eventually the tears came, and Kamil let them fall. The horse stood, patient as a rock. After the storm had passed, Kamil wiped his face on Hosanna's mane. For the first time since he was nine years old, he found that he could think of his father's killer without hatred and even think of his father without his heart contracting in pain. He murmured to Hosanna as an unexpected thought struck him. How could he be sorry that Richard had brought his army over? He did not need reminding that if the king had remained at home, he would never have met this red horse, from whom, Kamil felt certain, his new peace of mind flowed. He touched Hosanna's white star. 'What we did today, you and I,' he said, 'has made me my father's true son. And now that the Christians are leaving, Red Horse, you will surely be mine forever.'

It was a good thought and, as Kamil led Hosanna to the horse-lines, despite his weariness, he had a spring in his step.

19

Hartslove, 1192

Thousands of miles away, Ellie had not had a good thought since de Scabious had tried to blackmail her into marriage the previous November. As the winter had turned into spring and the spring into summer, and still no news came from the de Granvilles, her only thoughts were of escape, if only she had somewhere to go. Since her supposed 'poor behaviour' with Brother Ranulf, life had been horrible. After her disgrace, some of the servants were sympathetic, but the garrison knights treated her with increasing disrespect, except when Constable de Scabious was around. Now he felt he had the abbot's support, he was in no hurry to cement their union, since by spreading news of his own magnanimous offer to marry Ellie, predatory barons were no longer interested in carrying her off. He could relax and wait for the girl to come round, which she surely would. Marrying him must be better than becoming a nun. And that really was Ellie's only other option, for while Ellie had heard nothing, de Scabious did have news from the Holy Land, and it was to his advantage. Back in April, while on a trip to the coast to negotiate the purchase of some rich, imported cloth suitable for his wedding day, a man returned from Acre on the spring tides told him on good authority that Sir Thomas had died and that Gavin had suffered what everybody took to be a mortal wound. William, so the man said, had lost his horse and was shattered. In effect, the constable thought as he rode back to Hartslove, the de Granvilles were finished.

He passed on this news only to his most intimate circle of fellow malcontents. Before announcing it to the world, he needed to gather round himself a larger group of loyal knights and to oversee the placing of his own men in both the northern castles and the castles that dominated Ellie's dowry lands. He also needed to gain control over the de Granville stud. If the de Granvilles were generally known to be finished, landless knights would gang together to fight over their lands, safe in the knowledge that, unlike his father, King Richard had no real interest in England except as a bank and that it was safe to embark on a free-for-all. The constable needed to be careful.

By the summer he felt he was almost there, for he found he had a talent for attracting disgruntled men-at-arms. His major irritation was Margery, who kept winking at him and who he often found behind him when he thought he was alone. For a large woman she managed to be remarkably silent and invisible. Once, when he turned after talking to one of his most trusted lieutenants, he bumped right into her. He wondered how much she had heard, then dismissed her as too stupid to understand what was going on. Women like Margery only had one thing on their mind, and it was not castles.

Ellie could have no complaint about the constable's behaviour. Apart from his oiliness, which made her feel faintly sick, he did not try to thrust himself upon her, or keep her locked up. He was much too clever for that.

He needed to appear the height of courtesy and reasonableness. She did, however, find herself openly followed whenever she went out on Sacramenta.

After the hay harvest, she rode up to the abbey, but Brother Andrew shook his head sadly from inside the gatehouse and would not let her in. Of Brother Ranulf there was no sign. As she turned away, however, two monks came out to speak to the soldiers. The soldiers looked round at Ellie, who had reached the edge of the trees, then back at the monks. They looked doubtful. Then one shrugged and they dismounted. Ellie was puzzled. Nevertheless, taking advantage of their temporary distraction, she wandered into the wood. She was just gathering herself together, wondering how best to take advantage of her solitude, when she heard a noise.

'Psssst!'

She looked around her.

'Pssst!'

There it was again. She remained perfectly still, keeping her eyes skinned. In a moment or two, from behind a tree emerged fat Brother Andrew. He was sweating, even though the day was overcast.

'Miss Eleanor,' he said, putting his fingers to his lips. 'Just bring Sacramenta here. I daren't come out into the open.'

The mare walked obediently over and, delving into his voluminous pocket, Brother Andrew brought out some sweet bread for her. She took it delicately from his hand and chewed thoughtfully before pushing her nose in his pocket for more. Brother Andrew laughed.

'She is very like Hosanna,' he said. 'Or should it be the other way round?' He stopped when he saw that his remark caused a look of pain to cross Ellie's already careworn face.

'Oh, Miss Eleanor,' he said. 'I have stolen a minute or two, by getting those soldiers to wait while I have sent one of the lay monks to fetch some hides to be carried back to the castle. I told them to take their time. There now. Have you had bad news?'

'We have had no news, Brother Andrew,' said Ellie, trying to smile. 'And that is supposed to be good news. But we just don't know anything about Sir Thomas and the others. And meanwhile, I could hardly be in a worse situation.'

Slowly, she told her story and relayed to the monk the content of the meeting with the abbot and Constable de Scabious. Brother Andrew, who already knew the story, as did most of the county, allowed her to finish it before he said anything.

'If only you had come to me for your lessons,' he could not resist chiding, putting up his hand to pat Ellie's knee, then thinking the better of it and putting it down again. 'Maybe things would have been different.'

'I wanted to surprise you,' said Ellie dully. 'And anyway, you would never have got permission from the abbot, would you?'

Brother Andrew could not deny this. He found some more delicacies for Sacramenta to eat.

'What shall I do, Brother Andrew? You do believe that Brother Ranulf and I did nothing wrong, don't you?' Ellie asked.

'That depends on your definition of wrong,' said Brother Andrew as primly as a fat monk could. 'Brother Ranulf should have known better. But I do believe that you, Miss Eleanor, are as chaste as the day you were

213

born.' He twinkled up at her. 'Now, don't look so downcast. Have faith. If the worst comes to the worst, de Scabious may turn out not to be such a bad husband.'

Ellie opened her mouth to protest, but, before she could begin, Brother Andrew put his head on one side and looked very serious.

'Miss Eleanor,' he said as Sacramenta, finding no more titbits, chewed his sleeve, 'I know that is very hard for you to believe, and I shall pray that the worst does not happen. But the crosses that many people have to bear in these troubled times are very great. If you must marry de Scabious, you will have to bear it with fortitude. You have no option. A well-bred, unmarried girl like you cannot run about the country like a milkmaid. God has ordered society in a certain way, and you must maintain your place. If people like you start forgetting your station, why, where on earth will we all be?'

'So I must do nothing?' Ellie whispered.

'You must do nothing. But,' said Brother Andrew cheerfully, 'de Scabious is an unhealthy looking specimen. I don't think it will be long before you are a widow, and then, Miss Eleanor, the world is yours. Look at your namesake, our Queen Eleanor. Since King Henry died, she has done just whatsoever she fancies.'

From behind her, Ellie could hear the soldiers shouting thanks at the monks. In a moment, they would be in the wood.

'I suppose so,' was all she had time to say, before Brother Andrew, extricating his sleeve from Sacramenta's mouth with difficulty, put his finger to his lips once again and bobbed out of sight.

Ellie returned to Hartslove feeling a little better. At least she had a friend at the abbey. When she told Old

Nurse what Brother Andrew had said, Old Nurse sniffed, but then gathered Ellie into her arms and hugged her.

Shortly after this, de Scabious took to presenting Ellie with small gifts – a jar of spices or a semi-precious stone. Mindful of Brother Andrew's words, the girl did not throw them into the fire as was her inclination. She simply left them on the table in the great hall. She dared not openly antagonize de Scabious, for fear of what he might do. Old Nurse could not protect her if the constable decided to force his way into her rooms, and then she would really be finished. One day she saw Margery slip two of the jewels into her pocket. Ellie said nothing. If de Scabious thought that Ellie had picked them up, it would do no harm.

The only time she raised her voice was at the dinner to celebrate the grain harvest. De Scabious walked straight in and sat in Sir Thomas's chair.

'That is not your place,' Ellie said coldly.

The constable got up, nodded in her direction, and moved over. Ellie was shaking. In addition to getting her as a wife, she wondered how long it would be before the knights lost all sense that the castle was de Granville property and took to thinking of de Scabious as their overlord. Certainly, he was playing the part. There were more knights here than was strictly necessary and some she did not know. The constable seemed to be preparing for something. It did not take long before Ellie found out what it was.

At blackberry time, the constable sent for her.

'Miss Ellie,' he said, smiling at her in a way she found absolutely repulsive. 'You may have forgotten, but there is still trouble over the first Lady de Granville's dowry. I

215

am off north to see to things up here and shall be taking some knights with me. I will be gone for most of the autumn but will be back by Valentine's Day next year. I shall leave fifty soldiers here for your protection. You may have met some of them. These are troubled times. By the way, I think Valentine's Day a very appropriate day to get married. No point in putting off the inevitable any longer.'

Ellie was so relieved to hear that the constable was going that she almost smiled at him. He touched her arm and she tried not to recoil. If de Scabious thought she was coming round to him, he might tell the soldiers they must at least be polite to her. She could not bring herself to say anything, but inclined her head slightly in a not unfriendly manner. When he rode away with a large retinue in his wake, she watched from an upper window.

It was Margery who, after the constable had been gone for six weeks or so, confirmed her suspicions that the trip up north was more than just a 'maintenance' exercise. Poor Margery. Since the incident with Brother Ranulf, Ellie would not speak to her. At first Margery didn't care. Soon, so Margery thought, she, Margery, would be lording it over Ellie. Never mind being Eleanor Theodora de Barre, Margery would be just as grand when she was Mistress de Scabious. It was true, she knew, that the constable had said he was going to marry Ellie. But Margery knew what he was really up to. He would marry Ellie, repudiate her, keep her lands, then marry Margery instead. It stood to reason.

This had all been set firmly in Margery's head until the night before the constable left. As a 'leaving present', as she termed it to herself, Margery had crept, uninvited, into de Scabious's chamber. She had been sure that when she winked at the constable as she served the dinner, he had known exactly what she meant. They could not profess their passion in public, of course. But Margery knew. She just knew.

Or perhaps she didn't. She had found the constable snoring on a chair in front of the fire. She tiptoed towards him and tickled his nose. First he sneezed. Then, when Margery did it again, this time making what she thought were appropriately seductive noises, he opened his eyes, saw her face squashed up against his own and bellowed, 'Murder! Witches! Hags!' before throwing himself backwards. The chair toppled over and he and Margery had fallen into a heap together.

'Oh, Holy Virgin!' he panted when he had caught his breath.

'No, not the Holy Virgin, it's me, it's me,' Margery had cried, imploring him to be quiet. But when de Scabious caught sight of her coquettish grin as he was trapped beneath her, he bellowed again. 'Shut your mouth, woman,' he begged. 'And get out! Get out!'

'But I thought –'

'You thought what? That I really thought of you as a human being? You? Don't make me laugh. Look at you. You are not a woman. You are a lump of dough! Now get out of here before I drop you out of the window into the midden, where you rightly belong.'

Margery, howling, had scrambled up and backed into the corner. 'I thought we were to be married. I thought you liked me. I thought we were to take over this place.'

Quick as a flash de Scabious was on his feet. 'If I ever discover you have repeated any of the conversations you have overheard, you miserable piece of dung, I will have you flayed alive and your skin turned into – into – into – into casing for sausages!'

Margery had shut her mouth and fled. When she reached the women's quarters she found a place in a corner and lay, shivering. Occasionally she whimpered. Eventually, she fell asleep, her mouth open. Her last waking thought was that, if ever the opportunity presented itself, she would get her own back.

This had all been fermenting in Margery's mind and, after the constable had ridden away, she watched Ellie, wondering how best to approach her. She was not sure how much Ellie knew. Was Ellie aware that the constable was intent on taking over the de Granville lands? Did she know that the constable was as certain as it was possible to be that Sir Thomas and his sons were dead? It took some time for Margery to decide that the time was right. Then, catching sight of Ellie trying a new winter blanket on Sacramenta, she ventured to approach her.

Ellie stiffened. She could never forgive Margery for betraying her trust. Margery lumbered up to the horse, twisting her hands in her apron.

'Miss Ellie,' she said.

'I have nothing to say to you.' Ellie's voice was sharp.

Margery tried once more, received the same response and shuffled off. If Ellie was going to be so hoity-toity, well, she could just wait for de Scabious to arrive with dozens of soldiers and declare himself the new Count of Hartslove. Margery banged the pots in the kitchen until the cook shouted for her to find something else to do.

But the memory of de Scabious's contempt put fire into Margery's soul. She determined to try again. This time, she would start differently. So, finding another opportunity, she approached Ellie once more. Ellie was brushing Sacramenta's mane.

Margery walked quickly into the stable and began at once. 'I know you don't want to speak to me, Miss Eleanor,' she said. 'But I am only doing my duty.' Ellie turned away. Margery kept going.

'Did you know that Constable de Scabious has heard on good authority from a man returning from the Holy Land that all the de Granvilles are dead?'

Ellie stood, absolutely motionless.

'I overheard him telling his friends. He has known since April. And he has gone north to secure the castles. After that he will come back here as Count of Hartslove. There, now I have told you everything I know.'

Ellie turned, her face ashen. She dropped her brush, grabbed Margery and shook her. 'Are you sure about all this? If I find you have been lying, I'll have you flayed alive and your skin –'

'– Turned into sausage casings. Yes. I know. But it is all true. I swear on this horse.'

It was Margery who caught Ellie as the girl swayed, her legs giving way underneath her. 'Oh, sweet Jesus,' she whispered sinking into the straw.

'I'll get Old Nurse,' said Margery, suddenly feeling out of her depth. 'I'll just get Old Nurse.'

Ellie lay down beside Sacramenta. She could not take in what she had just been told. She closed her eyes and did not open them again until she could feel herself pillowed against the nurse's many rolls of fat.

'Old Nurse,' she whispered, 'they are dead. All of them. The constable knew and he never told us.'

Old Nurse began to rock backwards and forwards.

'There, Miss Ellie. There, Miss Ellie,' she said stupidly. 'What does the constable know?'

Ellie thumped Old Nurse with her fists and wept. 'Is that all you can say?' she sobbed. 'De Scabious does know. He heard it from a man at the coast. He has known since April and he never told us.'

Old Nurse did not reply. She could think of nothing but Sir Thomas's face as he left. 'God rest his soul,' she muttered, rocking harder and harder, taking no more notice of Ellie's pounding than of a fly. 'God rest all their souls.'

They sat, Ellie and Old Nurse, with Sacramenta bending low over them, for some considerable time. Then Ellie got up.

'At least we can do one thing,' she said, her voice hard. 'We can try to stop Constable de Scabious taking Hartslove. Sir Thomas's brother, the bishop, might help us if we can get word to him.'

'And how will we do that?' asked Old Nurse. 'Nobody from here will take a message to him from you without going to the constable first. They wouldn't dare. And I can't ride. As for that Margery – well, I wouldn't trust her.'

Ellie thought for a moment. She looked at Sacramenta. 'There is a way,' she said slowly. 'I don't know if it will work but we might as well try.'

For half the night Ellie was up trying to remember how to write. Which way round were the bs and ps? Her quill broke several times but finally she managed to scribble what she hoped was a coherent message. *It is not as elegant as the one I sent to Will with Brother Ranulf's help*, she thought regretfully. *But that can't be helped.*

She wrapped it in an old silken petticoat. Old Nurse secured it with a needle and thread.

The next morning Ellie sent for Sacramenta. She would go for a ride, she said. Two knights immediately called for their horses to accompany her. One came to help her to mount, but was pushed out of the way by Old Nurse.

'I'll help Miss Ellie this morning,' she said officiously and stood blocking their view while Ellie slipped the silk envelope behind the girth. Then Old Nurse hitched her on board.

Sacramenta was fresh in the November winds. Ellie crossed the drawbridge and rode down through the jousting field, remembering with an aching heart the first time Hosanna had shown his mettle and how she had loved being perched in front of Sir Thomas. Now all that was at an end. She urged Sacramenta to canter. She must not allow herself to drown in memories. Not yet, anyway. The knights dawdled behind as Sacramenta flattened herself to gallop through the fallen leaves. Speed, ah! That would help to clear her mind. Sacramenta increased her pace and they rushed faster and faster towards the river. As the mare's hoofs beat the ground, Ellie suddenly thought she heard the echo of other hoofbeats beside her. She glanced round. The knights were only trotting. The second horse she could hear was galloping. She could see nothing, but Sacramenta, too, seemed to stretch out her nose as if in a race. The wind tugged at Ellie's hair, and, just for a moment she felt she was flying. There was a whisk of red beside her. 'Hosanna?' The name resounded in her head. She could not tell if she spoke it aloud or not. But her invisible companion was not Hosanna. It was a flurry of leaves kicked up by Sacramenta.

Nevertheless, as the mare slowed down and Ellie chided herself for being so whimsical, she felt stronger.

Ellie's plan went quite smoothly, for the knights were idle and she was determined. When she reached the river, she leant forwards and muttered into Sacramenta's ear, 'Go to the abbey! I don't know if you understand, but you are the best hope we've got.' Then, slipping her feet from the stirrups, she slid into the mud and smacked Sacramenta sharply on her rump. Sacramenta grunted with surprise, but, to Ellie's relief, forded the river and was soon out of sight. By the time the knights caught up, Ellie had covered herself in mud. 'The horse fell,' she shouted. 'And now she has run off. I dare say she'll come home eventually. Can one of you give me a ride before I catch my death of cold?'

By evening Sacramenta had not returned. However, since Ellie did not seem to be worried, the garrison knights, after consulting the serjeant, did not go to look for her and played dice instead. By the next morning, they had forgotten all about her.

20

Jaffa, 31 July 1192

The Christians trapped in the citadel at Jaffa could see Kamil and Hosanna below. The tall tower offered the only remaining hope of safety, and not much hope at that. As Kamil looked up, he could see the Saracens' enemies leaning out to look down. He did not respond either to their taunts or their pleas. He was fully focused on his last task – taking the tower itself and forcing the Christians out. The marksmen he had sent had not been successful, and now Kamil thought more drastic action was required.

The slaughter in the city was by no means over, although the Saracens were in control. There were bodies piled on every street corner. Hosanna slipped with ease between groups of fighting enemies, avoiding stray arrows and crossbolts, bending and turning before Kamil even asked. The horse stepped neatly over the corpses that tumbled in the gutter. Kamil soon found himself engrossed in his work. As he ordered men to collect kindling (for the citadel might have to be fired) or defended himself from Christians on the run, he almost forgot that he and the horse were two different beings. Hosanna became an extension of his own legs and arms. They were as one.

However, as the day went on, something troubled Kamil. Something within him had changed. Even as he went about the business of war, which was his duty as a Muslim and a follower of Saladin, he was acutely conscious of the Christians' blood spreading like a stain down Hosanna's front legs. It stood out hideously against the horse's natural colour and Kamil hated it. Often Kamil looked for a water trough and washed the blood off. Sometimes he even found himself avoiding killing Christian men altogether and called for soldiers to take them into the custody pens he once would not have bothered to create. He was nervous of seeing the knight with the teardrop mark again, but he never did.

By evening, Kamil could see that nearly all the able-bodied Christians had reached the tower and were climbing further and further up. They refused to surrender, even though everybody knew that there could, in the end, be no other outcome. When the call for negotiations finally came, Kamil was not surprised to be asked to make an approach to Saladin on the Christians' behalf. The message was clear. The Christians declared that if Richard's army had not come to the aid of the city by three o'clock the following afternoon, 1 August, they would give themselves up.

Kamil galloped back to Saladin, who, having travelled more slowly, was now approaching Jaffa with the main body of the army. When he heard what Kamil had to say, he ordered his men to set up camp about half a mile from the city walls, where the orchards and gardens began.

'You have done well, Kamil,' he said. 'The answer to the Christians is that they have until tomorrow, three o'clock – although much good may the delay do them.'

The Saracens inside Jaffa were jubilant. They had won. Despite Kamil urging caution, for he was too much a soldier to take anything for granted, his men hoisted their green flags and pennants on the city walls in anticipation of total victory. Why bother to wait? Kamil pushed down his misgivings. What harm could a few flags do? Besides, his men deserved to celebrate. Richard, who the Saracen spies reported to Saladin, had arrived at Acre five days earlier, could never make it to Jaffa in time to rescue the Christian inhabitants. The city was surrounded.

Kamil rode out of the city and back to the camp. It felt good to dismount. He patted Hosanna, then handed him to a groom with instructions to feed him well. Kamil was exhausted. After sharing some dinner with the sultan, he found the tent allocated to him, undressed and fell asleep.

Neither Saladin nor Kamil had reckoned on Richard's fury. Two days after arriving at Acre, he received a message that Jaffa was under attack. Barely stopping to think, and leaving all his army's horses behind, the king set sail from Acre with a handful of knights and men-at-arms. Leaving Jerusalem for another day was one thing, but Jaffa, which would be vital for supply lines to the Holy City, must be protected at all costs. Losing Jaffa would make any future attempts on Jerusalem almost impossible. Richard could not countenance it.

Gavin and William leapt on board ship with the king. At the last minute, Hal scrambled up the gangplank, begging to be allowed to fight just once on this great crusade. He had no armour and only a small dagger, but he wanted to take his chance. William was reluctant but Gavin, remembering the frustrations of his own youth, told William that he should let Hal come. Anyway, it was too late. The ship was already sailing, followed by a small flotilla of other boats, all crammed with knights and soldiers.

Standing in the prow as the king's vessel travelled south, hugging the coast, William strained to pick up any clue about what was happening inland. Contrary winds made their progress agonizingly slow. Richard fretted that a journey calculated to take two days with an accommodating wind was going to take at least three.

The king was right. It was not until nearly midnight of the Christians' last night before surrender that the fleet reached Jaffa, and when the dawn broke, Richard's heart sank. They were too late. The green flags mocked him. The king stamped and swore.

It was Gavin who, straining his eyes in the thin light, saw movement at the top of the tower. He watched with increasing amazement, as a priest, waving wildly at the ship, jumped from the fortress into the sea. It was a massive leap. Unsure what this signified, Gavin indicated to the sailors that they should lower a rope and haul him in. The Christians were silent. What was going on inside the city?

The priest, gasping and his teeth chattering, demanded to see the king. Hal threw a blanket over him while Gavin fetched Richard.

'Sir,' said the priest, 'I have come to tell you that Jaffa has not fallen completely to the Saracens. There are many of us, even knights still armed, taking refuge in the top of the citadel. If you can move quickly to get us out and can provide enough fighting men yourself, the city may yet be saved.'

Richard, sensing a glimmer of hope, asked the priest how many Saracens he thought were in the city and what their state of readiness was. The priest told of feasts half-eaten, of Saracen horses unsaddled and soldiers sleeping in the streets. Richard made up his mind at once. 'We must attack from the beach and we must do it now,' he said. 'Every able-bodied man on this ship must wield a weapon.' He caught sight of Gavin. 'Are you ready?' he asked.

Gavin stiffened his back.

'I am ready, sire,' he said, pulling out his sword with his left hand.

'And you?' the king turned to Hal.

'Yes, sire.'

Richard smiled. 'I am surrounded by brave men,' he said. 'I shall not forget.'

William and Hal made sure Gavin was between them as they prepared to leap from the ship and make their way to the shore.

'Seems as good a time as any to try out my new skills for real,' Gavin shouted as all three plunged into the sea together. 'Even a one-armed man and a groom are needed now!'

When they surfaced, Hal was already holding his dagger high above his head. 'Hartslove and Hosanna!' he was shouting. Gavin and William, with terrified exhilaration, took up his cry.

The first Kamil knew of Richard's arrival was when Muslim soldiers began pouring out of the city gates through which they had only recently poured in. He was woken by screams. People were no longer praising Allah, they were begging for His help. By the time he had pulled on his clothes, run out to find Hosanna and was ready to fight, it was too late. The Saracen flags were being torn down. Jaffa was once again filled with fighting and, before breakfast, the red cross on the white background was flying again, hoisted by a handful of men whose bravery verged on madness. Kamil, although he tried his best, was helpless to stop this reverse. His mind was numb with shock and incredulity as he found Saladin to give him the bad news himself.

Saladin wasted no time in regrets. He immediately issued a challenge. There could be no more sieges, no more cat and mouse. The two armies should meet outside the city walls and fight a pitched battle. It was time to have definite winners and losers. Richard laughed when Baha ad-Din came to find him with the message. He was busy releasing the Christian prisoners and counting the Saracen dead. He made Baha ad-Din wait for an hour before he sent his reply.

'Take a message back to the sultan,' he said eventually. 'We cannot fight a pitched battle as we have no horses.' Then he went into the citadel to make sure all the fires were put out and the soldiers had made the city secure.

When Richard's message was brought back and read to him, Saladin sat thinking. Then he sent Baha ad-Din to gather the emirs together. He also sent for Kamil and asked him to help him dress in his most splendid attire. 'It was not your fault,' he said. 'The Christians are insane. We say many things about them, but they do not lack courage. Their faith is as strong as ours and they are formidable, even heroic, enemies. We cannot deny them that. But now the time has come for the last great effort. I shall go to our men not as a fellow soldier, but, for once, as their sultan.'

Saladin timed it perfectly. As the emirs assembled, the muezzin called the faithful to prayer. The sultan strode in, dazzling in gold. He took his place at the front and listened, with humility, to the imam. After the last words died away, but while the holy sentiments they had just heard expressed were still reverberating in their ears, Saladin turned to face his emirs and spoke.

'The Christian King Richard has retaken Jaffa,' he began. 'But he cannot keep it for long if our army is encamped outside. It seems that he has given up on Jerusalem for the moment. But this is not good enough. We must concentrate on making it impossible for the army of the enemy to remain here in any city, particularly those on the coast. But after so long in the field already, I do not believe we can afford another drawn-out siege either here at Jaffa or anywhere else. Instead we must fight and fight to the death.' Saladin paused, his eyes boring into the faces of his followers. 'But in order to obtain Allah's help,' he went on, 'We must fight by the right code of conduct. The Christians have no horses and, in a formal battle, we cannot use ours against men who have none. We must therefore send horses. That is the right thing to do. My plan is simple. We must send a horse for King Richard and for nine other knights. We will then use only ten horses ourselves. Everyone else will fight on foot.' Saladin stopped and looked about him. 'Is that agreed?'

The emirs, struck by the force of Saladin's words, after some consultation, nodded. Baha ad-Din sought permission to ask a question.

'But which horses shall we send?'

'We must send the best horses, the most beautiful we have, as befits the Muslim code of honour,' came the reply. 'Go and get them ready and I will choose which ones are fit for this endeavour.

With that, Saladin got up. Half an hour later he went to the horse-lines and walked along, picking out the animals that, in his view, would most please the Christians. He chose nine. Then he stopped, turned and walked directly over to Kamil. 'This one,' he said.

Kamil's heart turned to lead. The red horse had become more precious to him than his own life. With Hosanna beside him, Kamil became a better man than he could ever be alone. Saladin waited patiently for Kamil to answer. After a long minute, Kamil bowed his head. He was shaking. He could not help himself. But he did not need to be reminded in words of his debt to Saladin. Now he understood that the day of repayment that Saladin had talked about behind the rock had come. Swallowing hard, Kamil touched Hosanna's star. Then, standing straight again, his head once more held high, he gave his answer. 'Yes,' he said. 'My red horse will go. He will go in the name of honour, love and Allah.'

Saladin said nothing, but he touched Kamil's shoulder lightly with his hand. As he walked away, he looked back and delivered a further test, although his heart was bleeding for his favourite son.

'Kamil,' he said, 'you will be in charge of delivering the horses yourself.' Kamil did not flinch.

'As you command,' he said and called for brushes and cloths so that he could spend all night making the red horse's coat shine as never before.

21

At daybreak, Richard was woken by his page.

'Sire, something extraordinary is going on,' said the boy.

Richard, asleep in a house in the middle of the city, dressed quickly and, calling for his squire to bring his armour after him, went to the city gate. There he found a group of knights gathered. They were staring out on to the great plain. William was standing with Hal and left it to Gavin to greet the king.

'Look, sire!' he said.

In the pale, early morning light, something glittered on the horizon. As the glitter drew nearer, the knights could make out that it was a small group of mounted, unarmed men. They were led by a dark youth on a horse glowing red in the dawn. His head was bare. Behind him, three men were also riding, each leading three horses fully equipped for battle but with empty saddles. Behind them again was another man with one spare horse, an Arab stallion wearing only a bridle. The Christian knights stood silent. There was no sound from those approaching except for the jingle of bits and the muffled thud of hoofs.

Time seemed to stand still. William began to tremble.

He could hardly breathe. His eyes were glued to the young man and the lead horse. Gavin took his brother's arm.

'It probably isn't, you know,' he began, fearing disappointment so acute it would be unbearable. But his eyes were also glued to the horse, and his own heart was racing.

William did not hear a word Gavin said. As the cavalcade drew nearer, a few knights began to whisper. They were uneasy. Surely this was a trap? Some turned and called loudly for their squires to bring their swords. But Richard raised his hand.

'Be quiet,' he ordered. 'Be quiet.' And he, too, held William's arm to stop him from running forwards.

When Kamil reached the group of knights he dismounted and let go of the horse. Hosanna stood stock still, his head raised and his eyes dark and fathomless. William made a small noise in his throat, but Richard pushed him back while he himself went forwards and stood directly in front of Kamil.

Kamil gave a stiff bow. 'My master, the sultan, sends these horses to you,' he said to Richard, 'In the name of honour, love and Allah. We will fight today. We will use the might of our whole army. But, as befits the rules of conduct, as you will only have ten horses, we also will use only ten horses.'

Richard listened carefully, then gave a small gesture of acknowledgement. William waited, in agony.

'Tell your master, the sultan,' Richard replied, 'that I understand his gesture and I gratefully accept both the horses and his challenge.'

There was a pause while Kamil stepped out from behind Richard and looked down the row of knights. He ignored them but when, after what seemed like an age, he saw William, he walked towards him, slowly, his bearing proud. Hosanna, without being bidden, followed behind.

The two young men faced each other. Gavin drew back so that Kamil addressed William alone.

'I am returning to you,' he said, 'the red horse.' And with that he turned, took Hosanna's rein and placed it in William's hand. Kamil stood for a moment before saying something in his own language and touching Hosanna briefly on the neck. The ghost of a smile flitted over his face as Hosanna blew in his ear, and his voice was just a whisper. Then he called for his men to hand the other horses over to the Christians and stepped back. Catching the rein of his Arab stallion, he vaulted lightly on and, without another word or a backwards glance, galloped away into the distance.

William did not see him go. Before Kamil had even turned away, William's face was buried in Hosanna's mane as, in defiance of all knightly dignity, he threw his arms round his beloved horse's neck. The horse whickered gently and rubbed his head on William's back. Hal was beside himself. Gavin whooped and shouted. The king was wreathed in smiles. He came over to Hosanna and, under William's beaming gaze, patted the horse's neck.

'Happily returned, Hosanna,' he said and put his hand up to touch the white star on the horse's head. Hosanna himself seemed quietly happy to be reunited with his old friends. But, even as he basked in their love and attention, once or twice he looked into the desert and whinnied.

But the red horse's return did not herald peace and tranquillity. Battle was to commence within two hours. Back in his stronghold in the city, Richard quickly summoned the knights he wished to see mounted: the earl of Leicester, Bartholomew de Mortimer, Ralph de Mauleon, Andrew de Chavigny, Gerard de Furnival, Roger de Soucy, William l'Etang, Hugh de Neville and William.

The brothers were quiet as William, having been persuaded to leave Hosanna with Hal for a few minutes, went to find his armour in the great heap unloaded from the ship they had leapt from two nights before. Gavin took his exclusion from the battle with good grace. Of course there were some things it was impossible for him to do.

'We will need you afterwards,' the king said to him. 'Who knows what will happen.'

Gavin nodded and concentrated on helping William to arm himself for what might be the last time.

'This may be the end, you know,' he said, struggling with buckles made hard and rusty by the salty air and the weather. 'Saladin means this contest to be a fight to the death.'

William, his eyes shining, did not look remotely troubled. 'I know,' he said. 'But I will have Hosanna. If I don't make it back to ride over the drawbridge at Hartslove, you can tell Ellie we went down together, like true crusaders.'

Gavin tried to sound happy. 'I know you will do your duty by God and King Richard,' he said. 'But how I wish . . . how I wish we were at home now. To see you fight while I can only stand and watch; it is worse than torture. Much worse. I'm glad our father is not here to see it, too.' Gavin looked away so that William would not realize how upset he was.

William did not reply. He did not know what to say. What was about to happen seemed unreal compared with the extraordinary happiness at having his horse returned to him. He pulled on the long tunic he wore over his mail coat and adjusted it so that the crusading cross was straight. Then he put on his helmet.

'Do I look ready?' he asked.

The brothers embraced. 'God, the king and Hosanna,' whispered William.

Gavin tried to reply. He got as far as 'God and the king' but could say no more.

Then suddenly, William was gone.

22

The battlefield was set about a mile outside the city walls, where the plain opened out. Saladin and his emirs – among whom was Kamil – and Richard and his knights, faced each other at last. The Christian foot soldiers, their helmets gleaming in the morning sun, gathered themselves into round formations that the enemy would find difficult to break. Archers and arbalesters were lined up in rows behind them, each man ready to take the place of the man in front so as to fire a continuous stream of arrows and bolts. Saladin's army was arranged in seven lines, ready to attack in waves.

Looking out over the field, the silken pennants, the sparkle of steel, the men kneeling in rows and the knights rock solid in their circles, the scene was so fantastical that for a moment Gavin was reminded of all the colour and pageantry of the lists at Hartslove. But today was no game. He and William would not laugh about it at supper. The preparations for this battle might look like a ritual dance, but the reality was something much more terrible. The knights and horses might be proud, the emblems on shields and trappings reflecting the rays of the sun, and the emirs might be elegant, with their richly embroidered tunics, but soon the predominant colour would be red as the blood began to flow. Here, the trumpet that announced the beginning of the games at home would signal the end of men's lives. Who could know what the outcome of the day's slaughter would be? The only certainty was that where men now lived and breathed, corpses would lie. William's would almost certainly be one of them. Gavin did not know if he would be able to deal with this. *If William dies*, he thought to himself, *I will go back to Hartslove, free Ellie from our betrothal, make her mistress of her own destiny and come back out here to die myself.*

There was no further time for thought. At the agreed signal, Richard set his lance and his nine knights did likewise. William looked down the line. He named all the knights to himself, proud to die in their distinguished company. He felt as if he were in some strange, floating bubble. Only the gentle, familiar tug of Hosanna's mouth down the reins as he tossed his head and the sound of the trumpets brought him back to earth.

Finally, their lances pointing directly forwards and their prayers said, the Christian knights charged. At first there was just the dull thud of the horses' hoofs in the sand. Then, 'God and the Holy Sepulchre!' they cried in unison as the horses gathered speed. Their shout was taken up by the soldiers waiting behind them. William settled himself in the saddle and grasped his lance more firmly as Hosanna galloped straight as a die towards the Saracens, his ears pricked and his tail, a wave of gold, flowing out behind him.

For a second, the Saracens did nothing. Then all was tumult as the cry *'Allah akbar!'* threatened to drown out the Christians' roars. Kamil spurred his horse directly towards Richard. In the melee, all that could be heard was the clash of steel matched, almost at once, by the pitiful groans of the wounded and dying. Through the dust and blood, shouting and stamping it grew difficult to make out what was happening. His heart in his mouth, Gavin climbed on to the top of an upturned wagon and could just see Hosanna moving this way and that near the edge of the fray. William was fighting like a demon. To his alarm, Gavin saw that two of the horses sent to the Christians had been killed at once. The earl of Leicester was dead and Hugh de Neville was crawling away, belaboured on all sides by Saracens with maces. He could not possibly survive.

But Richard had seen off Kamil and his sword was flashing right and left to devastating effect. Gavin soon lost sight of his brother and after a few minutes saw the king crash to the ground. How Richard extricated himself from underneath his dead horse Gavin never knew, but he did, and, protecting his back as best he could, caught hold of the bridle of Bartholomew de Mortimer's destrier. The fighting around them stopped as, arguing fiercely, Bartholomew dismounted and handed his horse to Richard. Such was the extraordinary nature of the battle that Richard was courteously given time to mount before being brought once again into the heart of the fighting. Bartholomew, charging on foot, was almost immediately felled by an arrow through the neck.

Kamil was unconsciously doing his best to avoid William, but now attempted again to push Richard off his horse. Richard swiped at him, then the two were parted as other combatants assailed them. Saladin took Kamil's place, but was crowded out by Andrew de Chavigny. With a great shout, Saladin raised his sword and brought it crashing down on de Chavigny's shoulder. It sliced clean through his mail and deep into the flesh. The knight fell and did not rise. His horse, shaking the blood from its eyes, galloped back to Saladin's camp from whence it had come such a short time before.

The hail of arrows from the ranks of the soldiers grew thick and the thwack and thud of the crossbows was almost unceasing as Gavin shut his eyes and began to pray harder than he had ever prayed in his life.

The king was under threat again and again. It seemed a Saracen tactic to kill whatever mount he seized from another knight. Sometimes Richard was forced to fight on foot as he worked his way towards somebody, anybody, who had a horse. If it was a Saracen, he tried to kill the horse. If it was a Christian, he ordered the knight to hand the horse over. The order could not be disobeyed, even though this meant almost certain death. When Gavin opened his eyes again he saw both Gerard de Furnival and Roger de Soucy on their feet. Gerard was cut down at once. Roger, by some miracle, managed to get back to the Christian lines unscathed.

The ground was growing sticky with blood, and the air was filled with death. Those watching could see the combatants on both sides diminishing in number. Eventually, after a long struggle in which he managed to wound but not kill the sultan, Ralph de Mauleon also fell to Saladin's sword and William l'Etang's horse was struck by a crossbolt. Its leg shattered and its screams rose until Kamil galloped over and thrust his sword into the animal's throat. Through the red mist, Gavin heard somebody shout, 'William's down, the horse is finished.' He found himself beseeching God that it was the other William and his horse, not his brother and Hosanna. His guilty relief when he discovered his prayers had been answered almost overpowered him.

Eventually all the knights' horses, barring Hosanna and Ralph de Mauleon's, which the king had seized as the knight's dead body was pitched off, were slain. The battle thinned. Richard, taking stock, found William by his side. Together, they plunged in among the Saracens. As he raised his sword once again, Richard felt his horse stumble. He glanced down. Its flank was slashed. Before it could fall, the king leapt off. Kamil approached at the gallop. Now was his chance. With a silent cry of jubilation, he raised his sword just as Richard put his own above his head. A Saracen trumpet sounded. Kamil hesitated, his arm still poised. He could see from the corner of his eye that the sultan's troops were turning back, away from the city. Although all the mounted Christians, barring the king and William, were either dead or vanished from the fight, Richard's foot soldiers, with their arrows and crossbolts, were clearly in the ascendant. Kamil took no notice. He prepared his stroke. No matter what the soldiers were doing, he could kill a king. As he drove his sword down, Saladin was suddenly by his side, shouting. In obedience to the sultan's command, Kamil missed.

William, turning at the sound of the trumpet, saw Richard's horse fall and knew at once what he must do. As Kamil's sword hit the ground, he leapt off Hosanna and handed him over to his king. The time for the ultimate sacrifice had arrived and William was not found wanting. Richard took Hosanna without a word, and William silently helped him to mount. He touched his horse's white star, then stepped back. Kamil was watching and, without thinking, immediately placed his horse right in front of William. He told himself that he should not protect his enemy from the last of the arrows. But he never moved.

Now, apart from the cries of the wounded, silence fell. The whole world seemed focused on two men: the king and the sultan.

They faced each other without speaking. It was only as they steadied and, as if at a pre-arranged signal, began to charge towards each other that the deafening roar erupted once more.

Hosanna, galloping, sidestepping, turning and wheeling, was covered in sweat. Nevertheless, his hoofs seemed barely to touch the ground. He appeared to sense Richard's every thought, to understand every tactic as again and again Richard lunged forwards. Both men grunted as they raised their swords and attempted to find the opening that would finish the other off. Hosanna made no sound but, with a dexterity Richard had never encountered in any other horse, flowed round the sultan's stallion, leaving it flat-footed. Slowly, remorselessly, it became clear that the king was wearing the sultan down. Kamil, still mounted, tightened his grip on his sword. If Saladin was killed, then nobody would stop him finishing Richard off himself. He prayed that he could do it and spare the red horse.

Now the Christians began to shout that the king was the victor. Their cries filled Richard with new impetus and, suddenly, the chance was there. Just as he had been taught, Hosanna reared as Richard raised his sword to deliver the death blow to Saladin, the mortal enemy of Christendom.

It was for just this moment that a lone Saracen archer had been waiting. Taking deadly aim he fired one, steel-tipped arrow. It struck true. Richard's blow was never delivered. Saladin wheeled away, calling to the emirs to come after him. They all obeyed except one, who, leaping from his saddle and dropping his sword, ran over to where a red horse lay in the sand.

23

By the time Kamil reached Hosanna, Richard and William were standing over his body. William, stunned and speechless, was unable to take in what had happened. He was supposed to die with his horse. Then he had given him to the king. Now both he and the king were standing unharmed while Hosanna was lying with an arrow close to his heart. He did not hear Gavin calling his name. Even when Gavin ran towards him William could not move. Only when Kamil arrived did William make an inarticulate sound and begin pulling off his armour so that he could kneel more easily. Kamil dropped to his knees and took Hosanna's head in his arms. He did not bother to hide his anguish. William knelt down beside him and, as he did so, Kamil gently moved the horse's head into William's lap. Then he turned his attention to the arrow. The horse lay so quietly it was difficult to tell if he was breathing, but Kamil pulled the arrow out anyway. Hosanna quivered, then was still. William looked for Gavin.

'The ointment that Brother Andrew gave Ellie,' he said. 'It's here, in my pouch. Get it out.' Gavin, fumbling, did so. William laid Hosanna's head gently down while he opened the little casket and pushed its contents into the deep hole the arrow had made. 'Would the arrow have been poisoned?' he asked Kamil. He had to know.

Kamil shook his head. 'But it has gone in too deep,' he whispered. 'I don't know what can be done.'

Suddenly there was a thudding of feet, and Hal burst through. When he saw Hosanna lying motionless and the huge hole with blood welling to fill it, he was wild. 'There must be something we can do,' he cried.

William shook his head. But Hal would not give up. He struggled for something to say as he ripped off his shirt and tried to staunch the wound. But it seemed hopeless.

After a few moments, Hal rocked back on his heels, tears streaming down his face.

'Aren't we supposed to believe in God's power?' he cried at the king. 'We can't just do nothing. I prayed when I went unarmed into Jaffa, and God protected me. Maybe He could help Hosanna. At the very least we should pray. What else is there?'

All around them the groans of the wounded added to their despair. The glory of the battle had vanished and only its dreadful aftermath remained.

The king said nothing. William did not look at Kamil's face as he said, 'It does not matter to Christians which way they face when they pray, but I'm told it matters to you. Which way is Mecca? If we are all to pray together, well . . .'

Kamil hesitated then pointed. His face was expressionless.

Richard uttered a small exclamation and walked away. There were some things he would not do. But William, Gavin, Hal and Kamil, turning their backs on Hosanna, knelt together. Gavin, nervous and unsure, nevertheless began. God, Allah, Christ, Mohammed – it all seemed so much more complicated now. The only certainty was that they all, both Muslim and Christian, wanted the same thing.

'Here, Lord,' he said, hoping he was not going to offend anybody, 'Here lies a Great Horse. We ask that his death and the deaths of so many countless others are not in vain. We are in confusion. Show us Your will. Amen.'

Then Kamil began. 'Our hearts are protected from that unto which You, O Mohammed, callest us,' he said. 'In our ears there is a deafness and between us and You there is a veil. In our anxiety and sadness, let Allah show us the right path, the one of righteousness and piety.'

They all murmured their assent, then prayed silently, each lost in his individual thoughts. As they did so, behind them, Hosanna, gathering the breath that had been knocked out of him, opened his eyes and began to move. Slowly and with a great effort, he rose to his feet. When William and Kamil turned round, they found the horse standing, his nose on the ground, the blood from his wound making a small channel in his side. They all rushed to support him, linking hands, and, between them, shouting for others to help, they almost carried the horse the long, bitter mile back through the city gates and into a stable. The sun beat down, seeming to mock their efforts. On the way, Kamil whispered urgent instructions to Hal, and the boy scarcely nodded before rushing to find Kamil's stallion. He mounted and galloped through the dead and dying to Saladin's camp.

The sultan was pacing round his pavilion beside himself with worry over Kamil. How could the boy have stopped himself rushing to the red horse? Saladin was not angry, but he was terrified that, with the horse apparently dead, Kamil would not escape alive. When he heard Hal's unfamiliar voice, he rushed out just in time to witness his soldiers pulling him off Kamil's horse.

Baha ad-Din heard Hal's cries of indignation. He shouted at the soldiers and then, with his own hands, dragged Hal into Saladin's presence, shouting for an interpreter.

When the interpreter arrived, the sultan was standing over the boy, a fierce expression on his face.

'Ask him why he is here,' Saladin ordered. 'Ask him, where is my emir, Kamil ad-Din, whose horse he has?'

Hal could say only one word. 'Hosanna,' he said, urgently. 'We need medicine for Hosanna. The Saracen man has sent me. Please, please help us.'

Saladin stared. 'The Saracen man,' he said. 'Is he safe?'

Hal was beside himself. 'Safe? Of course he's safe. He's with my master, William, and Gavin and oh, please. Can't this wait? The emir says to send dressings and oil and anything you have. I know you can save Hosanna. He said so.'

'Kamil said so? What proof do I have?'

Hal was whispering now, all the energy draining out of him. Saladin would never believe him. But he answered the sultan anyway. 'I have no proof. But he did say so. He said it was for honour, love and Allah, or something like that. But he also said I must be as quick as the wind or the red horse would die. Maybe it is too late already.'

Saladin looked at Baha ad-Din and the old man nodded slowly. 'I think the boy is telling the truth,' he said. 'That horse . . . well, the truth seems to follow him.'

Nevertheless, Saladin did not make his voice any gentler as he turned once again to Hal. 'Honour, love and Allah. That's what he said?'

'Yes, oh yes,' said Hal. 'I swear by Hosanna.' He knew

that it was a sin to swear on anything but God. But to the frantic boy, even if what he had done merited hell it was worth it.

Saladin was silent for an eternal half minute. Then, clapping his hands, he summoned two servants and issued his orders.

In ten minutes, Hal found himself back on Kamil's stallion, leading a sumpter horse with packs bulging full of medicines and spices. Behind him, a wagon was making slow progress. Every minute the boy urged the packhorse to go more quickly. As he reached the gates of Jaffa, Hal felt as though he had been away for weeks, though it was in fact just over an hour.

William was waiting by the stable door and shouted to Kamil as soon as he heard Hal's voice. Kamil came at once.

'The sultan is good,' he said as he unpacked the wine, turpentine, cumin and honey, together with strong-smelling balms made of different oils and ground herbs.

'The sultan is good,' echoed Hal, rolling up his sleeves and doing whatever Kamil told him to do. Hosanna was already lying on a bed of thick reeds, and Kamil immediately began to plug his wound with some evil-smelling unguent, covering it with a silk bandage.

'We must use a poultice to get out any infection,' he said. William nodded. 'And we must keep the flies off.' For the next couple of hours, the two of them worked as one, cleaning the wound, preparing the poultice and trying to keep the horse cool.

In the wagon Saladin had sent slings and wood to make a litter. 'You can take the red horse home without him having to stand all the way,' explained Kamil. Home. William could not take in the concept. For the moment it seemed to him that his home was here, in this small stable in this foreign city, working with a man whom he had come here to kill but who was now joined with him in saving the life of a horse they both loved.

'You must thank the sultan,' William said quietly when the immediate activity was over and Hosanna was comfortable. As he sat looking at the horse, William took out a small knife, leant down and cut off a hank of Hosanna's mane. He gave this to Kamil.

Kamil took it and, as he did so, said softly, 'In the name of honour, love and Allah.'

William nodded. 'In the name of honour, love and Allah,' he repeated. At such a moment, William thought, surely God would not care by what name He was called. Without saying anything further, Kamil put the hank of hair in his belt, touched the horse's neck and got up. Outside, his stallion was waiting. Taking its reins, Kamil vaulted on, slipped unnoticed through the city streets and out of the gate. Then he urged the horse into a gallop and was soon lost to view.

24

After the great battle at Jaffa, the mood changed in Richard's camp. It was as if the sight of ships standing in the harbour all ready to carry them home served to remind the soldiers just how long they had been away. Two years of unimaginable hardship had taken their toll. This mood was reflected among the knights and soldiers left at Acre. There was no more talk of storming Jerusalem. Richard was glad.

Equally, as a relieved Saladin greeted Kamil on his return from Hosanna's sickbed, he also became aware that even his most ferocious emirs were not pushing for another assault on the city. The sultan listened carefully as Baha ad-Din reminded him that many of his soldier's farms lay in ruins because the men had put their duty to holy war above their work on the land.

But it was worse than that. Both armies had raided villages and destroyed crops without any thought for the people who lived there. Providing food for soldiers had become more important than worrying about hungry children. Furthermore, just to compound matters, both Christians and Saracens had taken pains to destroy what they could not use themselves in order to deny it to the enemy. The result was that in some Muslim villages,

Saladin was almost as unpopular as Richard. Baha ad-Din did not shrink from telling Saladin that, in his view, and in the view of many good Muslims, it was time to exchange swords for ploughshares – for the moment at least.

Richard had even more reason to go home. Before setting out for Jaffa from Acre, he had had news that his prolonged absence had put his lands and even his position as king under threat. At home, his brother John and King Philip of France were plotting. The English and Frankish barons who had not taken the cross were unsure whether it was worth keeping Richard's throne warm for him. If Richard did not come home, they did not want to find their loyalty misplaced and misinterpreted. It was becoming abundantly clear that Richard's subjects needed to see him for themselves.

However, there was just one more thing that the Christians had to do before going home. If they could not take Jerusalem as warriors, they would at least visit it as pilgrims. Swallowing his pride, Richard sent a messenger to Saladin to ask for safe passage for his men, which Saladin granted without hesitation. Richard himself refused to go, on the grounds that it would be humiliating for him to accept Saladin's charity. Accepting horses under the laws of chivalry was one thing. Accepting the 'safe conduct' pass that Saladin offered was quite another. Richard would go to Jerusalem in his own good time, brandishing his sword rather than leaning on a pilgrim's staff.

Gavin and William thought differently. As they walked together to perform one of their hourly checks on Hosanna, they agreed that to come all the way out and not see the holy places seemed wrong. They felt they owed it to their father and, although they did not say so aloud, each also wanted to be able to describe to Ellie something other than death and destruction. Picking their way through Jaffa's narrow streets, they passed men nursing wounds that would never heal and others in mourning for fathers, sons and brothers whose bones were whitening all over Palestine.

'We'll go to Jerusalem,' said Gavin, and William nodded his agreement.

He opened the door into Hosanna's stable and immediately his spirits lifted. Just a week after Hosanna had limped in at death's door, it was now a cheerful place. The horse's wound was healing well. As William ruefully remarked to Hal, Hosanna would always carry both the dent caused by William's sword, and a scar from the Saracen arrow.

Hal smiled. But Hosanna's scars were not uppermost in his mind any more. The only thing he thought of was home. The loss and then the return of Hosanna, together with the horse's almost miraculous survival, seemed to Hal to be as much luck as any horse could have in a lifetime. What was more, Hal thought to himself, I have survived, too. He had no wish to tempt fate any further and just wanted to see his mother again.

'Will you go to Jerusalem if we are given permission to visit as pilgrims?' William asked him, idly plaiting Hosanna's mane.

Hal considered. 'Will you?' he asked.

'Yes,' said William. 'After all, we have a lot to thank God for.'

Hal did not really agree. God, after all, had been as responsible for the bad things as the good. He considered saying as much to William but was suddenly shy. He was only a squire, after all, not a knight. What did he really

251

know about these things? He moved on to practical matters. 'Who will look after Hosanna while I am away?'

William laughed. 'I think the plan is that we should go in three different lots,' he said. 'Between you, Gavin and I, we should manage both to see Jerusalem and look after Hosanna.'

Hal nodded. 'It will be something to tell my mother,' he said, then, struck by a new thought, his eyes filled with a new worry. 'Assuming she is still alive,' he said. William patted his shoulder.

The brothers planned well. Gavin went in the first, Hal the second and William in the third and last company. Having seen Gavin and Hal come safely back, William set off under the leadership of the bishop of Salisbury, a holy man in whom everybody found much to respect. It was the second week of September and the skies were cloudless. As he put on the rough pilgrim's tunic Old Nurse had packed so long ago, William reflected on all that had happened since the Hartslove contingent had met the king at Vezelay in July 1190. He joined his fellow pilgrims near the front of the procession, obediently intoning Hail Marys as the bishop instructed. But his thoughts were far away. Things that had seemed so certain in the great hall at Hartslove seemed uncertain now. His father had not been invincible; his own horse, whom William had imagined would be loyal only to himself, had flourished in the hands of the enemy; his king had made mistakes and misjudgements. William shuddered as he remembered some of the sights he had seen. Was any city, even the Holy City itself, worth all that suffering, all those shattered bones, all that torn flesh, all the screams of agony? A city, after all, was just bricks and mortar. If God was so good, could this kind of thing really be His will? Then he shook himself. Here he was, on a journey to Jerusalem. He must think only of that for the moment.

Unhindered by the enemy, the journey to Jerusalem took three days. Most of the pilgrims were on foot and they marvelled at the difference between this journey and the terrible and fruitless winter journey they had endured. Although the sun's heat sapped their energy, without their armour they could travel in relative comfort. As they passed through the hills from which, two months before, they had begun their retreat to Acre, the soldiers and knights gave a small cheer.

William trudged along the dusty route trying to concentrate on Christ and His suffering rather than the mutterings of the men walking next to him. Many remained unconvinced that Saladin's assurances of safety could be trusted. Eventually William turned round and gently chided them for their suspicions. He himself had no doubts. A man who sent medicines for Hosanna would keep his word.

And for the most part he did. For while many of the Saracen soldiers spat and jeered at the pilgrims, they did not touch them. Nor were their threats and curses the reason why all the pilgrims felt a curious shiver as they climbed up from the valley and passed through the longed-for gates. At that moment the Christians almost forgot about the Saracens. The gates of Jerusalem! This was the city of the psalms, the golden city, the city of Solomon and the city of Christ's Passion. In this place, the meaning of Christianity had been forged.

William was almost overcome. For Jerusalem, his father had given up his life, Gavin had lost an arm and he had nearly lost his horse. In her defence, both Christians and Saracens had suffered more than any living thing should ever be asked to suffer. William looked about him. Jerusalem was a mess. The sun-baked, grimy streets were strewn with the detritus of a million lives and deaths, both human and animal. Inside erstwhile Christian churches, the Saracens had allowed animals to wander. Courtyards were now smoking middens. Bold rats scrambled busily in and out of crumbling, yellow, brick walls, squealing and fighting over stinking remains. At every street corner of this supposedly heavenly city were piled the crude instruments of death: smooth, heavy stones, jars of 'Greek fire', small mountains of crossbow bolts and many more vile products of man's imagination, all prepared for the Christian siege that never happened.

But, as William followed the trail of Christ's Passion, kissed the ground of Mount Calvary and placed a small ring made of Hosanna's hair beside the table on which, so it was said, Christ had eaten His last supper, he was moved beyond words. At this moment of uneasy peace and in this supremely special place, everything did make sense in an odd kind of way. William felt sure that, whether the crusaders were right or wrong, God looked on them with some kind of favour. 'It could not all have been for nothing,' he said to himself, and could see by the reaction of his fellow pilgrims that they were all thinking the same thing. No matter what those at home would say now or in the future, the knights and soldiers in Richard the Lionheart's army had done their best for Christ and deserved their reward.

Some pilgrims finished their devotions quickly, then regrouped again and set off, this time for Acre, where Richard had already gone to order the fleet to prepare for departure. But William found himself dawdling. He had heard it rumoured that, courtesy of Saladin, the bishop might be given a private opportunity to see the True Cross. It would be the opportunity of a lifetime. He sat down on a stone and waited.

As he watched the Christians and Muslims mixing together, their eyes suspicious, he allowed his thoughts to turn to Hartslove. Barring accidents on the journey home, it looked as though he could fulfil his promise to Ellie and ride Hosanna over the drawbridge. But then what? His brother's injury, although well healed, meant that he was finished as a knight. Gavin might be Count of Hartslove out here, but in England he would never be regarded in the same way again. The loss of an arm was too serious a handicap for a knight to overcome. William frowned as he reflected that once this would have caused him to rejoice. Not now. How close he and Gavin had become! But even this had its difficulties, for there was Ellie's future to consider. Would Gavin feel honour-bound to release her from their engagement? And if he did, could William, in all conscience, take advantage?

These thoughts disturbed William so much that when he saw the bishop and about a dozen other pilgrims being chivvied down a side street, he was glad to get up and follow them. The bishop was clearly going somewhere special. Maybe this was the moment William had been waiting for. The small group was being urged to walk swiftly towards a large complex of buildings. William hurried to catch up with them and was just in time to enter a small, richly painted hall before a heavy curtain was drawn behind him. The hall was furnished with two large chairs, one much more ornately decorated than the other. The pilgrims looked about them and the bishop motioned to them to be silent. After a few moments, the sultan entered through a door at the other end. He was wearing a silk tunic embroidered with suns and stars and was surrounded by men, among whom was Kamil. He looked so regal that even the Christians bowed.

Saladin gestured to the bishop to sit in the plainer chair and sat down himself on the more ornate throne. Iced sherbet and sweetmeats were brought. Most of the Christians shook their heads. William moved to stand behind the bishop, acknowledged Kamil with a small nod, and took what was offered.

After the servants had left, the sultan summoned the interpreter and began. 'We are enemies, your king and I,' he said. 'There can never be friendship between us. But I salute his gallantry. He is a brave man. Much blood has been shed on both sides and many bad things have been done since the Christians came to our land. But for the moment it is over.' Saladin sighed. 'King Richard has sent word that he will not visit Jerusalem. I am sorry, for I would welcome him here in the true spirit of hospitality. However, I understand the pride that drives this decision. In his place I would do the same. Humility comes hard to a king – although the man you acclaim as the son of God, Jesus Christ, found no difficulty in being humble. Is that not so, bishop?'

The bishop was uncomfortable. 'Sir,' he said, 'King Richard has no equal among all the knights in the world. And, if you don't mind my saying so, if the virtues of both yourself and the king were taken together, there would be no two men on earth who could compete with you.'

Saladin was amused. 'You speak well,' he said. 'I would

like to give you a gift in return for your compliment. What should it be?'

The bishop considered. 'I think it would be fitting,' he said in a hesitant manner, since he was nervous of being too presumptuous, 'Rather, I think it might be fitting,' – there was a small pause as he gathered all his courage – 'To have two priests say Mass at Our Lord's tomb every day.'

Saladin bowed. 'Quite a request,' he remarked. 'If I and my emirs agree, where will you find two priests who want to come and live in this city with us, whom you call dogs and barbarians?'

The bishop frowned. 'Well,' he said, 'I'm sure we will . . .'

William interrupted. 'Sir, my Lord Bishop,' he said, quite inspired, 'I know a holy man. He is a monk who is also an ordained priest. For much of his life he has longed to come here in the service of the Lord. His name is Brother Ranulf and his monastery is at Hartslove, where I live. He would come. I know he would and I know he would take whatever hardship it involved and offer it up for the good of the holy places.'

Saladin allowed William to finish before turning to Kamil. 'Is this the red horse's boy?' he asked.

Kamil nodded.

Saladin turned back to William. 'How is the horse?'

William turned to Kamil. 'The red horse is much better,' he said. 'We will take the slings the sultan so kindly sent for the voyage home, but I don't think we'll need them. He can now stand unaided, and the wound is clean and cool.'

'I'm glad,' said Kamil. 'Maybe when your Brother – what was his name? Ranulf? When your Brother Ranulf comes out here, maybe he could bring word about the red horse.' Kamil did not smile. How could he? He had thought the horse would be his forever.

'Better than that,' said William, 'Why don't you travel to England and escort Brother Ranulf back yourself?'

A muscle in Kamil's face twitched and he inclined his head. 'I would like that,' he said softly. 'Maybe it will be possible. We have much to tell each other, I think, about the horse you call Hosanna.'

The sultan rose. He was pleased and uncomfortable at the same time. You should not shed your enemy's blood unnecessarily, but becoming too friendly was dangerous. This conversation between these two young men, which he could not understand and which the interpreter was ignoring, must come to an end. 'We will see how these Masses you want are to be arranged,' he said shortly, addressing the bishop. 'Now it is time for you to go. The relic known as the True Cross will be brought out for you to look at.'

The bishop stood up, muttering thanks. Saladin curtly acknowledged them. As Kamil passed William, he hesitated, unsure, but when Saladin had left the room, he put out his hand. William grasped it. 'Honour, love, God and Hosanna,' he smiled.

Kamil nodded. 'We will meet again,' he said and touched the hank of Hosanna's hair now braided and hanging from his belt. He looked for a second as if he wanted to say more. But he dared not trust his voice. In the end, he just turned and vanished.

Moments later, two servants carried in a large plain box, roughly the size of a tall man's coffin, and unceremoniously dumped it on the floor. The bishop was trembling as they prised it open to display two pieces of wood, one about two metres, the other about one metre long, lying one on top of the other. The spaces in which Christ's followers had placed jewels were empty. All the Christians in the room immediately knelt. This was the cross on which Jesus had died. To an outsider it might seem a shoddy thing. But nobody who saw it that day ever forgot it and, on their deathbeds, it was on these plain pieces of wood, damaged by looters and dented by swords, that they focused their final thoughts.

William hurried back to Jaffa, full of his experiences. He told Gavin about his conversation with Kamil. Gavin looked disbelieving. 'Kamil will never come to Hartslove,' he said. 'Not unless we capture him and bring him in chains.'

'Maybe it is possible that we could be friends.'

'No, Will,' said Gavin. 'We can appreciate what he did for Hosanna without being real friends. War does strange things to us all. Things that seem possible out here are quite impossible at home. Forget it.'

William did not mention it again. He put Kamil out of his mind and concentrated only on preparations for the journey.

He, Gavin and Hal travelled to Acre with Hosanna. They took a week, walking slowly with the horse and stopping every time he seemed tired. The country was pleasant and the journey uneventful. Staying near to the coast, the waves lulled them to sleep at night, and during the day, moving slightly inland, they found plentiful fresh water and fruit. At Acre, which William had not seen since leaving after the slaughter of the Muslim prisoners, the loading of supplies had already begun. This was an easy task. There were only tiny numbers of people and very few horses to cater for. There were no siege engines or wagons to be taken apart and loaded, and the remains of the armour and equipment, rusty and almost beyond repair, made a pitifully small heap in the hold.

There were two worries. One was Phoebus, who William thought would not manage the journey. After much heart-searching, they decided to leave him behind with the Christians garrisoning Acre.

The other, and rather more major worry, was Richard, who had fallen ill. Hal, hopping with anxiety, could have kissed the king for declaring that his most trustworthy knights should leave him and return to England without delay. Once recovered, Richard declared that he would himself go straight to France and try to regain control of his territory there. Gavin and William should not, therefore, travel in his ship, but go without him. From his sickbed, Richard asked them to send news of England when they arrived. Gavin felt reluctant to leave the king, but Richard, to Hal's relief, insisted.

'Let's get you home,' William said to Hosanna, touching his star before leading him into the hold. Hosanna, stepping eagerly up the ramp, seemed to agree.

Looking at the quayside, the enormous scale of Christian losses was only too apparent. Once back in the belly of a ship designed for twenty horses, Hosanna found himself with room to lie down or even walk about. His companions comprised Dargent and only one other horse, an Arab one knight was bringing home to breed from. Hal carefully supplemented the esparto grass with reed matting and carpets for the horses' comfort. In between Dargent and Hosanna he also made a bed for himself.

Gavin and William grinned at each other when they saw Hosanna's 'bedroom', as they nicknamed it. 'Fit for a king's horse,' said William, as he lay down to test for comfort. He got up and, as had become his habit, ran his hands down Hosanna's neck. The eyes that looked into his own were luminous in the dark. In his own habitual style, the horse put his velvet nose into William's hand. As the great ramp swung shut, cutting off the warmth of the sun, William shivered and his hand automatically sought out the white star. Soon afterwards, his fellow travellers and all the sailors were visiting the hold, doing exactly the same thing.

On almost the last day of September, the sails were hoisted, the oars set and the ships slid out of the harbour.

'Home,' said William to Hal, as they got their sea-legs once again.

'Home,' echoed Hal, 'God willing.'

The journey back was helped by a friendly wind but was just as frightening as the outward journey had been. The ship's captain clung to the coast as much as he could, but in one huge storm, as the ships slid round the toe of Italy, eight sailors and two knights lost their lives.

'It is inevitable,' Gavin shouted through the racket, as William and Hal clung together, grappling with ropes and trying to secure the horses with slings. 'But we must remain strong. At least we are being pushed homewards rather than backwards.'

After the storm, the ship found itself alone on a tossing sea. Gavin was very sick, but the ship held her own against the weather and the horses survived. They stood with their noses almost in their bedding, but, although the Arab occasionally groaned aloud, they all remained upright.

Gavin suffered from acute anxiety and fearful nightmares, as well as sickness. The damp, muggy air below deck was suffocating. He woke each morning, drained and sweating, the stump of his arm throbbing with pain. On nights when the sea was choppy and he was tossed about, he heard himself calling out the names of the dead: Mark, Humphrey, Adam Landless, his father, both his warhorses. William could do little to help him. Eventually, he left Gavin alone and crept down to sleep alongside Hal and Hosanna.

'We will get back to Hartslove soon,' he kept repeating in Hosanna's ear. 'I know we will get back to Hartslove soon.'

In the second week of December, twenty of the returning crusaders, including Gavin, William and Hal, disembarked at Marseilles. Wearing their crusading crosses on their back, to show that they were returning from the Holy Land, they managed to pick up more horses and crossed France, grateful for the hospitality offered to men who had fought for Christ. The weather was dreary, and desperation to get home increased. They rode quickly, not stopping to celebrate Christmas, pushing the horses as hard as they dared. Hal had looked after Hosanna so well on the journey that the horse was almost back to his old strength and by the middle of January they reached La Rochelle. There, they hired a vessel for the last push up the French coast and across the English Channel.

Gavin called together the fifteen men returning to Hartslove. They were all that remained from the four hundred who had set out. 'Nobody can say we have not endured martyrdom,' he told them soberly when, after an interminable week during which the wind always seemed against them, the white cliffs of England eventually came into view. As the ship sped up the east coast to a port

262

from which the journey to Hartslove would not be so far, William was silent, gripping the rails. When, at last, the top of the abbey at Whitby was spotted by a sailor, all the men stood on deck, some in silence, some whooping with delight.

William turned to Gavin, trying not to allow his voice to crack. 'Home,' he said, 'we've made it home. Oh thank God.'

The weather was kind and it was a perfect English winter's day as men and horses clattered joyfully on to dry land. This was not the time to think of those who had perished at sea or how news of lost fathers, brothers and sons was going to be received. The men shouted to each other as they busied themselves finding transport home. Occasionally one or two would be found rooted to the spot, trying to take in the almost unbelievable fact that they were once more on English soil and that the whole hideous ordeal was over. Some wept openly.

The de Granvilles needed only one wagon and a few more horses for the last leg of the journey home. William purchased a carthorse by the quayside, and eight riding horses. They would return with eleven horses, having left with nearer eleven hundred. From other sailors, they tried to get news of Richard, thinking that he might have made for England despite everything. But no one knew anything. No matter. Gavin and William pushed thoughts of Richard away – the important thing now was to get back to Hartslove.

Just before they set off, a messenger sought them out. He had been hanging about the port for months, sent there by a monk, whose name he had forgotten. He had been paid well to find a ship's captain with whom to entrust a roll of sealed parchment addressed to Gavin de Granville in the Holy Land. The messenger had been idle. Now, it seemed, this Gavin had arrived himself. Disappointed at being deprived of his excuse to enjoy port life at somebody else's expense, the messenger nevertheless found Gavin and handed over the letter. Gavin's surprise betrayed the fact that he might be a brave crusader, but he was as illiterate as the messenger himself. The man smiled in a patronizing manner. Gavin ignored him, snatched the parchment and sent William to find a cleric.

'Hurry, Will,' said Gavin. 'We want to leave as soon as possible.'

William returned with a fat priest who took the letter, slowly smoothed it out and nearly drove the brothers mad before he ostentatiously cleared his throat.

'Ahem. Now, here we go. Which one of you is Gavin?'

'I am.'

'Yes. Well then.' The priest licked his lips.

'Oh, get on with it,' cried Gavin.

'Of course. But it is a tricky business, this reading.'

'It is a tricky business being a crusader.'

The priest cleared his throat again. 'Indeed. But not without rewards unavailable to a poor priest like me.'

Gavin looked at him. 'You want money?' he asked, incredulous.

The priest looked sly. 'Not for me, you understand. For my, er, my parish.'

Gavin leant over. 'Now look here, you fat parasite,' he said, 'I may only have one arm, but I could swipe your head off with one blow. My saddle was once hung about with Saracen heads. A priest's head would make a fine addition to my tally.'

William made a suitably fierce face as the priest, feigning an expression of pained innocence, settled his ample behind on a convenient chair.

'There's no need to be abusive. Right then. Let me see. This letter is from a Brother Ranulf,' he began.

William and Gavin looked at each other. Brother Ranulf?

'Oh dear,' said the priest, scanning the lines. 'I'm afraid . . .'

'Just get on and read it, will you.' Gavin bent forwards, staring at the words as if they would suddenly speak themselves.

'"Master Gavin de Granville",' read the priest nervously, following the text with a dirty finger. '"I am writing this on behalf of Miss Eleanor de Barre. She has sent word to me that . . ." Hutsliff? Hatsliff?'

'Hartslove!' exploded Gavin.

'Yes, Hartslove, quite right,' said the priest. 'Well, "Hartslove is under threat from Constable Piers de Scabious."' The priest stopped. 'I wonder if those are the same de Scabiouses who came from the small village of Malad –'

Gavin clenched his fist. 'For goodness' sake, man.'

The priest flapped his hand. 'So sorry, now where was I?'

'Oh yes. "He –" that's Constable de Scabious, you understand . . .'

Gavin put his hand on his sword.

'Yes, yes. Well, anyway, "he –" and I am back to the letter here,' – the priest was beginning to sweat – 'Anyway, "he has betrayed the trust of Sir Thomas de Granville, your father, on every count. We hear that Sir Thomas is dead. We hear that you are dead too, in which case, whoever is reading this" – that's me, isn't it? – "please send us word and return this letter." Not necessary, which is good news,' the priest smiled ingratiatingly but William and Gavin stared stony-faced, and he hurriedly continued. ' "But if this letter does reach its intended recipient, I must tell you that things are not as you left them. If you do not return quickly, more than the castle may be lost to you. I have sent for your uncle the bishop but he has, so far, done nothing. On your travels, wicked men may tell you bad things about life at Hartslove. But whatever you hear about Miss Eleanor, in the name of Hosanna, I swear it is not true. All I urge is that, if you are able, you ask God to give you a fair wind and hurry home. Brother Ranulf." ' The priest wiped his mouth.

'Is that all?' asked William.

'That's all,' he said.

'What can Ranulf mean about Ellie?' Gavin exclaimed. 'Should we send a message back or what should we do? Constable de Scabious will perhaps think again if he knows that we, at least, are still alive.'

William snatched the parchment from the priest's hands and traced the letters with his finger. Then he looked up.

'There's no point. Let's gather ourselves together quickly and get home. If de Scabious has taken Hartslove, news of our arrival would only give him time to mount a defence. Better to arrive unannounced.'

The priest looked at the brothers.

'No reply, then?' he asked, trying to hide his disappointment.

Gavin shook his head. 'No. No reply'. He tossed the priest a small coin and strode off, shouting for Hal.

The priest fell to his hands and knees to pick the money out of the dirt. *Oh well*, he thought, as he heaved himself upright again, *maybe some other knight would want to write a long epistle about the war. All this illiteracy combined with all this travel was such a godsend.* He could charge anything he liked for his services and the real joy was that nobody ever knew if he was writing exactly what they dictated or not. Some days, when the priest felt particularly happy, verbal flourishes just poured from his pen. When the man who was dictating looked puzzled by the length of the letter – and the huge cost – the priest would go into some long grammatical explanation which had the poor dupe's eyes glazing over. Sometimes, as a result, he even got an extra tip. But not this time. He looked at William and Gavin with distaste, then sniffed and lumbered off.

It did not take long to muster the Hartslove contingent together.

'We have lost our banner,' said William as he surveyed the group. 'We will have to have another made when we get home.'

It was time to say goodbye to the knights whose final destinations were not Hartslove. Some went off alone, all their companions having been lost.

One of the last to say goodbye was Gavin's old gambling companion, Roger de Soucy.

'Well,' he said. 'This is it.'

Gavin looked at him. 'You sound more as if you were going to a funeral than going home,' he joked.

Roger's eyes narrowed. 'The end of the crusade means that I am ruined,' he said, 'I have no money and no land. I am nothing until the king gets back. Even then he might not take me into his household.'

267

Gavin felt guilty. He tried to forget about Roger's gambling and remember only his bravery at the battle of Jaffa. The man had barely escaped with his life. Gavin thought for a moment. He should offer him hospitality at Hartslove. 'Roger –' he said.

But Roger interrupted. 'But I suppose things are worse for you,' he said. 'After all, a knight with one arm, well . . .'

Gavin flushed. 'I managed when we retook Jaffa from the sea,' he said.

'Yes, but out there we were desperate,' Roger replied. 'I don't think we've reached quite those straits here. Still, I suppose you are lucky in one respect: at least you have your brother to support you.' And with that he walked off.

Gavin felt as if he had been stabbed. He had stopped thinking about the loss of his arm as a real handicap. But he now saw only too clearly what William had realized in Jerusalem. Back in England, of course it would be seen as an overwhelming weakness. In the Holy Land, Richard had to make do with what was on offer. Back in his own lands, the king could have fresh knights, unscarred by battle and still at the peak of fitness. And then, Gavin went cold at the thought, there was Ellie. How stupid was he being? The domestic and personal difficulties that had seemed so inconsequential when far away and in danger of his life, now crowded in. Ellie. Whatever Brother Ranulf had implied in his letter about her, Ellie and he were betrothed. But why should she marry him now?

It was not until this moment that Gavin fully understood how much he had always accepted – no, he must be honest – wanted this to happen. True, he and

Ellie had not parted on the best of terms and Gavin firmly believed that she had always preferred William. However, he was still the elder son. Nothing could take that away. But now there was something else. Ellie would be horrified by the spectacle of a man with only one arm. He would revolt her, for truly his arm was a revolting sight. There was nothing for it. She must be released from her promise. As for Gavin himself, he would leave Hartslove to William and go back to the north where he had spent so many months in disgrace once before. Their uncle the bishop would have to help.

Gavin suddenly felt exhausted and, asking Hal to lead Dargent, got into the wagon. As the small cavalcade moved off, he shut his eyes and pretended to sleep.

25

Hartslove, end of January 1193

It was snowing hard, and Ellie was sitting by the fire in the women's quarters when a small boy on a hairy pony galloped over the drawbridge shouting that there was a party of knights and wagons coming up the road towards the castle. Ellie's heart began to race. It was only three weeks to Valentine's Day, when Constable de Scabious had threatened to make her his wife.

'Who are they?' she shouted down, but her voice did not carry far enough. She had no idea what to do. Since she had sent Sacramenta to find Brother Ranulf, she had heard nothing. At Christmas, she had seen the monk approach the castle, but he had been turned away by the garrison knights with foul language full of shaming innuendo. When Ranulf looked up, Ellie drew back so that he would never know that she had heard what they said. She felt that after all this time she could not ask about Sacramenta without arousing suspicion and began increasingly to fear that something bad had happened to the mare before she could deliver her message.

The good news was that de Scabious had not yet reappeared. But after Brother Ranulf's request to see Ellie, the garrison knights kept the girl a virtual prisoner. They were not openly offensive to her. If Constable de

Scabious had made a miscalculation about becoming count of Hartslove, they did not want Ellie bringing charges against them. So they kept her inside, not by force, but by ignoring her requests to be allowed to ride out, saying they were too busy to accompany her. When Ellie protested, they threatened to send for the man she least wanted to see.

Ellie spent the days trying not to let her fear show through. But at night, she sobbed on Old Nurse's shoulder as she contemplated life without the family with whom she had grown up. Old Nurse, watching Ellie's spirits sink lower and lower, was powerless to help. Margery crept about, almost as ashen-faced as Ellie.

Receiving no answer to her calls, Ellie now ran to her casement window and leant out, but she could make out no details through the swirling white.

'Old Nurse, Old Nurse,' she cried, as she picked up her skirts and ran down the spiral stairs, her hair swinging behind her. In the great hall she found four soldiers warming themselves. She hardly knew what she was saying.

'Get up,' she ordered. 'There is a party of armed men coming up the road. They have wagons and I don't know who they are or what they intend to do. Look sharp! Get the few archers and arbalesters we have on to the roof and into the tower. Haul up the drawbridge. But let nobody, nobody do you hear, let loose one arrow or one crossbolt before I give the order. Is that clear?'

The soldiers looked at her. They had to admit that the girl had guts, but if this was Constable de Scabious coming back, they were certainly not going to oppose him. He would be returning to Hartslove a powerful man.

271

Nevertheless, it was not safe to make assumptions. The approaching party could be anybody.

Ellie tried not to stamp her foot as the serjeant nodded his head in what he hoped was a non-committal way. 'Very well, Miss,' he said.

Ellie said nothing more, but ran to the door. What should she do if this was de Scabious coming as bridegroom? Never mind Brother Andrew's reassurances about a happy widowhood, she must fly, maybe taking one of the plough-horses for Old Nurse? At that moment, Old Nurse came bustling in. Ellie looked at her. It was impossible. A woman Old Nurse's size would need one of those elephants from Brother Andrew's book.

Old Nurse took no notice of the funny look Ellie gave her. She was panting. 'Miss Eleanor,' she puffed, pushing Ellie into a corner so that the soldiers could not see her. 'That boy, that shouting boy, did you see him? I was taking the laundry across the courtyard when I noticed he was carrying a roll of letters. I relieved him of them and said I would give them to the mistress of the castle. Here.'

Ellie snatched the roll from the nurse's hands, broke the seal and began to read. She turned from white to red and back to white. Old Nurse badgered her all the time, her voice getting louder.

'Miss Ellie, what does it say? Eleanor? ELEANOR?'

'Be quiet, Old Nurse,' Ellie begged. 'Please let me finish it.' She was following the letters carefully with her finger.

But before Ellie had time to finish, a commotion broke out. The old woman and the girl looked at each other, then ran out together, Ellie rolling the parchment as she went and stuffing it into her belt. All was confusion. The garrison serjeant seemed completely at sea.

'What is going on?' Ellie demanded, trying to catch a soldier and make him stand still. 'Is it friend or foe who is approaching?'

'That depends on who you are,' the man replied before shaking her off and running down towards the courtyard. Ellie and Old Nurse followed him. Whoever it was, there was precious little they could do.

They reached the gate to hear the porter engaged in a fierce argument with the garrison soldiers as to whether or not to raise the drawbridge. 'Put it back down at once!' the porter cried, and began to draw his sword. The soldiers gave in, and, as the great oak bridge settled back over the moat, Ellie stepped on to it and gazed down the road. She could see the approaching cavalcade more clearly now. It was neither Constable de Scabious nor Sir Thomas's brother, the bishop, come to help her.

Sitting at the front of a wagon was a crusader with his back to her. By his side, attached to the wagon, walked Dargent, his dark mane speckled white as the snowflakes settled. The flakes were so thick that the group had to come quite close before Ellie saw the glint of red that made her pinch Old Nurse's arm so hard it took days for the marks to disappear.

The noise from the castle died away. Nobody seemed to know what the appropriate response to this very impoverished-looking party should be. Out of all the people that might have turned up at Hartslove, these were the most hoped for and the least expected. Old Nurse touched Ellie's shoulder. 'Look!' she said.

Ellie tore her eyes away from the glimpse of red for a moment and turned her head in the direction of the river. From everywhere, like an army of white ghosts, people were running through the snow towards the castle. They

273

were led by the abbot and a party of monks, one riding Sacramenta. From deep in the valley, Ellie could hear the great abbey bell pealing. She felt as if her heart was trembling.

About ten metres from the drawbridge the wagon stopped. For a moment nothing happened, then Gavin stood up, the cross on his back sparkling as the snowflakes brushed it. As he turned, the space where his arm should have been was revealed to all, and a gasp went up from the onlookers. Ellie put her hand over her mouth. Old Nurse muttered, 'Glory be,' and took a gulp from the bottle in her pocket. But Gavin took no notice. Now he seemed to be calling somebody.

In answer to his shout, from the back of the group, came Hosanna. His coat gleamed copper through the snow, his mane and tail spangled with teardrops of ice. He held his head high. On his back was William, his armour burnished until it glittered and his bearing proud. The expression on his face, now lined and beaten by both his experiences and the weather, made those who saw him hold back a little. William had gone away a youth, untried and untested in the field of battle. He had returned, a fully-fledged crusading knight, having seen more in his short life than they were ever likely to see in theirs. The crowd fell almost silent. The monks, who had reached the moat, stopped and crossed themselves.

When Hosanna approached the wagon in which Gavin was sitting, he halted. Then, after a short exchange with William that was inaudible to everybody, Gavin slowly got out and took his place by the horse's shoulder. William did not dismount, but Gavin walked beside him as they covered the last few metres to the edge of the moat. They crossed the drawbridge together, Gavin's hand on Hosanna's bridle and William's arm raised in salute.

It was not until they reached the castle gate that Sacramenta's whinny rang out. When Hosanna responded, the crowd erupted, roaring in celebration. The returning men immediately broke ranks and merged with the crowd, finding loved ones and friends. Hal looked about him, then suddenly found himself swept off his feet by his mother, who was weeping and laughing at the same time. Other mothers, their hearts breaking, found no one.

In the shadow of the castle walls, Old Nurse took another gulp, 'Just to make sure I'm not dreaming,' and stood behind Ellie as the girl began to walk slowly forwards.

William looked down at her. He couldn't speak or move. His hand was still raised. Gavin let go of Hosanna's bridle and the horse lowered his head and blew some of the snow out of the girl's hair. Ellie laughed uncertainly and touched Hosanna's neck, her fingers at once finding the ridge and then the arrow dent. She hesitated, then, with a deep breath and a dazzling smile, broke the awkward silence.

'I knew you would come back,' she said. 'I just knew it. I have always believed it, haven't I, Old Nurse?'

Old Nurse, hoping she would be forgiven for 'forgetting' the nights Ellie had wept in utter despair, made a small harrumphing sound rather reminiscent of Sir Thomas. Then she blew her nose in her apron. 'If you say so, dear,' she said.

'What has been going on here?' asked William, slightly disconcerted to find that the first sentence he uttered to Ellie should be that one. He had lost control of his tongue.

A shadow crossed Ellie's face. 'Constable de Scabious

275

said you were not coming back,' she whispered. 'He has spread vile rumours. I am – well, I am supposed to be disgraced and unfit for anybody to marry.'

Gavin said nothing and Ellie did not look at him. She did not know what her look should say.

Old Nurse, who was patting William's leg, suddenly grabbed it so hard she almost pulled him off Hosanna.

'If either of you brothers believes the tittle-tattle put about by that man,' she said, 'you will be unworthy of your father's name. This girl, my Ellie, is purer than a nun in paradise.'

Before she could say any more, the abbot, running and smiling, appeared.

'My dear, dear sons,' he said, touching Hosanna's star. 'Welcome home. You are heroes and we want to hear all that has happened. What a time you have had! Did you see Jerusalem? Where is everybody else?' He caught the glance that William was giving Ellie and started to twitter. 'We have had our troubles here while you were fighting for Christ, you know, but your return is the most important thing.' He smiled encouragingly. 'Christ's enemies are not confined to overseas, as I don't have to tell you. But let us, at this happiest of moments, say only this, that all will be well now that you are back and that we must put all the unpleasantness that occurred here while you were away behind us. I am afraid I have not behaved very well.' He turned to Ellie. 'I was too trusting of the constable. In the end it turned out that he knew – or he thought he knew – more than he let on to me. His motives in dealing with you, Miss Eleanor, have been less than pure.'

Gavin and William looked rather bemused. Neither could take in what the abbot was saying.

Unable to take his eyes off Ellie, William said the first thing that came into his head to shut the abbot up. 'The king is not back with us,' he blurted out. 'We don't know where he is.'

'Oh,' Ellie said, in tones of surprise, 'but I do. The king is in prison in Germany. He was captured before Christmas.'

They all stared. 'In prison?' William repeated. 'How did you find out?'

'Because I can read,' said Ellie, pulling the parchment Old Nurse had given to her earlier carefully out of her belt. 'And even write a bit, too.'

'I know,' said William.

The abbot coughed.

Ellie was embarrassed. 'Well, never mind about any of that now,' she said, then ran forwards to call for hush. The snow continued to fall steadily. Ignoring it, Ellie climbed on to the stone mounting block at the side of the horse-trough, the one that had once, in another life, been the scene of William's humiliation. Then she spoke loudly and clearly so that everyone could hear.

'My friends,' she began, unrolling the letter. 'We must give thanks for the return of the Hartslove crusaders, or what remains of them, from the Holy Land. But the king's journey home has not been uneventful. From the cell in which he is currently held by Duke Leopold of Austria –' the crowd gasped, '– Yes, the returning crusader king has been betrayed. But anyway, from his prison cell, King Richard has sent special greetings to his faithful knight William de Granville, now Earl of Ravensgarth.' The gasp turned into a roar. Ellie held up her hand to indicate that she had not finished and began to read slowly but clearly from the parchment. ' "The new earl has the right to build five castles on the lands formerly belonging to Bartholomew de Mortimer. He has earned his new status through the gallantry of both himself and his horse Hosanna during the course of the crusade but particularly at the battle of Jaffa." That's what this letter says.'

William started. 'An earl?' he said. Ellie raised her eyebrows as he turned to Gavin, standing beside him. Gavin leant heavily against Hosanna, his mind reeling. Here was the beginning of his new life. With the loss of his arm, he had lost everything.

Ellie cleared her throat. 'I haven't finished,' she said and continued reading. '"I also bequeath to my faithful counsellor Gavin de Granville, now Count of Hartslove, the horse that I won from Isaac Comnenus. He must come and claim it from me when I return home. Furthermore, I instruct him to come and be part of my household, for he has proved a valuable counsellor and a true friend."'

Gavin put his forehead against Hosanna's shoulder for a moment. He could feel the horse's warmth through the cold. Then he steadied himself and slowly raised his left arm. The crowd waited in some trepidation. Even with King Richard's kind words, would he be happy that his brother now outranked him? What could William have done that deserved such a great honour? Would Gavin be resentful? He had been such a hot-headed, thoughtless young man when he left for crusade. Maybe this would spell the end of peace at Hartslove. What a shame that Sir Thomas had died! What would this new arrangement mean? Without the crusade to unite them, would the two brothers soon be at war? And then there was the business of Ellie. What would she do now? It was with bated breath that the crowd watched Gavin, still leaning against

278

the red horse. They shimmied forwards, as he began to speak.

'I give you,' he said, his voice wavering only a little, 'I give you William, Earl of Ravensgarth.' Then he repeated it more strongly. 'I give you William, Earl of Ravensgarth, a true earl, a true brother and a true son to our father.'

The crowd broke into spontaneous applause. Gavin leant against Hosanna again and the horse breathed gently into his face. Gavin smiled. He knew what to say next. He held his arm up and once more demanded silence.

'But let him never forget,' he went on, suddenly fluent and not shaky at all, 'that this honour is not his alone. From now on, a chestnut horse will be incorporated into the de Granville coat of arms. For when the story of Richard the Lionheart's crusade is told, when our myths are made, let us remember that this is not just a story about men. Without our horses we would have been nothing. So, my friends, I commend to you not just my dead father, a fine crusader, and my brother, William, together with all crusaders living and dead, but also the memory of our horses. In particular I commend to you this horse here, this horse called Hosanna, who represents all that is gallant and noble and who has never been found wanting.'

At this the crowd set up a chant. 'Hosanna! Hosanna!'

Gavin nodded and looked about him. The horse was being touched by everyone who could get near him. Hal had extricated himself from his mother's bear hugs and slipped up to Hosanna's head. Eventually Gavin found himself looking at Ellie. She looked at him, straight in the eye. All her past confusions died away. She knew just what to do. She knew, with all her instincts, that this man needed her. She was horrified by his arm. She was nervous of the future. But she knew that if Gavin's life was not to be ruined entirely, she must bind it in with hers. The next few moments, she felt, were of vital importance.

Moving away from William and Hosanna, she touched Gavin's shoulder. Tears mixed with the snow on her cheeks. Gavin swallowed hard. Not pity, surely? He could bear anything but that. But it was not pity he saw in Ellie's eyes, or in the arms that were stretched out towards him.

Suddenly Gavin felt his terrors lift. He moved towards Ellie and she did not shrink away. 'Have you understood what has happened to me?' he said, slowly and deliberately. 'I am not sure you have got the right brother.'

'I understand exactly what has happened to you,' she replied softly. 'And who's to say you have got the right heiress?' She began scrabbling around in her pocket. Triumphant, she brought out the little wooden dog Gavin had returned to her at their unsatisfactory leave-taking. 'It has been right there since you left,' she said simply.

Gavin took it and shut his eyes for a moment. Then he clenched it in his fist as he turned to William and shouted in almost his old style, 'A dunk in the horse-trough for the new earl, and shake down a thick bed for his Great Horse.'

William threw back his head and laughed. Then, finally, he dismounted and the two men clasped hands briefly before moving forwards and going their separate ways.